CW01594612

Delaware's

Top Captain

a novel

Sean Davis

outskirtspress
DENVER, COLORADO

This is a work of fiction. The events and characters described herein are imaginary and are not intended to refer to specific places or living persons. The opinions expressed in this manuscript are solely the opinions of the author and do not represent the opinions or thoughts of the publisher. The author has represented and warranted full ownership and/or legal right to publish all the materials in this book.

Delaware's Top Captain

v1.0

Outskirts Press, Inc.
http://www.outskirtspress.com

ISBN: 978-1-4327-7547-6

PRINTED IN THE UNITED STATES OF AMERICA

This book, my first book of many more to come,

I dedicate to my three handsome children, my sons.

Corey Davis

Dashawn Davis

Najee Jamison

The shining armor that they are today, with us four together…

"Only the strong survives"

I love you guys always,

Your Daddy

In Memory of
Shamika (Meka) Johnson
1970-2007
R.I.P

Acknowledgements

First and foremost, I thank God for this unique gift HE has given me to write this book. My thoughts coming from above. You have blessed me in so many ways that I don't know where to begin, so with that, I thank you forever.

Janet Davis, my mother, my beautiful black Nubian queen. Thank you for believing in my dreams; also I believe you're the best cook in the world. I love you, Mom.

Ms. Em, you grasp my story. Thank you for believing in me since day one. Without you I wouldn't be the upcoming author that I am today and that you knew I would be today. I once told you that I will master this profession they call writing. Keep doing your thing, my devoted publisher. You're very special to me. Thank you.

JoAnne Brice. You're that Easton, Maryland chick that knew where I was heading in this business. If it weren't for you baby, for the foresight that God has given you to give to me, that I could write this book. You wouldn't be reading this book today. Remember the Evening Night Out letter that you asked me to write you? That's how this all began. Ya know what I'm talking about sexy. Love ya. Smile!! You're probably laughing right now.

Gina Crumpler. My dear baby sister, even though you're older than me. Thank you for believing that my dreams were definitely coming true. You never doubted me. You helped me in out so many ways. Your precious time to me, while working those long, crazy hours with Wilmington Dart Bus Company. Keep on driving that bus baby sis, and smile. I love you too.

This book is dedicated to my beloved sister, Shamika Johnson, whom passed away as I was writing this book.

Diane, Ms. Em's assistant. You believe in my dream also. You once said to me, "Keep smiling, stay humble, stay focused and before you know it...you'll be a published author." You kept me smiling and laughing throughout this whole process. It's crazy because I think that this world is half yours gurl. You live in it to live and smile just because. Thank you. Keep smiling.

I also thank you my oldest brother, Randy Davis. My youngest brother, Minister Troy Davis. My oldest sister Derrial Davis. Don't worry Kenneth, Tamika (R.I.P.) and Masina, I love you three always; smile for me.

I give shout outs to all my friends; Steve Barley, Rob Jamison, Kai Flower, Harold Ellington, Tyaire Collins, Javon Hudson, Bebe Willis, Geese, Hag, Gus, Moe, Verna Matthews, Pierre Carter, Malik Matthews, Joseph Jamison (Jo-Jo), Pooh, Mike Johnson, Valaine Anderson (Lady), we go way back to 1994. Kenny Mac, stop stressing man, and Eric Ferrell. Wilmington, Delaware I got nothing but love for yall, especially the Bucket Projects on the Northside of Wilmington, one love Posse. Those of you that I forgot to mention...I truly apologize.

All my peoples that are on lockdown, keep y'all heads up. 2 C Pod, 2 Q Pod, Dorm-1 and Dorm-2 (Key Program), H.R.Y.C.I

R.I.P. Cousin Edward, Uncle James, Grandmom, Keith, Cousin Kenny Davis (Southbridge still lovin ya), and Shamika Johnson. Teardrops to LaTanya (Toni) Badson, still missing you girl.

To all my fallen soldiers of Wilmington who passed away leaving us all memories to cherish. Inside we cry.

Thank you to all of my supporters, your support means so much to me. Let's do what we do when we do it.

Last but not least, the three very special women in my life who will be there and around always and forever; Karen Pinchney, you held my son Corey close to your heart while I was absent and I thank you so much for that. I love you guys.

Nichole Wilson, Dashawn is our king, our pride and joy. You also held him close to your heart in my absence and I thank you so much sweetheart. I love you guys, too.

Crystal Jamison, Najee has his own posse already. You know we gotta stop 'em, smile. You, my dear, you also held my son close to your heart while in my absence. Thank you Crystal. I love you guys.

To the three of you ladies together; Hell ain't got shit on us because we put one another through so much I can't begin to explain, but it was I that caused all the turmoil that I put you ladies through. You three have nothing but love for me. Y'all are always going to be the mothers of my sons and I will always be the father of your sons. So keep smiling. I have so much love for yall.

Chapter 1

23rd and Church Street

"Bolo the Pitbull" more like Delaware's Top Captain, a second voice came roaring… "What can I do to assist dumb and dumber this time". I leaned against the door of my white Lincoln Navigator.

"You drug dealin creep," the first voice said as he yanked my Black & Mild from my mouth. Smiling, I said, "You wanna be a top cop, detective, or whatever the fuck they call you down that donut eatin shack of yours". I paused while grabbing his wrist. "You lay another fuckin' finger on me and I'll have your entire family chopped up in one hundred pieces, now dare me, you skunk". He freed his wrist from my grip.

Det. Maddox and Carmine are the two most intelligent men on the city's police force. As always, there is a good cop and a bad cop. Maddox is the good cop. Black man with a husky build, and stands about 5'8" with a low cut. Money talks when it comes to Maddox; especially when I need some invaluable information.

Now Carmine, a white man that has a chubby 5'3" frame with a bald head. He's the skunk that I call him. His body smells like a fat man that has not washed his ass in weeks. He once had a gun with seven bodies on it and claimed it was mine. The judge dismissed the case because his fingerprints were the only prints on it.

"Bolo…Bolo", Maddox interrupted as he wedged his body in between us. "We just want to ask you some questions" he said. "And what one questions is that?" I asked sarcastically.

"Did you have anything to do with ------------"MOTHERFUCKER, YOU KILLED MIGUEL LOPEZ"? Carmine interrupted with a 9 mm pointing in my face. "WHOA…WHOA…" Maddox shouted, grabbing the nose of the gun. "GET YOUR ASS IN THE CAR", he snapped!

"SKUNK!!" I shouted. Detective Maddox just shook his head as he walked towards his car, "I'll holla at you later", he said before speeding off.

I sat in my Navigator wondering what could have happened to Miguel.

"Welcome to my domain Mr. Lance Jones", Miguel said as he extended his arm, motioning me to come inside. Nodding my head, I said, "Nice place you have here".

"Thank you Lance" he replied as he handed me a bottle of Dom Perignon. "Have a drink", he said as he sat down.

"Thank you, sir" I said as I paused before gulping down the full glass.

"You are my only commander here in Delaware and I appreciate all of the business you handle for me. Needless to say that you take care of my entire operation; enemies as well."

Miguel operates at least eighty percent of cocaine distribution in this city. He's Spanish American, 5'8" with a stocky built, wavy black hair; wears tailor-made pinstripe Versace suits. His home is decorated fabulously. The living room had a four-inch thick Persian rug, and a very expensive Corinthian leather sectional with silk curtains.

Miguel and I met about three years ago while at the Auto Action in Atlantic City. He walked up on me while I was admiring a baby blue fifty-seven Chevy, which he now owns. From that day forward, I became his right hand man.

I leaned back, resting my head on a white plush leather headrest and said, "It's my job sir…to protect you, your family and your empire."

"Lance, you've been loyal to me since day one. I respect that to the utmost". Miguel sat up while grabbing his remote control. I noticed a 6-inch Panasonic Plasma TV slowly disappearing into the left side of the wall.

"WHAT THE FUCK!" I shouted watching Miguel stand smiling, then walking over to a huge black safe. "Man you must have about thirty million dollars in there". Turning the music down, he said "not even close". Lance grinned as he tossed me a few stacks of new $100 bills.

"Over $90 million is in this safe" he boasted as he closed the safe and the plasma TV reappeared.

Immediately I said to myself, 'Here I am sitting in this muthafuckin house after three years of meeting him and my pay is only $30,000 a month, now something's fucked up...really fucked up. Wow'. My thoughts were racing. 'This nigga got everything I ever wanted and its right at his finger-tips, or should I say, a push of that red button on the remote control.' Crazy thoughts continued to invade my mind, 'and after all I put myself through protecting him, his assets, his money, his family and his empire. The countless murders, the lives I've taken, including seven police officers along with some of their families in three different states. What's mine is mine and what's his I WANT.' The thought of him calling me Lance and not Bolo enraged me! Let the games begin.

Cindy:

"We haven't met down here in quite some time Bolo', she tapped three times on my shoulder. "Give me the address and how many are in the house", she added. "One" was all I had to say before she reached into my coat retrieving a golden manila envelope Mission accomplished...and she walked off.

Several months later, Bolo had a female companion of Miguel's deliver roses to his residence not knowing the unthinkable was about to happen. Just how far will Bolo go to protect his own family from the dangerous streets of Wilmington?

Then comes Sophie out of the clear blue. They met at a casual worker's night out party held at the Hotel DuPont. She seductively walked up to Bolo and kissed him. Her purpose, what are her reasons for wanting to bring Bolo to his knees? What part does she play in what's about to happen to Bolo's favorite cousin, Dawn?

Word quickly spread about what happen to Dawn, someone Bolo would lay down his life for. Bolo's enemies, along with penny pushing drug dealers are all out to get him, while not making themselves known to his vulnerability. The Wilmington police, the Senator, Governor, and Mayor are having many sleepless nights because of the corruption Bolo brings to the State of Delaware. Countless unsolved murders with many being their own brothers in blue.

It gets worse, Bolo's lawyer went astray because he was seen talking to the F.B.I. His mind is set on one thing and one thing only…REVENGE!

Stepping away from a black Toyota Camry that was rented the day before, there was a Spanish man standing in his doorway nodding his head and smiling at me as if he knew who I was. The lady that I am, smiling back at him while walking with a dozen red roses cuddled in my arms. I began feeling his eyes searching my body from neck down, continuing down to my pink polished toenails.

"Hello, may I speak with Mr. Miguel Lopez please?" I asked, while standing a few feet away from him. His mind began racing with all kind of ways he could handle this perfect framed figure.

"Yes, I'm Mr. Lopez," he desperately answered, still smiling searching my nice curves with his fake 'I want you so bad' eyes.

"I'm here to deliver these beautiful roses to you sir." I held them high in front of my face knowing that his eyes are all over my body. "They'll need to be placed in some water." I added.

"Come in please," he kindly stepped to the side while pushing the door further open for me to enter.

"Thank you. Your kitchen would be…?" I heard him mumble something before he spoke, he slammed the door behind us.

"I'm sorry fat ass, it's straight back that way on your left," he pointed to a black narrow hallway.

Walking pass an oval glass cocktail table with stacks of money and large amounts of what seems to be cocaine. I sense this man is into some real big shit; maybe some kind of Kingpin. Turning my back toward him, while looking over my right shoulder, than placing my hand on my hips. I noticed his manhood rising beneath his expensive black terry cloth robe.

"Naughty boy, you better watch your mouth Miguel sweetie; it can get you into some serious trouble!" I yelled with the thought of him moistening his lips at me, making me want to throw up all over his beautiful, money green, and marble kitchen floor.

"I love trouble! I live for trouble baby," his voice echoing proudly, thinking he might get some of this warm, wet pussy that he's been yearning for since the second I stepped out of the car. As wet as I am, I just might give him a sample for a small price.

"Stop it, you're making me wet." I peeped around at him, whispering, while blowing him a kiss. The sweet smelling aroma that's coming from between these golden thighs would make any man drool and pay any price for what he desires. "Okay, you asked for it big boy cause here I come." Once again, I peeped around the wall throwing satin pink panties at him.

"You naughty girl you, come in here so I can taste that wetness that I've been lusting for." Miguel yelled over the loud sound of jazz traveling freely through the house. His voice ricocheted, telling his mind that what he was about to experience was going to be the best yet. Flashing a single rose, I began displaying my right thigh to get this party started.

"You ready baby, cause here I come!" I prepared myself while placing a rose in my mouth.

"Yes, yes, yes," he screamed vividly into the open air of his living room. "I'm waiting," another scream came bouncing off the walls.

"Close your eyes honey and keep them closed," rose pedals began tumbling down off my breasts and down to the expensive, white Persian rug.

"Baby, they are already closed," he eagerly shouted, quickly closing his eyes at the sight of me walking toward him. I began caressing my breasts and running my fingers through my jet black, shoulder length hair; standing over-top of him...CLICK-click! I raised my gun. "Now didn't I tell you that your nasty, filthy mouth was gonna get you in some shit one day, muthafucka?!"

"Who the hell are you bitch?" His eyes widened as if he witnessed a family of ghosts. His manhood quickly submerged between his legs. His hands holstering his body as he anticipated reaching for the chrome .357 by his side.

"Your death certificate, asshole." I snatched my wig off while pointing my black 9mm Smith & Wesson directly at his temple. This was definitely the moment I've been waiting for. Especially with all the shit I've been through since the day I met Miguel, from killing off his enemies to protecting his family at any or all cost.

"Bo...!" was the last sound that came out of Miguel's mouth before his brain became a beautiful portrait of red liquid dots decorating the wall. I can imagine what he was thinking when he noticed it was me, his right hand man, dressed as a glamorous female.

Tap-tap-tap-tap.

Awakening to the heavy tapping on my windows. I cautiously adjusted my eyes to see two gunmen pointing their guns directly at my head and chest. My first instinct was telling me to grab one of my nine millimeters, but the nigga on my passenger's side was shaking his head as if to say, "I dare you muthafucka."

"GET THE FUCK OUT...NOW!" shouted the grimy nigga on my side. He yanked open the door. "FUCK" the other nigga shouted as he opened up the passenger's side. "THAT'S...BOLO," Peanut muttered as he held both gun at the passenger's temple. Gus added, "Delaware's Top Captain", while digging his gun into the driver side's back.

"Gentlemen, gentlemen, gentlemen," I said calmly as I slowly stepped out of the car. The expressions on their faces changed when they realized who I really was, pissing and shitting themselves. They stood trembling, like it was winter, in the middle of a 90 degree summer day. Lil' Timmy and Lil' Tyrone, two that wanted to be stick up kids.

"Bolo, man we..."

"Shhhhhhh!" Timmy watched as my gun came even with his heart.

"Bolo, we sorry man. We tryin to get paid, but we didn't know it was you." Tyrone cried.

"Tryin to get paid with my money, huh?" I smirked.

"Nah, nah, nah Bolo." They both cried like bitches.

"Bitch ass niggas, shut the fuck up...shitty asses".

Gus and Peanut hit the twins so hard that you would think there were born as conjoined twins, the way their bodies clashed together when they hit the concrete. "I tell you what," I pulled a wad of cash while tucking my heat in my waist. "I respect you little ass niggas for being the stickup boys that you are." I watched both of them stand to their feet. We all eyed an old lady from across the park as she walked her dogs. Several cars whizzed by. I nodded my head to Gus and Peanut to give up what money they had on them when Peanut abruptly said, "It's over four thousand here, Bolo."

"Three thousand plus, Bolo." Gus added.

"Well, well you little niggas lucked up, it's over 10 stacks here." Bolo handed the money to Jimmy.

"Damn, thanks Bolo", he smiled. "Bolo, we sorry man"Tyrone coughed.

"Enjoy your money gentlemen", I laughed as I hopped back into my car.

Psst! Psst! Psst! Psst!

Five years later and I'm still being labeled as the most notorious drug dealer in Delaware's history. Many say that I'm just a man tryin to make ends meet, but to the enemies, the police, my local government and those nickel and dime niggas hatin on the hustle. I'm Lance "Bolo" Jones-

DELAWARE'S TOP CAPTAIN.

Rob Base "It Takes Two to Make a Thing Go Right"...was blasting in the air as me and my crew walked into the Hotel DuPont's Golden Ballroom. It was packed, wall to wall. "Whatcha think Bolo?"Ty asked as he reached into his Armani jacket for a Cuban cigar.

"Well gentlemen", I shouted over the loud music as I surveyed my surroundings. "Will yall look at this fellas?" We all stood watching this beautiful, black, Nubian sista walk seductively pass us wearing the hell out of this strapless, sparkling dress with jet black hair to her ass.

"Damn, it's so many beauties in here tonight!" Kev shouted, tossing his white Versace hat in the air, then recovering it behind his back.

"Let the games begin!"Ty shouted as we all went our separate ways.

'*Let the games begin*', echoed in my head as I thought about how I slashed Cindy's throat for neglecting to mention to me that she was training to be a cop.

Once at the bar, it was quite amusing watching the sistas enjoy themselves, professionally dressed while some were clinging onto their significant other. There's one particular female that I have my eye on and definitely has my undivided attention. She is sitting directly across from me. I watch her as her left index finger traced her candy apple red lips, while gently licking her tongue as if she wants to feel my manhood in her mouth.

Her movements escalated while blending to the sounds of The Whispers, '*This is what I'll Doooo, to get you in the mood…*' She then motioned her lips to say, "I'm yours if you want me baby. I'll do whatever you want me to do for you". A soft whisper echoed in my ear. Was my mind playing tricks on me, I thought, as I turned to the right and noticed a light skinned sista sporting a Toni Braxton cut, brown eyes, with fake ass dangling diamond earrings down to her shoulders. "Hello" she smiled while brushing up against me. How could this wanna be gold digging bitch have the nerve to place her hand on my tailor made three thousand-dollar Armani suit?

"Hello!" I smiled back at her kindly, not wanting to show or tell her what's really on my mind.

"Hi, my name is Tuesday," her girlish voice confirmed she was in her teens, eight-teen or nineteen at the most, her eyes blazing for attention.

"Hello, May I help you to a drink handsome?" the white petite blonde hair barmaid interrupted while smiling, knowing that I was about to explode at any minute. "Thank you." I whispered as I glued my eyes directly on her pretty, sharp smile. "Yes, ma'am, may I have a Hennessey set-up with a few pieces of lemon and a side of orange juice."

"Coming right up, sweetheart!" she literally rushed away to make my set-up as if she knew what was about to go down.

"Tuesday, what brings you out on this lovely Saturday night?" I asked.

"Well, I came out wanting to meet some of your characters, have a few drinks and possibly get into whatever we get into tonight!" Her body language quickly erected, alarming me that this pissy adolescent is willing to give up her pussy to a stranger that hasn't even mentioned his name.

"Here you go handsome. That'll be twenty-five dollars." the beautiful blonde said, shaking her head shamelessly at Tuesday. "Thank you and keep the change," I said as I handed her a crisp $100 bill, then walked away smiling, wondering what was on Tuesday's mind. Who in their right mind would name their child Tuesday, the third day of the week?

"You bastard, he is so ignorant!" Tuesday blurted out at me. Out of all the gorgeous women that I came here to meet tonight, a teenager looking for a quick lay happens to push up on me. "Hey Bolo!" a woman spoke as she tapped my shoulder. As I looked slightly to my left, I noticed a sexy, caramel sista with sandy brown, curly hair and sparkling eyes the size of three-carat, princess cut diamonds.

"Mercedes sweetheart, how are you doing?" Blushing at the sight of her eight-teen inch split on the side of her dress, baring her curves.

"Fine Bolo. Thank you for the invite" she replied. Chuckling as she sat down crossing her legs. "You're very polite as always" Mercedes said.

"Thank you." I said while grabbing the cocktail waitress arm to bring a Corona Lite Beer. "Very special also" Mercedes added crossing her arms, her bright smile, telling me that she desperately wants to go home with me tonight as she said with a kiss, "I'm off this weekend, so don't ask me who I'm going home with tonight cause the answer is YOU!"

Mercedes once stated to me, "Every time I plant a juicy wet kiss on you, you make my pussy soaking wet." This will definitely be a night of blazing fireworks for the first time between Mercedes and me. "You're the only person that I know that traces her tongue around a bottle like your sucking a dick."

"Bolo, honey can you imagine what's gonna happen to you tonight?" A cherry rolled off her tongue, bouncing off the bottle and into my glass. "How's that for starters?" she added, grabbing my arm tightly.

"I-I see baby" I whispered as she caressed my manhood as it stood straight at attention "Come on, let's dance," she said excitedly. I jumped up accidentally brushing against her curves. I can imagine what she thinking about when she smiled at me.

"He's already awake and ready for action," she said, whispering in my ear while running her wet, warm, tongue around my earlobe. How can I say no to a beautiful sista that has a body no man can refuse? Especially with an ass the size of a twenty pound butter ball turkey, skin smoother than silk, pussy print that is screaming out my name, I can hear the syllable over the bass of the music.

"Mercedes…listen to you girl," my voice rattled, as I felt somewhat embarrassed pulling her closely to me.

"I hear you the shit here in Delaware, Bolo" she said, leaning back a little, focusing on my lips. "Delaware's Top Captain" she said as she leaned forward once again.

"They talk people talk, everybody talks," I replied, chuckling to hear the words to Janet Jackson's *Control*.

"My place, twenty minutes after the party" she laughed, pushing me away by my shoulders. "Enjoy the rest of your night." Mercedes whisked away, turning around and looking over her shoulder while patting her ass twice, as she strolled down the catwalk; leaving me alone to fantasize about how I would handle her.

Mercedes is a well-educated black sista who's independent and can hold her own. Once she became pregnant and lost the baby to a serious car accident. After that she lost her self-respect, self-love along with her self-esteem. With the help of a few friends of mine, she's back where she left off, but more powerful than before.

"Damn Bolo, what was all that about?" Kev asked, escorting this white chick that has her arm tightly secured around his. "Mercedes been wanting to hook up with you for a long time," he added, whispering something in the blonde chick's ear.

"Just a little pussy date man," I smiled, 'It's all about Mercedes tonight' I thought as they watched me light a cherry Black & Mild. "What about you and that broad Rhonda, her cousin?"

Kev motioned his friend to leave his presence with a kiss. "Now and then" he said. "I had to pull away from her because she said she was falling in love with me," he acknowledged, "Plus she wanted to have a baby."

"Family man, huh? Hell No," Bolo said. "That's not good for business," he said, sliding the Hennessey bottle over towards him.

"Rule number one…no kids in organization" shaking my head. I noticed the chick in the strapless grey sparkling dress walking pass and smiling at me. "Rule number two...no rings on those fingers."

Kev shouted out, "I'll holla at you later Bolo!" He read my mind as I continued for searching my target as she vanished into the huge crowd on the dance floor, laughing. "Be safe in the motherfucka" I sipped the last of my Hennessey, than made my way into the crowd of dancing machines doing the electric slide.

"*Take it back now yall. Two hops this time. Two on the left, two on the right. Cha Cha now yall. Slide to the right, slide to the left, take it back now yall.*"

Someone called...now Cha-Cha. He called once more as I landed right in the back of my target, looking directly at her fat ass. Spinning around "Would you like to dance?" she asked as the music changed to Freddy Jackson's *You are my Lady*. She pushed up on me than began spinning away tracing her curves and smiling, with her straight black air covering half her face down to her chin. Body squirming slowly to the floor she quickly rose, caressing her breast. Her eyes were directly focused on my body language "Well?" she motioned her lips while spinning around once more.

"Sure, why not," I smiled, both index fingers motioning for her to come closer to me.

"I'm Sophie" she said, "Your name is?" her back pressed against my chest as she glanced back over her right shoulder. Cherry lipstick giving away the aroma of sweetness of her breath as she breathed.

"Bolo," I whispered, wanting to slide my tongue into her mouth that was breathing the cherry scented aroma. "They call me Bolo, Sophie," he added.

"Nice to meet you too Sophie" my eyes followed her hands slowly working her thighs as she let go, leaving mine to comfort as well. "Are you alone?"

"No, I came here with two of my girlfriends," she replied, turning around to face me. "What about you, Bolo?" Her fingers pressed against my lips.

"I'm here with two of my best friends who flew in from Florida this morning" my tongue crept out, pulling her finger back to its resting place.

"Very warm," she moaned, eyes rolling to the back of her head. "Dinner on me."

"When, where, and what time?" I asked, questioning her sincerity, whispering in her ear. The moment I slipped Sophie's fingers into my mouth was the second her body language gave into me. Her mind was telling her that she had to have me no matter what. The first few minutes of our conversation was when she first walked past me smiling. "I'll keep you informed," Sophie said, her eyes matching the purse hanging off her shoulder.

"Will you?" I nodded, "Can't wait for that day to get here already." It was a confession waiting to happen along with my deep tone of voice.

I'll have something very special planned for you Bolo" she paused, grinning at a couple kissing. "I can't wait to see how well you handle this baby" as she crumbled the paper while placing it in my hand, then resting her head on my shoulder as R. Kelly's *Slow Dance* began playing,

Several hours later, I dropped Kev and Ty off to their drop offs, then headed in the opposite direction, Detouring, I made a left on 11th & Walnut and began punching numbers on my cell phone. DESTINATION REACHED!

"I knew you would find your way here tonight, sexy" she said as she stood with the door wide open. "Now that you're finally here Bolo, why don't you make yourself at home" her body covered with all lace, pink, satin Victoria Secret.

"I'm here baby," I stepped in smiling. "I wouldn't miss this opportunity for the world." My tongue quickly moistens at the sight of her matching lipstick.

Pouring chocolate down her cleavage, slowly making its way down to her belly button. "Meet me upstairs," said Mercedes, pulling her bra completely off, then wrapping it around my neck.

"On one condition," my tongue met the chocolate dripping off the bra strap. "If only you let me have my way," I added. My dick stood at attention, wanting to jump out from captive, looking at her already, hard nipples also standing at attention. Kissing. "I'd love that. Now get!" she patted my ass while laughing and watching me come out of my clothes.

Seconds later, the lights were dimmed as the sound of smooth jazz fills the air. Mercedes stepped into the bedroom, butt-naked, licking her glossy lips while stroking her left nipple. Her right hand massaging her inner thigh with her fingers submerged, slightly, in her pussy, as she walked up to the end of the bed.

My mind is telling me to just grab her and start giving her the business, but my subconscious told me to hold off for just another second or two. "Damn, you have all the right curves." I watched her hips spread wide like an Eagles wings as she placed one knee on the bed, staring at my dick, ready for whatever.

"So I take it you like what you see baby?" she asked while her eyes focused mainly on my stiff, hard dick. "How well can you handle this, Bolo?" Softly she spoke as we both watched her lips slowly come down over my manhood.

"Mercedes," I moaned, my eyes widen at the sight of her tongue working magic on the tip of my dick. Sighing, "You do this well baby."

"Baby, baby, try this please" she whispered as she climbed on top of my face. "Yes, Bolo, eat this pussy, oh yea...yea!" Crying, she slithered down my body, sliding her clit on top of my hard slab, working those hips back and forth...up and down. Heavy breathing, sex in the air, bodies sweating, both reaching our climax while screaming one another's name at the top of our lungs. Slowly drifting off to sleep, she whispers, "Thank you baby."

Home, I woke to the sound of a woman exploding into my answering machine. Her voice growing louder while the ray of sun touched the tip of my eye lashes, forcing me to fumble for the phone. "Hello," I asked grumbling, laying on my back waiting for the impatient voice to respond.

"Where have you been, Mr. Lance Jones?" Her voice piercing my ears as she paused patiently, waiting for my next sound.

"Hey Auntie," I replied, trying to avoid her questions. "You better answer me now boy!" she shouted, bursting into laughter. "Auntie, I spent the night over this chick's house," I pause, smiling as she continued questioning me. '*Mom, he said you're gonna pay for what you did to him*' a familiar voice grew closer to the receiver.

"What the fuck did she just say to you Auntie?!" I asked cautiously, not wanting to startle her. "Bolo", she avoided my question. "Bolo my ass!" I began getting angrier.

"Mom, is that my cousin Bolo?" Dawn interrupted.

"Yes, Dawn," Auntie Ann responded with her voice growing low and fading.

"Let me talk to him please," Dawn eagerly shouted.

"Hey girl", I said. From a distance I could hear Auntie tell Dawn that '*she better not say anything to me*'.

"When will you be here cousin Bolo?" Dawn asked, choosing her words carefully. "Hello to you too!"

"Sorry cousin, hi!"

"Now that's better, I'll be over there this afternoon," I said, "I need to run to the bank first."

"Okay then, I'll see you when you get here." She quickly hung up the phone.

Thinking about what I just heard my cousin Dawn yell out before she took the phone from her mother, I began wondering if my family is in some sort of danger. Aunt Ann and my cousin Dawn are the joy of my life; they took me in when my mother passed away from years ago. This dangerous drug game that I'm in requires a lot of protection for my family and those who I love, including my crew. Our enemies are those who abide and uphold the law.

Jealously will always hang over your head as the black clouds ready to let loose the rain. Dawn's voice sounded unusual when I called the house. Frightened and quick to hang up, something she never does. I fell back for about another 15 minutes, then jumped in the shower and was out the door headed for the bank.

As I entered through the revolving glass doors, from a distance I noticed a fine, petite, white woman with shoulder length blonde hair walking towards me. Her eyes, the color of a clear blue sky, wearing a brown, wool suit. "Hello, my name is Constance Waters", she said, extending her hand. "Welcome to Wilmington Trust, how may I help you today?"

"It's a pleasure meeting you, Ms. Waters", I replied, desperately wanting to know more about her. "My name is Lance Jones" the warmth of her hand when I held on to it, shot an electric bolt through my body. So far she has my attention. Her body language is telling me to watch her as she strolled down the aisle to watch everyone adore her moves.

"Mr. Jones, why don't you and I step into my office so that we may have our privacy?" She led the way as I followed right behind her. Sure enough, all eyes were on us as if we were newlyweds abut to make a grand entrance into a ballroom of celebrities... "Nice office you have here Constance."

"Thank you, Mr. Jones", she quickly responded. "Call me Bolo, if you don't mind please." I spoke softly, her eyes followed me to the large framed office window.

"Sure," he voice lowered, "Why don't you have a seat over here please", she added, motioning me to sit across from her. My senses tell me that Constance handles her business very well, certificates and awards covered her walls proudly. "Thank you". Constance cleared her throat, then tapped the yellow writing pad with her gold point pen. "Please sit Bolo," I obeyed her order as I sat down. "How may I help you?" she asked again, tilting her head downward, glancing over her the gold frame glasses she retrieved from her side desk drawer, eyes directly on my lips. "I'm waiting", she added, with her ballpoint pen read for motion as if she was prepared to write a documentary about my life.

Leaning slightly back into the chair, crossing my legs, anticipating how I want to address my business proposal to her. "Constance, I'd like to open an account, if that's possible."

"Now Bolo, anything is possible as long as we both set our minds to what's best here in the banking business." she said, her eyes glowing, welcoming a new found client. "Now were getting somewhere." I nodded in agreement.

Reaching into the white cabinets behind her, she turns hand me some papers. "Then why don't you fill those out so we can get the process rolling" her voice jumped with excitement. Shaking my head in disgust I mumbled.

"Gosh I hate paperwork."

Laughing, "now-now, let's start off with a positive attitude", she leaned back shaking her head. "How much will you be depositing?" Her questions rose in mid-air while watching me fill out paperwork

"Three hundred thousand for starters." I raised my eyebrows looking at her expression as she sat straight up in her cherry wood business chair. Choking, she quickly pushed her chair back and rushed over to a cream colored marble counter and grabbed a clear pitcher of water. Taking baby steps back over to her desk, she says, "Bolo, please beware that I'll have to report anything over ten thousand to the Internal Revenue Service (IRS)", stressing to me that her mind was willing to accomplish any and everything to make this deal go through.

"Yes, Constance, I'm very much aware of that and that will not be a problem at all, "Bolo responded confidently.

"Bolo", she paused, "shall we move forward with your deposit?" her smile shined like a full moon above a dark, black sky.

"Only if you accept this extra $50 grand for yourself to keep this off the record", I smiled, reaching into my black briefcase. "You're in the banking business Constance, therefore, you definitely know what to o and from the man certificates and awards on your wall, you do your job well. "

Chuckling, "I- I will handle everything for you Bolo"; she turned my briefcase around facing her. "Now that our business here is complete, why don't you give me a call tomorrow around three o'clock." We both stood up as she handed me her business card. As she led me out of her office, she tapped me on my shoulder and whispered, 'I'm looking forward to hearing from you Bolo", she paused, then continued with, "Along with a dinner date".

"Have a nice day Constance," I replied laughing, as we shook hands to confirm our newly formed friendship. Cell phone ringing, I ran to my car to save an anonymous call while my cell phone battery went dead. Finally, back at my car, connecting my phone to a charger, I answered, "Hello."

"Dinner at my place next Sunday", she said sighing. "How about six o'clock sharp?"

"Be there" I said, chuckling. I began driving down 11th St. heading towards the "Bucket" (one of three Northeast housing projects).

"Oh Bolo", she said, "Punctuality is very, very important to me."

"Sophie, I'll ---". Then before I could finish my sentence the phone went dead.

Conscious mind, I began to remember where I saw Sophie's face... my ex crime partner, Miguel Lopez, had a family portrait hanging on his wall in his family room about five years ago. How could this be so? The three years that I've known him, he never mentioned anything about Sophie. What is her plans with me, maybe to bring down my organization?

Damn! I approached the projects and while parking my car on the corner of 25th & Thatcher, I watched as everyone began to disperse in all directions. The white and blue jumped out vans, along with a black, unmarked vehicle behind them.

"Bolo", yelled Kev, walking as fast as he could towards me as if he was in a walk-a-thon. Then I heard "get down! Get the fuck down!"

"What's up Kev," I asked, we embraced each other like we haven't seen one another for days. I quickly asked, "Is everyone okay, and where is Ty?" We watched as a few small timers were being handcuffed.

"Everyone is cool Bolo," he said, pointing towards Ty coming down the street with a big ass Kodak smile on his face.

The Bucket is one of the areas I control in the city, with estimated sales of $18K a week. "Listen up guys, from now on, I want all perimeters locked down, so it's your job to hire the most effective crew to secure my area", I said while leaning back on my car. "Make sure they are well fed and that they have a nice stack in their pockets." They both agreed with dedication pouring out like the rain dance Indians invented.

Kev said, "Don't worry Bolo, we'll get right on it", his eyes alarming us to something coming up the street. Slightly turning to my left, my peripheral alarmed me of a police cruiser and a black unmarked patrol car pulling out from around the corner towards us.

"Pretty white BMW Bolo," Det. Bailey shouted before his car came to a complete stop in front of us. I quickly shot back "You kinda wish it was yours, don't you Bailey?" as I plucked my Black & Mild on his car's windshield. "I'll be back!" he shouted as he sped away towards 26th street, just missing a green Lexus parked on the corner.

Bailey was a big, black, husky cop, with a low crop haircut, who was once left for dead in an alley two years ago while walking his pit bulls on the Westside. Once someone beat his three hundred pound ass with a wooden baseball bat, immediately he became second in command on Delaware's vice squad. Terrorizing the city is what he does best, especially after he was unconscious, his dismembered dog in so many places. They called off the search when they couldn't find the dog's head, which alone was hanging on a utility pole.

"Call Jay and tell him I'll be there in about twenty minutes", I said as I slowly pulled away from the curb. "Peace out" I tossed his fingers in the air.

Two of my most dedicated soldiers, I said to myself, along with Jay, who I was about to go holla at on the Eastside.

Kev, I met at a summer football game; when this dude came out of nowhere and called him a pussy after he scored a touchdown. One hundred eighty pounds, all muscle, dark nigga, about 5'7" with a low cut. He walked up to this guy, knocked him the fuck out, then knocked his girlfriend out for calling him a punk motherfucka. Since that, his elevator never left the lobby, if you know what I mean.

Now Ty, him and I use to work together for Daisy Construction. We were hauling mortar to the bricklayers in a wheel barrel, when suddenly a brick came crashing down on his foot. Luckily he wore steel toe boots that day. Three guys who were working above had been laughing and joking at us; that definitely got Ty mad, bad enough it was over ninety-five degrees out. Next thing I knew, all three men were found dead the next morning, shot to death, execution style and all covered in mortar.

Light skinned, 5'4", medium build with corn rolls down to his shoulder; that's Ty for you…a lady's man.

"Jay, what's up my man?" I asked, extending my hand out the window before coming to a complete stop. "Bolo," he said, "I just got off the phone with Ty and Kev" he waited until I turned my car off before opening the door for me. "Jump out van and that dog faced Bailey" he added, laughing as we high fived.

"They should be over here sometime soon, so you duded need to be on point."

"We ready!" he stated, "Every perimeter is secured", glancing he watched a dope fiend trying to get his attention.

"Good, I see your cousin Shannon is back in town."

"And already asking to make some money", Jay interrupted, motioning a fiend to one of his helpers.

"So it is, let him get a piece of pie. More recruits means more money and a tighter safety net for the organization."

"Bolo, speaking of cousin", Jay hesitated, his eyes giving him away that he's really worried about something. "She's our family man, please find out what's really wrong with her because she's been acting really weird, like she's afraid of someone or something." Dawn never acted this way.

"Family it is Jay; I'm on my way over there right now". I hopped back in my car. "I'll holla at cha later on tonight man." Angrily, I sped away thinking about what my cousin Dawn yelled out before her mother handed her the phone... '*Mom he said that he is gonna make you pay for what you did to him*'.

Not paying attention to where I was going, I ended up on Gov. Printz, so I made a U-turn then headed back over to the Eastside. The entire time I was thinking about Jay's facial expression, a man that would do anything for the love of his family. He's slim, baldheaded, 5'7" tall with a brown complexion and definitely crazy. One night I watched him walk up to this man standing alone outside the KFC on 26th street, shot him three times, then walked away like nothing happened. Later that night, Jay told me that the man he shot and killed caused his mother to have an accident, which resulted in the man calling his mother a bitch.

Clifford Brown Walk, CB-Dub, is the block my Auntie and Dawn live on, which is where the most drugs are being sold. You got dope fiends combing the streets searching for their next fix, dragging their off-springs along with them in the open drug market. Kids dressed as rag dolls, wondering where their next meal will come from. For now, they'll have to work with the creamy, slimy snot running out their noses, catching it with their bottom lip and allowing their tongue to slop it as if it were fresh lemonade.

One woman was on her knees sucking a niggas dick while looking at the clear, glassine, plastic bag with a powdery substance being waived in her face. "Get the fuck up and get the hell outta here!" I yelled, watching the, both run like scared cheetahs. The problem with dope fiends, they'll do anything to catch a quick fix.

Door opening..."Cousin Dawn, let me holla at you for a minute" I said as I stepped in the house. "Yes, cousin Bolo", she replied, her voice escaped her shallow petite body, placing her gold herringbone necklace around her neck.

"Where is your mother?" I asked. "She's at work now" she said; her mind racing with the words, *hurry up and get this shit over with.*

"When we were on the phone this morning", I paused watching her sit down next to me, "You came in yelling something out, which I truly need you to clarify."

"Hmmm mmm", she mumbled, tilting her head slightly while keeping her eye on her crossed legs. Her heart was pounding uncontrollably, waiting for the next question to explode in her ears. "She told you not to tell me whatever you yelled out to her this morning and you know how much I love my family", I stressed to her.

"Y-Yes I do, "Dawn said, her body wants to jump up and run towards the door.

"You know that I will not allow anyone to harm or threaten my family, not you, not your mother, no one that I love", I said. I watched a single tear fall from her eye."

"I-I know, cause they say everyone is afraid of you"

"It's not about that right now, Dawn. It's about keeping my family safe from any danger, especially when someone threatens them." I said. The sight of her shaking, tensing as if she wanted to blurt out crying makes me even madder.

"Cousin Bolo, I'm scared he might break in the house one day and hurt me or Mommy" Dawn frantically shouted as tears rushed down her blushed cheeks, knowing she wasn't supposed to tell me what happened.

"Come here," tears falling from my eyes, I grabbed her as tight as I could to calm her down. She continued saying, "Mommy, she told me not to say anything, but her ex-boyfriend Rick, pulled a gun out on her", she paused, tightening her grip around my waist then added, "He-he said that he'd kill Mommy, then smacked her so hard that she almost knocked over the fish tank", she said as she buried her face deep into my arms.

I yelled, "WHAT THE FUCK!" I then pushed Dawn and told her to get the hell out of the way. She balled into the fetal position and began shaking uncontrollably.

Before I left the house, I promised Dawn that Rick will never come near them again once I get my hands on him, or my crew get their hands on him. I hit everyone as I was walking out the door…steaming! Rule number one, never lay a hand on my family. Rule number two, never, ever threaten my family or there will be serious consequences.

Chapter Two

"Jay", Kev said, pulling his mask down over his face. "This nigga should be alone unless he got one of his bitches up in here with'em."

"Shit, Kev" Jay chuckled. "You aint gotta say no more because whoever up in this muthafucka gonna get it, one way or another." They both slipped into their black leather gloves. "So let it be."

Dressed in all black, they began slowly creeping along the side of house 817 on 23rd street. A perfect night for the soon-to-be dead man and whoever was in his company. Rain danced mercilessly on parked cars as it poured from the sky. Thunder roared while lightening illuminated unseen places making them a shadow in the dark. Once they were within inches of entering their target house, Kev, reached for the door knob and said, "Bolo said this nigga always leavin his door unlocked."

"What an easy one this will be", Jay said, smiling.

Buck is wearing only boxers and a t-shirt with his head buried deep into a few lines of coke. He kept tilting his head backwards from the rush he was encountering. Laughing at the Tom & Jerry cartoon her was watching, suddenly he noticed a slight movement from his peripheral vision. Trying to reach for his glock, he heard Kev say, "Move another inch muthafucka and you're brains will be all over this pretty maroon carpet you just installed."

"H-How you nigga get the fuck in here?" Buck's eyes widen, imagining his brains all over his new carpet.

"H-H-How the fuck you think we got in here?" Jay imitated Buck as he stood over top of him. "Door was unlocked nigga. And you won't be needing these" he said, as he dumped the shells from Buck's gun.

"T-Tell Bolo I-I got h-his money." He motioned to a few scattered hundred dollar bills beside him.

"Fuck the money Buck, where's the product? Where's the fucking product?" Kev stepped forward pressing his gun into Buck's temple.

"C-Come on K-Kev and J-Jay man," tears began to pour from his eyes, "don't d-do this."

"Your time is ...."

"Buck, honey, who are you talkin-----------AHHHHHHHH!" a half-naked woman screamed while dropping a clear plate of crack cocaine

"BITCH, SHUT THE FUCK UP!" Kev shouted, blowing Buck's brains all over the place.

"Noo--------"

Mission accomplished. Jay and Kev made a call to Bolo for further instructions on what to do next.

"Peace, I'll see you guys tonight. Tomorrow night rather."

Sunday evening. 6:30p.m. Sophie stood standing in her doorway, smiling at me while checking her watch and shaking her head, then looking back at me. "Perfect timing" she said, standing behind a dark colored screen door still smiling.

Chuckling, "Punctuality remember" I stepped out my car.

"Smart ass"

"Thank you" I begin admiring her silk-laced above the knee burgundy robe she was styling. Her hips protruding like a like a wild flower; jet black hair pulled back into a ponytail. Manicure hands, nice polished toenails matching her robe. The sight of her breast, plump with erected nipples, fell under my eyes.

Laughing, "Bolo, get your ass in here and have a seat", she began, stepping backwards with her robe completely wide open. My manhood quickly stood at attention noticing her perfectly groomed public hairs while fantasizing what's behind door number one.

"Beautiful place you have here."

"Thank you Bolo" she said, stepping up to me. "Please excuse my appearance, I've just gotten out the shower." Whispering as she grabs my hand.

"You're excused Sophie" I muttered, not knowing what her next move may be.

Moving closer she says, "Let's get shit straight Bolo, I wish that I could give you this pussy right now, but you won't ever get it baby so you can search this all you like" as she pulled her robe above her butt cheeks. She patted them once then kindly walked over to the stereo singing Luther Vandross, *Amazing*.

Once she disappeared into the kitchen, she blurted out, "Why don't you give yourself a self-tour, Bolo?"

She didn't have to tell me because I was already on my way upstairs. I can definitely say that Sophie has great taste in making a house into a home. Her bedroom was decorated with a wooden, queen sized canopy bed set, black satin sheets with ruffle gold trimming, and curtains to match. 36" plasma television and bathroom decked out in all pink and white satin.

Back downstairs, I made my way into the kitchen to see how she was coming alone with dinner. The beauty of Sophie standing over the stove cooking her homemade gravy, for the fried pork chops that'll be served at dinner, spinning her around would make a man's dream of paradise. "Don't even think about it, Bolo" she said, her mind telling her that I wanted to caress her ass.

"What?" I replied, laughing than stood by her side.

"Don't what me. Would you like a glass of wine?"

"Yes, please." I begin pouring two glasses of wine while she switched from the gravy to stirring the mac and cheese.

"Teaser" I added, pushing her slightly away from me then walking to the back door.

"You'll never get it darling. I'm way too dangerous for you."

"Actions speak louder words."

"Someday smart ass, I'll show you how dangerous I can be." She rolled her eyes and motioned for me to tie her robe again.

"Whatever, Sophie" backing away from her. "Can I use your phone, please?"

"Here" she yelled, snatching a black cordless phone off the wall. "No bitches, Bolo" laughing.

"Taking the phone into the living room, I kicked off my shoes, making myself comfortable. I noticed a black Smith & Wesson 9mm handgun resting in a tinted glass case in Sophie's cream-colored entertainment center. '*Oh well, if she says she's dangerous then I'll put her ass to the test one day.*' I mumbled, searching numbers on the phone to call Cousin Dawn. The way Sophie pulled my dick out my pants and began massaging it to a full erection blew my mind. Her body language and facial expression spoke loud and clear to me. *Damn I want you inside of me, let alone suck on it and feel you cream all over my face.*

"Hello" Dawn's voice burst through the headset, waiting for someone to answer.

"Hey girl, why you're not answering your cell phone?" I asked, sipping on some wine.

"Cousin Bolo, it's in my bedroom on the charger" she replied, laughing with someone in the background. Will you take me to the mall to get a better phone, please?"

"Dawn, we'll go to Christiana Mall tomorrow to buy you a better phone. One that has a more powerful battery to go along with it." Pushing me away lately, she quickly yells downstairs to her mother to pick up the phone.

"Hello"

"Hey Auntie, you're okay?" I asked.

"Yes" she paused, "Why you ask me that?" her voice faded away, echoing the troubles that she's going through with her ex-boyfriend Rick.

"Can't I ask my favorite aunt how she's doing, or if she needs anything?"

"Yes" she replied laughing, thinking that I don't know what she's going through.

"Nephew," she said, "You just gave me two-thousand dollars the day before yesterday, let alone giving Dawn some money" her voice came alive

"Well tell Dawn that I'll be picking her up tomorrow at eleven o'clock, so please be ready."

"Okay, love you nephew" she said.

"Me too, cousin Bolo" Dawn blurted out.

When I was almost six or seven years old, my Aunt Ann took me to some hospital to visit my mother. Once there I heard my mother ask my aunt to take care of me, meaning until she got out the hospital bed. I couldn't understand how she just closed her eyes and never opened them again. That was before she said that she loved me with her whole heart. Now, Dawn, she's my favorite cousin, very beautiful. Her fine, straight black hair touching the back of her butt cheeks, so light in color you would think that she was a white woman. She had hazel eyes, sexy, petite, 120lb frame, and she could be shy and emotional.

"Woman, when is that food gonna be ready?" I asked Sophie, smacking her ass.

"Stop, Bolo" she replied, spinning around. "You better be patient and go answer my door, if you don't mind" she placed her hands on her hips, eyes rolling up and down at me.

Doorbell ringing repeatedly. "Hey Bolo", Crystal and Bianca smiled at me as they quickly rushed into the house pas me.

"Who is that baby?" Sophie asked, yelling from the kitchen.

"Your two crazy girlfriends from the Golden ballroom" I replied, sitting back down to enjoy my glass of wine.

"Delaware says you're crazy Crystal." Bianca rolled her eyes. Her attitude distinguishing a smile.

"Bitch, what are you talking about? Who is?" Crystal arrogantly shouted, standing next to Bianca with hands on their hips.

"Hey my two bitches" Sophie spoke softly, her girlish tone of voice gave way when she walked into the living room closing her robe. The second she came walking into the room, immediately Crystal and Bianca turned to me, rolling their eyes, then focused back on Sophie.

"Wa-wait a minute, bitch, what the fuck you two been doing in here?" Bianca pointed at me and Sophie then crossed her arms, rolling her eyes at us.

"Bitch, Bolo is not, will not, lick, suck, nor stick his dick inside of this good, wet pussy…ever" she replied, walking over to massage my shoulders.

Laughing, "We heard that girlfriend" they both high-five each other, while looking at me.

Bianca gave me the eye of a woman that get what she wants, pretending to fix her blue jean skirt alarming me that her pussy is already moist. *When I get the chance Bolo, this pussy will be all in your face.* Crystal traced her lips with her tongue, *I can't wait to get you all alone big boy, cause what I have for you, you'll fall in love with it.* While nodding her head at me.

"Bolo honey, you won't mind if Crystal and Bianca have dinner with us, will you?" Sophie asked, pouring me another glass of wine. "Cause you ain't getting none anyways."

"Girl, what's up?" Crystal asked Sophie, then walked over to the stereo to change the music to contemporary jazz.

"Nothing, but what I have planned for my baby, Bolo" Sophie paused, nodding her head at the smell of the aroma that filled the air. She sat on my lap.

"Excuse me you wanna-be love birds." Bianca interrupted. "I have to use the ladies room."

"Me too" Crystal blushed, following Bianca to the stairs.

Shaking my head, "There's only one bathroom up there" I responded sarcastically.

"I'll wait until she comes out, smartass" Crystal shot me a killer look, then went upstairs.

"Damn, she told you, Bolo" Sophie laughed, watching her girlfriend disappear into mid air.

"You better get her Sophie." I said.

"I will honey, as soon as I finish in the kitchen." She said, chuckling, then skipping into the kitchen. Back in the living room I began making myself more comfortable once again. There was something different about her entertainment system. Something missing. Her gun. It was missing from its case. I paid it no mind. Poured me another glass of wine, then dazed into some more cartoons.

Somewhere around a half hour to an hour, I awakened from a daze and suddenly felt death in the mist of the evening air. I noticed their eyes begin searching my masculine body slumped deeply into an unconsciousness. All sporting army fatigues with black silk bandanas covering the beautiful texture of their skin. Black, Diehard working boots on and ready for battle of some kind. Each of them wearing well-fitted black gloves to match their boots.

"Damn" I mumbled while watching Bianca brandish her polished chrome .357 magnum with a black grip handle. Crystal by her side with her raised sawed off shotgun just below her right breast. Looking to my left, just slightly over my shoulder, I noticed Sophie with two black Smith & Wesson 9mm handguns pointed directly at me as she emerged from the kitchen. That explains the missing gun. "What the fuck is happening here" Once again, I mumbled under my breath while reaching for my black .40 Caliber Glock.

"You make another move Bolo, and I'll take your head off like a bowling ball rushing to hit its target," Sophie's voice began to grow closer to me. *Make our day* is the expression they all had in their eyes, as if to tell me to just move one more time. *Damn It*! I grunted, as I gently placed my hands on the throw pillow that was wedged between my thighs.

"Damn, what nigga?" Bianca mocked me as she noticed my heart jumping out of my navy blue Versace sweater.

"What should we do with his punk ass girl?" Crystal asks, cocker her still raised sawed-off shotgun she held tightly in her hand. Had I known their weapons weren't ready for action I would've blown all three bitches heads clean off their bodies.

"Let's see now. He runs eighty-five percent of the cocaine distributed here in Delaware. We don't want his money. Maybe he gave an order to kill someone that I truly love and miss. But we didn't invite him here for that," says Sophie.

Wondering who she was inquiring about, I interrupted, "Invite me?"

"Shut the fuck up Bolo, or shall I call you Mr. Delaware's Top Captain," she squatted in front of me while pressing her nose against mines. The warmth of her double mint breath made me melt where I stood. Her eyes became so seductive and I could tell she wanted to just cut me loose. "Your sorry ass is in for a rude awakening." She head-butted me then walked toward the kitchen. How could this be happening I asked myself? "Bring his ass to the kitchen table" Sophie ordered, then walked into the kitchen.

"Poison he will get" Crystal reached down to grab my gun while pressing the shotgun against my manhood who already ran for cover.

Bianca yelled, "Get up now!" Once I reached the kitchen I notice a candle lit dining room full of red roses and a strawberry aroma scent filling the air. Right now my thought is to run towards the kitchen door despite all the gunfire that will be trailing behind me.

"Have a seat muthafucka" Crystal pressed down on my shoulder so hard I bounced back up to meet the butt of her sawed off shotgun pounding hard on top of my head. Searching the dining room table that's decorated with expensive Chinaware, there was a setup for four with about two to three ounces of a white, powdery substance resting on a plate in front of me. In my mind I begin interrogating myself of what I slipped on or forgot in the past to get me in this life threatening moment.

"What the fuck is happening here?" I asked. Shaking my head at the three of them with their guns still drawn on me.

"Didn't I tell you," Crystal gripped my jaws, "to shut the fuck up!" She gritted her teeth.

"Oh yes, you will be eating your fuckin dinner baby" Bianca slammed a silver antique spoon down on the plate as the white substance jumped up at me, ready to terminate me as well. They all began encircling the table, stopping one at a time to whisper a threatening death sentence into my ear. Then Sophie stopped dead in her tracks. Bianca on her left and Sophie stopped dead in her tracks. Bianca on her left and Crystal on her right, guns marking their targets.

She said, "Sorry it has to be this way baby, but let me formally introduce you to my protégé's. Crystal and Bianca." She paused as they laid their weapons on the table. "Just to let you know how dangerous we bitches are." All laughing as we all watch Sophie sit on my lap facing me.

"So you're the mastermind of all this shit, huh?" nodding her head. "You planned this whole damn thing. Didn't you?" I asked, as our lips met for the first time. My mind telling me that I seriously need these beautiful, dangerous bitches in my organization while I shook my head smiling.

"Yes baby, and your ass was so damn scared, Bolo" we embraced not wanting to let go. Here comes my manhood back into action probably smelling the sweet aroma of Sophie's pussy as he rises to the occasion. "

"Crystal and Bianca, shame on the both of you" I retrieved my glock from Crystal.

"What can we say", taunted Crystal, placing both hands on her hips.

Sophie kissed me slowly, "She's so wet down there Bolo, that she can feel him slowly rising baby. On top of that, she don't like me wearing panties."

"How wet is she?" my tongue searching her lips wanting to know more about the wetness of her desires.

"Wet enough that neither your dick nor your tongue will get at her."

Winking her eyes, Bianca said, "Are you ready to eat your poison, Bolo?" as she prepared a toast for us all.

Chuckling, I asked, "Do you really think that I would come alone?" I paused. "Let alone die all by my lonesome?" Then I forced my gun into her waist.

"Huh?" Sophie looked deep into my eyes as a teardrop slowly trickled down her blushed cheeks and in between her nicely exposed cleavage.

"Yeah! Now you two make one more fuckin move and I'll blow her insides all over this fuckin room." I motioned for Crystal and Bianca to put their guns down. *I should have blown your fuckin brains out myself while I had the change you bastard.* Crystal was thinking as she motioned her lips then rolled her eyes at me; as if looks would kill, I would've been dead long ago.

Stuttering, "B-Bolo, w-we were j-just p-playing with y-you" Sophie said. Her body trembling uncontrollably.

"WHAT?! NOW SIT YOUR STINKIN ASSES DOWN!" I shouted to Bianca and Crystal with Sophie's gun that I grabbed off the table. They quickly sat down at the table placing their hands on top. "Y'all ain't shit!" I yelled, daring one of them to even breathe a word from under their breath. There was a silence as the phone began ringing, leaving an echo of many whispers chasing an unseen ghost.

"But Bolo..."

Laughing, "Don't Bolo me you scared asses. Let me formally introduce you to my dedicated warriors." I snapped my fingers twice as we all watched Ty, Jay and Kev surface from the kitchen with their weapons drawn. Sophie rolled her eyes and sucked her teeth. While burying her head into my chest she asked in disbelief,

"Bolo, how'd you manage to do that?

Nodding my head slowly up and down. I asked, "Remember when I went to the back door to get some fresh air?" eyeing all three women shaking their heads.

"Oh my gosh, yes!" Sophie grabbed my ears while sucking my bottom lip.

I stood up to say, "That's when I left it unlocked for my notorious crew." We watched as my boys returned their guns back to their waist side.

"Girl, he's damn good" Bianca and Crystal blurted out proudly.

"You mean he's a good professional" Jay stood next to Bianca.

"Whatever" Crystal laughed.

"Professionals we are" Kev bumped shoulder to shoulder with Crystal. Ty just stood back in the corner laughing at all of us.

"All this time Bolo, you had us thinking that you were scared and here you are with back up like the President of the United States" Sophie sat back down on my lap.

"Now Sophie, Bianca and Crystal, the shit y'all was putting me through in the living room... I was about to have my men come in while y'all had me on the couch, but Sophie baby, you had them escort me into the dining room." I said, nodding my head and smiling. Everyone laughed.

"Damn it!" Bianca yelled, her head moving slowly to the sound of jazz fading in the background.

"Ladies," I interrupted while leaning back to allow Sophie to work her magical tongue in my mouth. "Will you please get more chairs?" allowing her tongue to move slowly around my neck as we all prepared for a delicious meal.

That next day, Dawn and I had a nice day spending time together at the Christiana Mall. After dropping her off, I headed on over to my stash house on Tenth and Bennett street. Cruising down Fourth Street I began wondering about the portrait of Sophie and Miguel hanging on the wall of her family room. My mind began racing a hundred miles a minute. *Is it that she knows that I used to work for him knowing that I was to protect his family? What was her business with me? Was it to join my organization and bring it down to the ground? I'll definitely hire my own investigator to see who she really is and see what she wants with me.*

Stash house.

"Ty and Jay" I paused, shaking my head at the sight of them wearing no protection gear. "No masks or gloves gentlemen?"

"Hell yeah" they yelled in unison, eyes opened wide at the sight of my presence.

Jay said, "We just sat back down at the table Bolo."

"Nice, nice, nice" I replied nodding my head while examining the blue wrapped packages containing kilos of pure cocaine.

"One hundred fifty five" Kev added, extending his arms openly over the table as if to be performing a magic trick. The expression I had on my face quickly ejected Jay from his chair to say, "The extra fifty-five is from the amount that we purchased and to keep us as their loyal customer."

"Well thank you, gentlemen. Now if you guys don't mind, and I know you won't, why don't you split the extra fifty-five? Then help yourselves to an extra, umm, thirty thousand a piece" I stood up smiling.

"You ain't got to tell us twice Bolo" Jay leaned back into his seat.

Kev, Ty and Jay were all satisfied with what I instructed them to do next along with a mission that had to be completed that night. The minute I jumped in my car and pulled away, my cellphone began ringing distinctively displaying a picture of a pair of black 9 mm handguns. "Hello?"

I need you to come down to the riverfront. Warehouse number four, now" Sophie's voice rising high as a kite flying through trees.

"Now?" I replied, turning onto Tenth and King Street.

"YES BOLO, PLEASE!" she shouted, "WHEN YOU ARRIVE BIANCA WILL DIRECT YOU WHERE TO PARK" then added, "HURRY UP DAMN IT." The roughness of her voice barked at me as if there was pit bulls in the back seat of my car. What's so damn important I don't know? Maybe it's one of those tricks she had up her sleeves. Turning up King Street through MLK Boulevard I noticed Bianca standing afar. Closer and closer I get, she places her hands on her hips, sporting a brown, two-piece, suede suit and shaking her head as if the President of the United States declared war on the drugs on the State of Delaware.

"What's up, Bianca?" I asked, my eyes burning from the sun ray beating off the hood of my car.

"Hey Bolo" she replied, tapping her feet repeatedly on the ground, "park next to my car please" she directed me to the burgundy XJS Jaguar which was parked next to Sophie's 318i champagne colored BMW.

Silence. Not a word was spoken as I glanced in my side view mirror watching Bianca walk up to open the driver side door for me like the polite young lady that she is. "Well, well, let's see what you ladies have in store for me this time", breaking the silence as I stepped out of my car.

Soon we entered the door to the warehouse that was half the size of a college football field, and cold as well.

"A big ass surprise, Bolo" she smiled leading the way through a small, grey, rusty door. Her walk was all about the illusion of neon catwalk and she fantasized as if there were professional photographers taking millions of snap shots of her.

"OH SHIT!" I shouted, reaching for my weapon. "WHAT THE FUCK IS HAPPENING IN HERE?" I asked, walking closer to see a medium built Chinese man sitting naked in a high gloss wooden chair. Sophie standing directly behind him, her mind seriously wandering in the in the coolness of portrayal.

His hands, feet and mouth tightly secured with duct tape. His eyes bearing down on my black 9mm hoping a slug doesn't come flying at his head. One thing for sure, we can't leave him alive knowing that he'll be a clean and faithful witness.

"Sophie...Crystal...Bianca..." I hesitated as I became closer and closer, a familiar face getting clearer and clearer to me. "What's the meaning of this?" Bianca standing beside me as I begin to get angrier and angrier.

"This whatever you want to call him, Bolo," Sophie spoke as she began punching her victim in his face, "he tried to interfere with our business. He's our enemy so he has to be dealt with!" her voice trailing through the open air of the empty warehouse.

"What the fuck business are you claiming?" I asked under my breath while gritting my teeth and shooting her nasty look. As I watched the three of them slide on a pair of black leather gloves. I began to wonder.

Grunting, I faced the so called enemy to see that he's already seriously beaten by the deep, three inch gashes on his arms, swollen eyes and busted up knees. "HANDLEYOUR FUCKIN' BUSINESSTHEN SOPHIE!" I shouted, recognizing the Chinese an as SenatorYang Wa Fu.

"Blow torch" she said, extending her hand out to Crystal while snatching a one- foot blow torch from her hands. "How's this muthafucka?" torching the enemy's knees as his muffled screams rang out.

"I'M NOT IMPRESSED! FINISH HIM OFF NOW! SHOOT HIM DAMN IT!" I shouted once again, startling them all.

Sophie jumped back then yelled, "Give me that damn gun." Rolling her eyes a me while snatching the gun out of Bianca's hand.

BOC! BOC!

"You bastard!" she yelled angrily, blowing the Senator's brains clear against the concrete column that's supporting the foundation to the warehouse. His eyes were so swollen though he managed to open them widely as if to say *I'll see you in Hell bitch*.

Later that evening while walking into my Cousin Dawn's bedroom, she emerged from her walk-in closet butt naked only to stop in front of her six foot gold frame mirror. She watched, admiring herself slipping on a pair of satin lace baby blue panties.

"Hey cousin Bolo" she spoke softly; glancing at me wile tracing her well fitted panty line

"Hey girl, what's up?" I replied as I walked over to the mirror watching her check out her abs.

"Going to the movies tonight with my girls, then out to eat at the Golden Dove. Wanna come?"

"Nope" I responded, watching her grab a matching baby blue bra. Facing the mirror once again, her medium sized breasts waiting for the comfort of her bra. Her eyes staring at me like little puppies looking for milk. '*Please let me have a boyfriend and I promise I won't have sex with him.*'

Dawn can't have a boyfriend because she's too beautiful for someone to even think about sexing her back.

"Dawn!" said Aunt Ann.

"What mom?" smiled Dawn, resting her hands on her hips.

"What's up with those tight ass jeans, Dawn?" was all she could get out. Crazy thoughts were running through her mind when she saw her daughter dressed in a pair of tight, blue jeans with a baby blue see through top and matching heels. Her long black hair dangling down her back.

"Mom, what are you gonna say when cousin Bolo let me have a boyfriend, let alone when me and my girls are chillen out in his hot tub next weekend?" Dawn replied, grabbing a thin, dark blue jacket.

"DAWN!" she shouted, watching Dawn run out the house then jump in her car.

"Well Auntie," I said, hunching my shoulders at her.

"BOLO" she shouted again as I began imitating Dawn running out the house.

Chapter 3

Mr. Smith how could you have done this to me. I've treated you like family since the very first day you took me on for counsel. Your best client, not to mention I pay you very well even when I don't need your advice. Now you want to bail the fuck out because you got into some shit that you can't clean up? Well, all I can say is thanks for your representation and now, your services are no longer rendered.

Lawyer, client confidentiality huh? I can imagine Mr. Smith being in the comfort of his new family...the Delaware River.

Later that night, around 2:00 a.m. I asked Sophie to meet me at the corner of Parma Avenue on a somewhat deserted street behind Bowl-A-Rama in New Castle. Just near a few manageable houses that are kept neat while some are abandoned and waiting to be claimed. A full moon illuminating the darkness of the sky as a falling star dashes beneath its glow. Suddenly emerging from around a five-foot tall bush as instructed, Sophie greeted me with a warm peck on my cheeks.

"Hey Bolo, you asked me to meet you here?" she asked. Her voice was rattled from the coldness of the night.

"Sophie, I have something that I need to show you." I replied, sensing the tiredness in her uncomfortably raw voice. "We need not mention any names when we enter."

Her mind began roaming about as if she stepped into a dream cloud. Her silky black hair was pushed back neatly into a ponytail supported by a black ruffle hairpin. As if in uniform, she wore black jeans and a black, long sleeved cotton shirt with her gun holster under her arm. "Got it." She said while pulling her gun slowly from her holster, looking directly into the clean, black sky.

Click, click!

The sound of Sophie's Smith & Wesson cocked ready for action as we slowly began creeping quietly into a light grey, small abandoned house. "Oh my God baby," she sighed, turning to face me. "The whole family?" she asked, wide- eyed, hands concealing her mouth.

"You asked me what I could do for you," I replied gruffly taking her by the wrists. "This is what I do when I want to do it, no witnesses, no compassion, and no nothing dammit." Gritting my teeth, I leaned forward and planted a kiss softly on her forehead.

"But- but the whole family?" she asked once again. Her girlish voice crackling gave way the teardrop reaching the corner of her eye.

"You don't do anything until I tell you, you understand me?" I avoided her question, looking pass her teary eyes and onto the family I kidnapped. The crazed look in Sophie's eyes when she saw a black family of two male adults, a female adult wearing only a pair of brown cotton panties along with their two teenagers dressed only in pajamas; I can see why she's so damn disturbed. The whole family was duct-taped and blindfolded, ready to be executed one by one over one man's jealousy.

"Yes," replied Sophie, releasing a quick sigh. "Why's there a tin bucket of water under that one?" she pointed.

"It's not water…its acid."

"Oh shit…acid!" she yelled, shaking her head knowing what's about to go down.

"Calm down baby. He disrespected me, my family, and most importantly he abused and threatened to kill them as well." I landed a hard right punch to my main target's chin and the grunting sound that Rick made when I punched him repeatedly made both teenagers piss their pants. "Why don't you do me a favor, baby?" I asked, standing behind both teenagers. "Take these two into small room because I don't want them to hear what's about to happen." I pounded down on both their shoulders watching them jump from the closeness of my voice.

"I'm on it." She replied, tapping them both while untying the main knot that bonded them together.

"Hey you," I called walking over to Sophie. "I kidnapped the family to show you that if I want a family, then I'll have a family." I smiled, whispering in her ear.

"I get the point now, sweetie." Sophie replied, smiling at me while slipping on her black leather gloves. "Come on you two."

"By the way, I don't harm innocent people." I said, removing the duct tape from the couples' mouth.

A frightened family, the Malloy family, became discomfitures when I gathered them all I their living room and told them that they were being kidnapped. Both of their sons and their daughter tried to make a quick run out the kitchen door, but was caught by a few of my men that were waiting for them as well. Their parents practically begged the hell out of me to take their lives instead of the lives of their children.

"Whoever you are, thank you so much for saving our lives and the lives of our kids," her voice wept as if her kids were already released.

"Like I said lady, I don't harm innocent people," I said while placing an old rusty chair in front of them. "You two listen very closely, you hear me?"

"Yes, Yes," they replied, jumping at the slightest of Sophie's touch to remove the duct tape from their hands.

"I told them that it wouldn't be nice if they tried to escape," said Sophie, walking over to Rick. "They said that they wouldn't think about leaving their parents behind."

Back to focusing on the couple whom separated from my main event. I watched Sophie begin punching on Rick as her own human body bag. Very petite, about one hundred and forty pounds, she sure knows how to handle her business. I can imagine Sophie beating on a man her size because he'll never have a shot at the title. Suddenly she stopped, pausing at the sound of my voice.

"Listen very carefully because I'm about to place the both of you back there with your kids," I said as I sat back down in the chair. "In one of the corners you'll find your clothes, so please feel free to put them back on. Then I must warn you that if any of you attempt to walk out either of those door, you will be immediately shot and killed."

"Yes sir."Thy agreed in unison.

"AND!" I shouted, "Once you hear three knocks on the door," I paused, knocking on the wooden chairs three times, "Your family will be free to leave fifteen minutes after and not one minute before."

"Oh my God, Sir, thank you so much."The woman cried out, her voice ricocheting throughout the coldness of the abandon house.

Standing up pushing the chair away, I motioned Sophie to escort the two back to the room where their kids were waiting. I instructed the couple not to enter any door, especially the one with the red tape on it, and then left them one hundred thousand dollars for their troubles.

"What are you smiling for girl?"

You have an emotional side to you darling," said Sophie half teasing.

"Yeah, so what!" I replied, "I don't harm innocent people. Now lower his ass in the acid please."

Rick began to scream, muffled only slightly by the duct tape. One day Rick decided to leave my aunt for another woman, then later on that month returned to her house threatening her and my cousin Dawn with his gun. For a man of Rick's character, a short, good looking black man of two hundred pounds with broad shoulders, he could have had any woman he wanted. His hands would lay a woman flat out on her back in a split second if he punched her.

"Oh shit!" Sophie yelled, "Look at his eyes bulging out!" She watched me snatch the blindfold off Rick's face. "He knows he fucked up now," she added, stepping back to my side. The sight of me made Rick shit his pants.

"You ever slashed someone's throat?" I gritted my teeth while staring at Sophie, then slashed Rick's throat from left to right. Then I had Sophie knock three times on the door to let the family know to wait fifteen minutes and not a minute before, so they could go home.

Once we were outside and Sophie was jumping behind the steering wheel of her car smiling, she paused to say, "I'll call you when I wake up later on Bolo. Maybe you and I can have brunch together." She held the palm of her hand to her cherry lips while blowing sweet kisses into the cold morning air. I watched Sophie slowly pull away from me shaking her head as if to say, *you are so crazy boy*.

Later on that morning it began pouring down rain just as I pulled into a driveway on Silverside Road, in front of a beautiful, burgundy, stone front, two-story home. Complete with a two car garage, it rested on a well-manicured 1.5 acre lot.

"Welcome to the queen's castle." Constance smiled, pleasantly holding the door open for my arrival. "Was it hard to find?" she asked.

The heavy rain began pounding down on my head harder as I managed to reach in the back seat of my car to retrieve my black briefcase. "Hello princess," I replied, closing my door, then running towards the house. "Hard to find but easy to see." I stepped inside and turned to eye the one-piece, pink and black satin nightgown stopping just above her knee. Her neat, blonde hair dangling behind her back.

"Bolo, please excuse my appearance."The expression she gave when we made eye contact was telling me to be patient and I might get what she wants me to taste. She smiled.

"You have breakfast yet?" I asked, taking my mind off the pleasure she wants to secure me with, then opening my briefcase for the business that I came here for. Constance walked over to her entertainment system, picked up a cd cover, placed the cd in their place and walked away.

"No" she said.

"Then we'll have pancakes, bacon, and eggs."

"I'd like that"

She looked over her right shoulder smiling and singing along with Etta James' *At Last*. I can imagine what was on her mind when she glance at my hairy chest displaying from my unbuttoned Versace blue shirt.

"By the way, why don't you make yourself at home!" She yelled, her voice carrying through the music of Etta James. I made my way upstairs and helped myself to a self- tour of what Constance called, her castle. Nice cherry oak canopy bedroom set dressed with butterfly silk lined with matching drapery covering her windows. Making her home my home was what I will do by starting a nice, hot shower.

One hour later, I was singing along with Freddie Jackson's *You are my Lady.*

"Must be nice in there, Mr. Jones," Constance whispered, peeping through the pink and black striped shower curtain. She glanced down at my manhood and shook her head at the sight of running water trickling down my muscular body.

"Yes, it is naughty girl." I replied laughing while stepping out the shower, watching her facial expression as her eyes wandered from the top of my head to sneaking peeks at my nine inch swinging dick between my thighs.

"I'll see you when you come back downstairs." She quickly backed up, grabbing the doorknob, then ran to wherever she was heading. Her body almost went into complete convulsions. She ran out of the bathroom like a marathoner losing their course. Back downstairs relaxing and listening to her mix C.D, I watched Constance walk into the living room, then quickly turn back around into the kitchen.

"Bolo!" Constance called, her voice softly echoed as she walked back into the living room still shocked from the sight of my nakedness. The thickness of my thick, wet, soapy nine inches still lingering in her mind. "Would you like to join me with a glass of 1983 Jordan red wine along with our delicious breakfast?" she asked.

Sighing, I tilted my head back slightly over my left shoulder to see Constance standing a few feet from me, holding an antique silver tray with golden brown hotcakes, bacon and scrambled eggs. Sitting on the tray next to our steaming food, two glasses of red wine. What surprised me the most was the sparkling of her antique tray, but the lace trimmed, see through, silk, hunter green night-gown that she changed into.

"Ah- sure," I muttered, searching her seductive curves supported by her vanilla cream toned smooth legs. Her nipples were raised to the occasion making themselves well known.

She walked up to me.

"Why don't I have a seat next to you?" her ass cheeks began hopping in slow motion as she whisked past me. The fragrance of her expensive White Diamond perfume, instantly hypnotized my ability to focus on what business I came here for. *Fuck!* I silently screamed inside. I looked at Constance; she looked at me than suddenly she smiled, breaking the tranquility of silence.

"Baby are you okay?" she asked, preparing my food while slicing the hotcakes into bite sized pieces. *HELL NO!* I screamed inside, once again noticing the tip of my dick emerging from its where about.

"Yes, I'm okay Constance." I quietly answered, squirming and trying to keep my dick from fully creeping into view from beneath the navy blue terry cloth robe that I borrowed out of her walk in closet. Her body language; our facial expressions definitely spoke out telling the both of us that we better get this brunch over with. My dick completely emerged as warm, sticky fluid began covering it. Constance displays a diminutive smile while searching it position. Her moistened lip prepare her tongue for whatever action it may come upon.

"You will be when I finish with you," her voice low as she spoke, lowering her red candy lips around all nine inches of my hard slab.

"Damn," I moaned, coaching her to perfection, massaging her head as I ran my tender fingers through her silky blonde hair.

"I want more," she announced, her hazel eyes gazing up at me. "Give me what I want and now." It was like her body felt my cry for more pleasure as the warmth of her pussy lips seduced the stiffness of my manhood.

"YES –YES!" We both shouted, closing our eyes while experiencing every wall that she had erected being torn down.

As I begin to walk out the front door, Constance smiles at me while tossing her CD case and singing along with Aretha Franklin's *NaturalWoman*. While cruising down Concord Pike after being stuck in a traffic jam, the Sun decided to peak out from the afternoon's grey clouds. McDonalds is crowded, which I believe is being robbed. Police cruisers along with unmarked detective cars made it pass just in time as an officer stops traffic to direct it to a secondary street.

My cell phone rang, "Hello."

"Hello Bolo, it's me Bianca."

"Bianca, you have such a lovely voice," I said, my smile raced to display the whiteness of my bleached teeth. Thinking about·what I would do with her alone, "What's wrong?" I asked.

"Thank you sweetie, everything is fine on my end." Her voice sent a signal to me that she had time to talk. "Where are you?" She asked, probably wondering where R. Kelly's *Bump and Grind* was coming from.

"I'm in my jeep stuck in this damn traffic on Concord Pike, coming from a business meeting with my banker." I paused, thinking about how Constance and me worked up a sweat all over her house.

"What's up?"

"Sophie asked me to call to you to see if you were still going to the Crystal Palace tonight? Also is it possible that you could come over to my place to see what's wrong with my television?" She asked, her voice sharpens my ears as if I were auditioning for the handy man job.

"Bianca I just pulled into my driveway. So can you please click over then call my house phone on your three-way please?"

"Sure" she said.

I ran into the house almost falling down in a huge puddle of water. That tells me that my yard keeper is not on his damn job. "Comcast just can't do anything you ask them to do" I said, throwing my briefcase on my coffee table anticipating her next words cautiously.

Bianca was silent, carefully choosing her words, "No. But you'll get the job done correctly. You can give me the pleasure that I've been looking for Bolo. Not to mention once you're inside me, I promise you that she'll come flowing like the Niagara Falls." She began laughing so loud you would think I walked into a comedy club.

Bianca. Listen to you girl" I laughed along with her. "What do you have on?"

"Face it, Bolo. She doesn't have to know about a damn thing about what you and I decide to get into. She's not giving you the pussy so you might as well come and fuck me and experience all you can experience." Her voice, her tone, seriously caught my attention.

"Listen to you" I said, stripping butt naked to go take another shower.

"I'm due. I'm definitely backed up with so much cum inside me…"

"Bianca, Bianca," I quickly interrupted. "Actions speak louder than words. I'll be there tomorrow to give you all that you need and want."

She yelled through the phone. "THANKYOU!"

The thought of Bianca going behind her girl Sophie's back. Her voice. Niagara Falls. The whole nine yards, I began tapping the number pad on my cordless phone wanting to tell her to meet me somewhere secluded. *Damn!* I silently whispered. If Bianca had envisioned about me, then I could only imagine how Crystal was feeling, especially the way both of them watch me. I got dressed and headed to my Aunt Ann's house.

"Hey cousin Bolo" Dawn said as she sat down on the love seat. "Where are you going looking all sharp?" she asked.

"Me, my crew and a few chicks are hanging out tonight at the Crystal Palace" I said while sitting down next to her. "Where's your mother?" I asked, grabbing the TV remote out of her hand.

"She went to Atlantic City with three of her girlfriends" she said, smiling calmly while snatched the remote back. "You know they found that top notch lawyer of yours in the Delaware River."

"So what? I was gonna fire his ass anyway. I believe he was turning his back on a few clients of his."

"What are you gonna do about another one?"

"Well Cousin Dawn," I turned to face her. "I don't need any more of these crooked ass lawyers to back me up on shit."

"I heard that" she said, turning away from me to the television set.

Standing up to leave I said, "Look, I have to get going to pick everyone up by nine o'clock." I handed her five one-hundred dollar bills.

"Thank you cousin Bolo. And please be careful tonight." Dawn said, kissing me on both my cheeks, then escorted me to the front door.

Later on that night at the Crystal Palace on Philadelphia Pike, a long line awaits our arrival as the white ultra-stretch limousine comes to complete stop in front of the black stone faced building. Highly noticeable, *Crystal Palace* in huge, neon letters on the front of the building. An astronomical crowd of men and women of all nationalities waiting patiently to enter into the world of fantasies. A place where dreams come true.

"Hey Bolo sweetie!" an unidentified Chinese woman spoke to me while planting a wet kiss on both of my cheeks.

"WHAT BITCH…AND?!" Sophie gritted.

"Calm down baby." Laughing, I quickly grabbed her hand yanking her backwards.

"Bolo, my man," said Chris. "Good Evening." He glanced back at Crystal while rubbing his bald head.

"Watch it Chris cause looks can kill you," I said, tightly grabbing her hand. Whispering lightly, "She'll kill you at the drop of a shiny silver dime."

Chris sat down, shocked and lost for words, not knowing what was about to come out of his mouth next. "Cat got cha tongue muthafucker!" I leaned forward screaming directly in his ear.

"Damn" his voice weakened. "How many?" he asked, stepping back while snatching his hand away.

"Seven. Make sure we get a booth for seven." I said, handing him four, crisp one-hundred dollar bills. Chris expression was telling us that he wants us the hell away from him. He quickly motioned for someone to seat us.

"Kev, will you please order seven bottles of Dom Perignon. And lots of lemon on the side.

"I'm on it Bolo." He replied, watching Ty and Jay follow behind him.

Looking back at the women all dressed in strapless one-piece dresses, I noticed the three are watching this beautiful black sista dressed in an all-white body suit. Black boots hugging up to her knees and jet black hair down to her waistline. Seductive brown eyes that will hypnotize a man in a split second. Once seated, Bianca quickly jumped up. Her body language displayed serious trouble and her hands were on her hips.

"THERE GO THAT STINK BITCH!" she shouted, eyes directly on the woman wearing the all-white body suit.

"DAMN RIGHT GIRL!" Crystal jumped to her feet. "YOU BETTER HANDLE YOUR BUSINESS CAUSE THAT BITCH AINT GONNA KEEP DISRESPECTING YOU," said Crystal.

Raising my eyebrows, I looked at Sophie and shaking my head in confusion. "What is all that shit about?"

"You'll see later on, Bolo" she replied, grabbing my arm as we headed for the dance floor.

"You're amazing Sophie, and very beautiful might I add."

"Thank you Bolo. You're very handsome also" she said, leaning back a little to admire my two-piece black Armani suit.

Kev, Jay and Ty are smiling at us as they make their way back to the booth with all seven bottle of Dom Perignon. Crystal blending with the crowd, spinning around as if she were dancing professionally, heading straight to Sophie and me.

"May I cut in please?" Crystal asked.

"Sure girl," Sophie responded, unwrapping her hands from around my neck.

Crystal gently pressing her body against mines slowly. Her eyes searching every inch of my face, she began tracing my lips with her right index finger. Her left hand bracing my neck as if she wanted to force her black licorice lips on me.

"Thank you for everything Bolo" she said, kissing my chin while sneaking her wet, warm, tongue slowly into my mouth.

"You're welcome Crystal" I said softly as we danced a few songs away.

The Deejay cut in, voice echoing over the mike, "I like to give a shout out to my man, Bolo." He said. A bright, white spotlight burst into action on Crystal and me. "DELAWARE'S TOP CAPTAIN!" he shouted. Everyone stopped dancing to follow the bright, white spotlight. A few of the people on the dance floor whispered. *Oh shit, that's Bolo, Delaware's Top Captain*.

You Muthafucka. A silent scream came raging from my firing eyes as if I was ready to blaze my target.

"Come on Bolo" said Crystal, grumbling while shaking her head dangerously. The deejay noticed the fire spitting out rapidly from my eyes as he quickly eliminated the spotlight then disappeared into the darkness of the on stage curtains. His mind completely discombobulated.

Later on that night as the club began closing, the owner of the Crystal Palace stops me and my crew at the door. "Hey, Bolo my man," he extends his hand out to me, "I apologize for what my stupid ass deejay said earlier tonight."

"He wasn't thinking straight Carl. So apology accepted." I said, embracing him then walked off.

Once I motioned Jay, Kev, and Ty to ask the limousine driver to pick me and the ladies up in front of the building. One woman argued with her boyfriend or husband while banishing a small piece of white paper in his face.

Click. Click. I looked to my right and then to my left to see who had a gun in their hand. When suddenly Bianca dashed toward the woman wearing the all-white body suit. Gun raised.

BOOM! The gun sounds off as the woman's body tumbled to the ground. People disappearing and screaming, running in every direction that will lead them away from danger. "GET THE HELL OUT OF HERE NOW!" I shouted, pushing all three women into the limousine before it came to a complete stop.

Chapter 4

Two hundred kilos of pure uncut cocaine well packaged and ready to be distributed all around the city of Wilmington Countless stacks of money that definitely needs to be vaunted. Scales to weight the product. Glassine backs ready to be sealed. Chrome .357, sawed-off shotgun and .44 caliber glock all resting on a ten foot wide cherry wood antique table. Not to mention a brand new black baby Oozy with two- one hundred shot banana clips begging to be fired at will.

The three of them, Kev, Jay and Ty all protected by the light-blue mask and latex gloves, taking extra precaution not to inhale the aroma of the cocaine, nor allowing it to even seep into their pores. *Why was the front door unlocked?* I asked myself.

"Bolo, what up my man?" Kev asked, standing up to acknowledge my presence. His eyes wondering about Jay and Ty, then back to me.

"Good morning gentlemen" I spoke, searching for an eye connection between Jay and Ty.

One thing I've learned about the men in my organization, with their honesty and loyalty, they will never ever lie to me. Holding or hiding anything. I can tell by their body language and most importantly the motion of their eyes.

"Hey Bolo" Jay grunted, head and chin resting on his chest. His eyes were directly on the weighing scale with not a drop of residue laying on it.

"Bolo" Ty took in a hard swallow. "What's up?" he asked. His sunken body at sitting at the tip of the chair. Once he moves, he's on the floor. His peripheral vision positioned and waiting for my next move or any sounds to come screaming out my mouth.

"Well fellas. What do we have here?" I asked, smiling while placing my 9mm Smith & Wesson in front of me.

Breaking the code of silence is what I've also learned about the men in my organization, only to steer away their guilt. They probably were wondering how I got into the house without the motion detector alarming them of someone's presence.

Laughing. "Bolo, we never let the money get high like this" Jay said, cracking a smile at me.

"Yeah, he's right Bolo." Ty responded, shot me a smile while hoisting himself up in the chair. Since everyone is relaxed of my presence we all begin counting the stacks of money on the table.

"You're definitely right Jay and Ty" I replied, lighting a vanilla flavored Black & Mild. "Kev and Ty, how are my perimeters over in the Bucket projects?"

"Everything is everything, Bolo" said Ty reaching into his coat pocket, pulling out a Cuban cigar.

"Bolo, we also added a few more people to our squad" said Kev. "Especially the corner house on twenty-third and Locust Street." He removed his mask and gloves, then covered up the two hundred kilos knowing that this money need to be counted first.

"Damn, you guys are good. How ya'll manage to pull that one off?"

Kev definitely felt the tension rising. So he had to say something that I wanted to hear, to get my mind off of me asking why was the front door unlock, especially with two hundred kilos, guns and countless money wide open on the table.

"Yeah" Kev smiled, knowing he had more to say. Her name is Trina, Bolo." He nodded his head watching Ty and Jay drop their shoulders.

In silence they waited patiently, for the next sound to come out my mouth, then I asked, "Trina. Tell me about this mysterious woman named Trina?"

Ty quickly jumped to his feet smiling, then said, "Bolo, she came to me and Kev asking could she be of any help to us and our organization." He watched Jay walk over to the stereo system with a C.D in his hand. "Basically a stash house is what she was saying. Helping with locating the police while they're in the area." He sat back down.

"We said damn right" Kev said, leaning back while twisting the top off the Hennessey bottle. "So she gave us a quick tour of her house. We told her that we will be paying her rent and all the utilities that she has, plus." He took a sip from the bottle. "Some good money in her pockets every week, then gave her a nice one thousand dollars for starters."

Well excellent job my men have accomplished for the organization, recruitment as well. Very impressed, I am. Keys to Trina's house, weapons stashed there. I was delighted to hear that Trina didn't do any drugs. Family...no drugs, money, women, nothing will come between my men and our organization.

"Jay, my man. Why don't you give us a report for the eastside?" I asked.

"Here's what it is Bolo, Ty, and Kev." He walked back over to the table and sat down. "The chick that I was telling y'all about last week. Deja's her name." He motioned to Kev to hand him the Hennessey bottle. "Well she's down with everything. She even has her girlfriends making money for her while handling my business." He blew into the air feeling the vivid sting from the Hennessey. I laughed out loud.

"Perimeters, Jay?"

"All perimeters surrounding Ninth and Clifford Brown Walk are locked and secured," he said.

Something one has to learn in this business of selling drugs is that you have to pay very close attention to what each individual is talking about or there will be lives at stake. It can cost you your life as well.

A few hours later we all began drinking champagne, talking about guy stuff. We talked about how Bianca just walked up to someone and blew their brains clean out their head. Sophie, and how she killed Yang Wa Fu, the Senator for the State of Delaware. Crystal, we have yet to witness what she's capable of doing.

"Bolo!" yelled Jay. His eyes grew the size of the United States silver dollar.

"OH SHIT!" we all shouted, reaching for our guns as two masked me suddenly burst into the dining room with their weapons drawn.

"DON'T MOVE MUTHAFUCKAS!" they shouted, pointing their guns directly at our heads.

I looked at my men; they looked at me searching for a solution out of this shit. My organization, my crew, our lives. How could this be? The front door that I left unlocked, never reset the motion sensor and never once had I checked to see if the back door was unlocked.

"Move and I'll blow your fuckin brains all over that coke," a voice screamed. Another one emerges from the kitchen. "You'll be a dead man snorting all you can snort," he said, making his presence well known. Although, which one of us he was talking about, I don't know. I asked myself, *What the hell is happening here?* No one knows about my stash house but me and my crew. One lesson I taught my men was not to fear no one, always stay calm in the most dangerous of situations.

I slowly began moving my eyes about to Jay. He's too drunk to even say a word, both hands on the table. Ty finally dropped both stacks of one hundred dollar bills he was counting. Kev, he's shaking his head wishing they would focus on something so he could make a fast break to his back up gun taped to his back. Me, I'm distraught right now. So I say, "What the fuck is this?"

"Shut the fuck up Bolo, cause you can get it first!" The one that came from the kitchen pressed his gun heavily against my temple.

"You bastards" I whispered.

"One more word out you, punk ass, and your boy here gets one" he walked over to Ty, then shoved the gun into Ty's neck.

Time to negotiate. "Look. Y'all can have all this shit. The money. The coke. Take it all" I said, looking at the three of them.

"Mr. Delaware's Top Captain" he said, coughing, then placing another gun to my chest. She only wants a kiss from you" Bianca laughed, removing her mustache.

Kev yelled, "Bolo, you had this shit set up the whole entire time!" he watched Sophie and I share a passionate kiss.

"Damn Bolo, you had us," said Ty, bending over to pick up the money that fell on the floor.

Jay laughing and nodding head. “You’re on point, Bolo. Definitely on point” he said.

“Good morning gentlemen” Sophie, Crystal, and Bianca said in unison while shaking their heads. Silence. Everyone’s eyes are now focused on me knowing that I have a few words to say. The women all standing behind my men.

“Kev, Jay, and Ty” I said, walking over to turn the music completely off. “Consider this a lesson learned fellas. The last two times I came here, you guys had the back and front door unlocked.” I sat back down at the table, “So I came up with a plan to scare ya asses and to teach you niggas a valuable lesson as well.”

“Y’all niggas have all this money and coke on the table in the fuckin open, with both doors unlock” Crystal smacked all three upside their head. “Are yall fuckin crazy?” She laughed rolling her eyes.

Sophie said nothing but watched Bianca’s next move as she says “Yall fools have a death wish or something” Bianca also rolled her eyes, then pushed all three of them, almost knocking Kev out of his chair. Then, after I had my talk with my men, the ladies all joined in on some champagne while discussing a trip to Atlantic City tonight.

Later that afternoon, I arranged for a limousine to pick me, my crew, Sophie and her girls up at Kev’s house over on Twenty-six and Washington Street at about eight o’clock tonight. For now I have to run a few errands. But first, check on my aunt and cousin Dawn.

My aunt Ann is sitting down on the floor with her back up against the ruffle brown sofa constructing a puzzle in the form of a city or state. My cousin Dawn is nowhere in sight. “Hey Auntie” I said, sitting down next to her but on the sofa.

“Hey nephew” she replied, looked up at me, smiled, then back to working on her puzzle.

“Where’s Cousin Dawn?”

“Right here cousin, Bolo” Dawn said coming from upstairs. You know they found Rick’s ass in an abandoned house with his throat slashed. His feet submerged in acid" she sat next to me.

"Really?" I said, leaning back, placing my left ankle on my right knee.

My Aunt Ann took a deep breath inhaling, then exhaling. "We don't have to worry about that bastard anymore" she said. Her voice had a sign of relief as it floated through the air."

"What do you mean by that?" I questioned.

A teardrop rushed from her eyes and quickly made its way to the puzzle she was constructing. "Bolo, he hit me, pushed my baby and threatened to kill us both with his gun." She rested her head on my leg and started crying. Her cry was so uncontrollable that she fell asleep right on my leg. I looked over at my cousin Dawn as a tear slowly moved down her cheek and pulled her close to me to tell her everything is alright. Then I comforted them both while she fell asleep.

Leaving the house, I watched as Dawn's friend Rhonda started to walk in. Since both my Aunt and Dawn were both asleep, I wanted to ask Rhonda a few questions. One was why she was inquiring about me.

"Hey Bolo" Rhonda's girlish tone of voice softened my ears. "How long they been asleep?" she asked, staring at my aunt on the floor and my cousin Dawn on the sofa asleep.

"For about a good twenty minutes or so" I said, closing the door shut. "Dawn told me that you were inquiring about me. Care to answer that. Now that we're face to face with each other?"

"Yes, I was Bolo" she said. "Come follow me and I'll show you what I've been inquiring about." Rhonda led me right upstairs to the guest room. She tapped a red button on the CD player then walked back up to me while singing Barbara Mason's *Yes, I'm ready*. Pulling down my pants she dropped straight to her knees.

I left Rhonda back at my aunt's house smiling and day dreaming about how she'll have all nine inches someday soon tearing her walls down. Once I returned to my home sweet home, the place I can come relax and get away from my surroundings, I checked my phone messages before jumping in the shower. I had a perfect evening ahead with my crew, Sophie and her girls.

Constance called so I'll see what's up with her for tonight.

My house phone rang. "Hello?"

"Hi handsome. How are you doing?" Constance asked.

"Fine, Constance. I was about to call you," I said, undressing while making my way to the shower. "What about you?" I asked.

With a short laugh she said, "I need to be in your arms right now Bolo. What are you doing?"

"I'm about to jump in the shower. Me and my crew are all headed to Atlantic City in about another two hours."

"Why don't you meet me in my office Monday morning and I'll make your stay very welcomed" she laughed.

"Cool because I have more business proposals that I would like to address to you." I stepped in the steaming hot water, being careful not to get the phone wet. "Some real estate investments that I need you to check into for me." I paused. "What do you have on Constance?"

"I have on some burgundy laced satin panties that I want you to invest in when you get to my office." She continued to blow air through the phone while turning up the volume to Adina Howard's *T-Shirt and Panties on*.

"Really?"

"With the matching high-heel pumps that you brought me."

"Constance"

"See ya," she whispered.

"CONSTANCE!" I shouted. The phone went dead. I looked down at my manhood, threw the phone on the floor, and turned the shower knob to the cold position.

Later that evening, we all headed down to Atlantic City to gamble and have as much fun as we could have. We all toast individually to one another. Less than two-hours of being at the Taj Mahal Hotel & Casino, Sophie won five thousand dollars. Then she and I took a nice stroll on the beach under the twinkling stars.

"I'm ready to go home, Bolo" said Sophie, resting her head on my shoulder.

"Call Kev and the rest of them, and tell them to meet us back at the limousine while I take this call, please." Sophie walked ahead of me knowing that I needed my privacy in taking this incoming call. "Hello."

"It's me cousin Bolo" Dawn said. Her voice was hoarse. I glanced up into the darkness of the sky. Hoping that what she has to say isn't bad as a falling star dashed beyond.

"Dawn, what's wrong baby?"

"They were just shooting around here." Her soft- spoken words carried fear through the phone.

"Who was it Dawn? And what were they shooting at?" My voice touched Sophie's ears, as she quickly turned around, confused.

She inhaled then exhaled. "Shooting up in the air. None of them were form around here" she swallowed. "But they were in an all-black van with no windows on either side" she said. "One of the back windows was shattered though."

Twenty minutes later.

"I'll be there in an hour or so, Dawn" I opened the door for Sophie as she stepped into the limousine.

Once back in the limo, I explained to everyone what was going on around in my cousin Dawn's neighborhood. I asked them to be on the lookout for the black van that she described to me. Once we were on the Atlantic City expressway everyone began falling asleep to the sounds of James Brown's *Please, Please, Please*. Sophie was sound asleep, cuddled under my right arm. Bianca curled under my left arm, placed my hand on her soft, milky breast. Kev, Jay and Ty also sound asleep.

Crystal. Her eyes bulging while following Bianca's hand disappearing into my pants. She shook her head to hold back any sound that wanted to exit her mouth. She covered her mouth as she watched her manhood slowly work its way into Bianca's wet, warm mouth as a miracle was performed.

Leaning, I tilted my head backwards and mouthed to Crystal, *You're next baby*. As I closed my eyes, she whispers, "I'm ready."

Chapter 5

Lights are dimmed. The Miracles, *You really got a hold on me*, quietly floated in the background. Flat on my back I laid butt naked between black, silky sheets, soaking a cherry flavored Black & Mild and taking small sips of Dom Perignon. Suddenly at the blink of an eye, she appears, standing at the doorway of her bedroom. Sporting a full-lengthed, brown terry cloth robe with white laced trimming, her sandy brown shoulder length hair blended perfectly with her caramel skin tone.

"Don't move," Sophie said. "So we meet again."The strap from her robe came loose, displaying her bare naked body. Fine curves, trimmed pubic hair and nipples pointed straight out; her eyes were as sexy as they want to be. "You miss me?" she asked.

"I've been waiting for this moment for so long" I replied, watching her slowly move around the bedroom lighting scented candles.

"Will you take care of her tonight?" Sophie asked, standing at the bottom of the bed at the base of my feet. She smiles while tracing her lips with her manicured finger. Eye-to-eye we read one another's body language.

"Yes" I said.

"It's all yours, Bolo" she said, kissing me. She slowly glided her warm, wet pussy over top of my nine-inch hard dick.

Seconds into making love Sophie pulls back from kissing me, holding my waist as I held her. Her expression told me to give all that I had to give her.

She shouted. "FUCK ME!" her girlish cry echoed through the sound of the music playing Jackie Wilson's *Lonely Teardrops*. Slowly, we fell asleep.

Later that night I wrote Sophie a virtuous letter telling her how much fun I had being in her company. I then went over to my Aunt Ann's house, took a nice hot shower, then jumped in my cousin Dawn's bed since she wasn't coming home that night.

"Nephew is that you?"

"Yes Aunt Ann. I'm spending the night." I said.

"Talk to you in the morning." She said peeking into the bedroom, wearing only a blue towel wrapped around her body smiling.

"Nasty ass" I yelled at her, then ducked under the covers.

"Back at you" she shouted. Her voice met someone else's as they began laughing out loud.

Hours later my cousin Dawn came walking into the bedroom not recognizing that I was laying in her bed half sleep; let alone butt naked. She only had on a golden set of panties and bra.

"Cousin Bolo, I didn't know you were here" said Dawn, while sitting down on the bed next to me. "Let me tell you all about my girlfriend, Brandy." Sucking air between her teeth then crawled into bed with me.

"I'm naked girl."

"So what? We're cousins."

I shook my head at her, "What about Brandy, Dawn?"

"Ya know, you fucked her cousin Mercedes." She leaned back, and then rolled her beady eyes at me. "Mercedes was telling Brandy all about you. Brandy ran to me and asked can she come over and meet you." She submerged beneath the covers while resting on her left elbow.

"Wow" I responded as we continued to gossip about all of Dawn's girlfriends. I kissed her on her forehead then off to sleep we went.

8 a.m. and the morning sun rays beat upon Dawn's face awakening her to my presence. She quickly jumped up, running to the window blocking the cool wind from bouncing off the walls to her half naked body. "Good morning stinky" I said, smiling at her while pulling my shirt down to my waist. "You slept alright last night?"

"Yes. Is Mommy here?" she asked, stretching and yawning her way to her seven-foot, oval shaped, gold framed mirror.

"No. But she said to be here at the house by noontime and she'll be right back." I grabbed my jacket while slipping on my right shoe. "That chick

Brandy called too."

"She did?" Dawn turned around to face me while pulling her bra off, then slowly pulled her panties down to her ankles. "What she say cousin Bolo?" Her eyes glued on my lips, waiting patiently for the next sound.

"Call her when you get up." I turned away from her, about to leave the bedroom. "And who wants to see ya naked ass?" I added.

"We're family. You know you like my fat ass" she ran and jumped on my back. "I love you cousin Bolo" she added, as she bit my neck then kissed my cheek.

"See you, Dawn. Call you later." I tossed her back on the bed, smacking her ass. She smiled, laying there for a few seconds not noticing her legs were spread wide open. Quickly she yanked the two-tone comforter over her body.

Just a few blocks away from my Aunt Ann's house is where one of my stash houses was locate. Straight don Tenth and Bennett Street. Kev and Ty should be almost finished up on whatever kilos remained. They were dealing with the very last kilos of cocaine when I walked into the dining room.

"Hey guys. What's up?" I asked Kev and Ty while waiting for Jay to spring from the kitchen, basement or make his way to acknowledge my presence.

"Hey Bolo" they answered. Both stood up as we high-fived then embraced.

"Where's Jay?" I asked.

Kev sat back down and looked up at me. "His girl Tamika wanted him to take her to her mother's house because she didn't feel like driving today" he said, reaching for the pack of glassine bags from the corner of the table.

"Bolo, when you get time, Trina wants to see you," said Ty as he grabbed his coat and looked at Kev.

"Amillo said that the next time we score, he's giving us an extra twenty-five on top of the two hundred that we're buying from him." Kev smiled.

"Cool. Give Dexter a call for me please and let him know that I'll be over in Riverside shortly."

"Gotcha" Ty responded, nodding his head, and then punching the number keys on his cell phone.

Minutes after driving down Eleventh Street, I looked ahead to see the Wilmington Police set up a roadblock for whatever reason. I began slowing down so I could place my weapon cautiously under my seat. Two officers motioned me to stop just to get a glance in my car, then off I headed over the Twelfth Street Bridge to the Riverside projects to see Dexter.

Fucking stick-up boys. Broad daylight. It takes a lot of guts to stick someone up with a gun in broad daylight. On top of that in front of KFC. I secretly placed Dexter into the Riverside housing projects to get close to the so-called penny-pushing drug dealers. Very soon, my product an only my product will be flooding these dirty projects. I turned onto Twenty-Ninth Street from Governor Printz Blvd and made another right onto Claymont Street. Dexter smiled at me as I pulled up alongside him.

"Bolo," he said, opening the driver side door for me. We looked down the street at a white woman emerging from her dark blue Toyota Corolla. "Everyone is coming to me for weight now."

"That's what's up Dex," I said. We both watched an ambulance wail pass us, continuing towards Vandever Avenue. "I definitely have plans for Riverside." I said.

"I'm down for whatever," he replied, shaking his head at the white woman biting her nails and staring at the both of us.

"Dex" she whispered. Her cry is calling for some attention. She continues to tap her feet impatiently.

"Your services are needed," I said. I held my door open as I watched the white junkie look away from me. "Handle ya business lil bro and be safe."

Dex said, "Peace." He walked away mumbling a few bad words at her. She jumped back from the roughness of his voice.

Since I'm on this side of town I might as well make a stop over Trina's house to see what's on her mind before I head home. I figured I'd call Sophie to see if she's down for dinner tonight.

Standing in her doorway smiling, Trina began slow dancing to the sound of Roger Troutman's *Computer Love* while patting her ass with her left hand. I rolled all my windows down until the song ended. She rolled her eyes at me then began unfastening the string to her tan colored sweat pants. Now she had my full- undivided attention.

"Hey smiley face," she said. "I thought that would get your attention." Janet Jackson couldn't even compare to what Trina was packing. She watched me roll my windows back up.

"Hello Trina" I said, feeling horny. "Are you trying to seduce me?" I asked. Closer and closer I walked towards her standing in the doorway. I watched as her sweat pants slowly crept down her heart shaped thighs. Pink laced cotton panties with little designs on them peeked through. I managed to step behind her, tracing her panty line while working my fingers into the warm wetness of her pussy.

Low voice, eyes weakened, she slowly turned around. "No" she moaned. "You're seducing me Bolo." Her mouth opened. We begin kissing and sucking her body fluids off my finger until we couldn't taste it anymore. Pushing away from each other, we were both sedated.

"You were all over the channel six news last night." Her eyes motioned me to sit down.

"I'm not impressed, Trina" I said, holding her hand as she sat next to me blushing. Her Toni Braxton hairdo gave away that my men were taking very good care of her. The grey police scanner she held in her hand signaled that there weren't any activities happening at this present moment.

"How's everything?" I asked.

Looking at the scanner, she said, "To tell you the truth, Bolo. They haven't been around since about seven o'clock this morning. Probably wondering why no one is in sight when they do come around here."

"Good. We need to keep them in suspense, chocolate." Her skin tone the exact color of a Hershey's chocolate bar. Eyes a native Chinese would be jealous of. "I see my men, Kev and Ty are taking good care of you." I said. She walked over to lock the front door. Then she glanced at me while stepping onto the first step and nodded her head. I followed.

Once in her bedroom, both naked, she gently laid on her back; legs positioned hovering above her shoulders. The only words that came out of her mouth was the sound of Linda Jones' *Hypnotize*.

Red Lobster on Concord Pike was so crowded I had to pay a black couple two hundred dollars to take their place in line. Sophie gave me a dumbfounded look then cracked a smile. She was willing to wait anyway rather than face the wind chill to find a car. The waitress grabbed two menus and motioned us to follow her to the smoking section.

"Would you like anything to drink?" she asked.

"A bottle of 1980 Merlot red wine please." I said, watching Sophie sit across from me speechless. "Would you care to address your proposal to me?" I asked.

"Yes ma'am. We'll have two slices of your delicious chocolate cake. That will be all." She paid me no mind about the question I asked her. I watched as she kindly carried on a conversation about the expensive pearls wrapped around the waitress' neck.

"Thank you" she said, "I'm sorry, Bolo." She reached over to tag my chin. I watched this small, petite black toss her food smack in the waiter's face then walk away smiling at him.

"Did you just see what she did to him?" I asked Sophie.

She totally ignored me, something I definitely disapprove of. I was thinking about having her and her girlfriends join my organization, which would be excellent.

"Bolo. Me and my girls would like to join your organization." Sophie said.

"WHAT!" I shouted. Everyone in the smoking section had their eyes on me.

"We want to join." The seriousness in her voice. Her voiced softened. She took a sip of her wine and waited for my next response.

"Join my crew. Me. My boys. My organization?" I bit down softly on my bottom lip waiting for the waitress to place our chocolate cake in front of us both. "What can you and your so called friends possibly handle in my organization?" I asked.

Dangerously she said, "We can handle whatever comes our way, Bolo. We're willing to abide and follow any and all rules that you down on us." Her expression was so serious that I felt a chill rush through my body. Everything around me went silent. A baby in the background crying her heart out broke the silence between Sophie and me.

"What?" I asked, lighting a Vanilla flavored Black & Mild. I took a long puff then blew it straight in the wind to form o's. "Three bitches that think they're gangsters, want to join my organization. Bolo's crew." I flicked the ashes on the floor then shook my head.

SMACK! As the sting registered on my face, she whispered. "You bastard. You call me a bitch one more time, Bolo. I'll forget we ever met. Let alone sucked and fucked. Now try me." Her voice in defense. Her well-manicured hand submerged back under the table. Leaned back, she rolled her eyes.

"I apologize for calling you a bitch which slipped out." *Click-click*. "But if you ever, ever lay your fuckin hands on me the wrong way, Sophie. I'll blow your pussy away as if I never stuck my dick in it. Let alone ate it." I said angrily, pressing my gun against her pussy print.

Sophie and I soon apologized to one another, then continued to enjoy our chocolate cake. She went into her black velvet purse and showed me a picture of her standing next to two Spanish men. One was my ex-boss, Miguel Lopez. What was her motive? Her purpose for wanting to join my organization?

"Well. Will you consider my proposal baby?" She asked, massaging my throbbing jaw.

"Yes." Just then my cell phone rang.

"It's Tamika," she said.

"Baby what's a matter?"

"Bolo, please come to Christiana Hospital. Now!" she screamed through the phone crying.

"FUCK!" I shouted. "Emergency at Christiana Hospital."

"Go, Bolo. I'll have Crystal and Bianca come pick me up, then we're coming out to the hospital," said Sophie as she kissed my cheeks while she punched numbers into her cell phone.

Minutes later while heading south on Concord Pike trying to find the most efficient route to Christiana Hospital, I began wondering what Jay could have gotten himself into this time. Jay has his own private contracting business which he oversees twenty-one employees. One day last summer, he accidently punctured his right leg with a powerful nail gun. Tamika had to rush him to the hospital; luckily she was there at the time. I pulled up to Christiana Hospital.

Tamika immediately ran up to me crying as soon as she noticed me stepping off the fifth floor elevator. Black mascara streaked down both her cheeks and astronomical amount of blood covering her well fitted, dark blue jeans and her white, ruffle trimmed blouse. The expression on her face spelled out death. I embraced her and tried to calm her down, wanting some answers to the questions I was about to ask her.

"Calm down Tamika. Calm down and tell me what happened." I said. Wiping the mascara off her cheeks, she rested her head on my chest as we sat down. She began telling me what went on with my man, Jay.

"Jay honey, are you about to go somewhere?" Tamika asked.

"Yes baby, I have to handle some business just around the corner!" Jay yelled back from the kitchen.

"Don't be long please cause I want you to take me to my mother's house."

Next thing I knew, Bolo, we were both outside. I asked him to hurry back. That's when I asked him did he ever see this dark green Impala with tinted windows." Tamika said.

"Maybe it's someone that I know." Jay glanced over his shoulder at Tamika.

I yelled, "JAY LOOK OUT! LOOK OUT BABY, THEY HAVE A GUN! That's when I heard three gunshots. His body jerked then he fell to the ground. The car sped away" she said. "Then, Bolo I rushed him here to the hospital. Just before he passed away we said that we loved each other."

Passed away. It echoed in my mind before I asked, "You don't have any idea who they were Tamika, that killed Jay?"

"No. But I'll put the word out."

"DAMN IT!" I shouted.

Sophie, Bianca, Kev, Ty and Crystal all walked down the hallway shaking their heads at the sight of Tamika's bloody shirt. Each one had both hands covering their faces. The women cried as they walked straight to Tamika to comfort her at the nurses' station. I sent Kev and Ty to give my condolences to Jay's family and not to worry about any expenses. He was like a brother to me and I missed him already. My revenge on his enemies. I promised to mail their body parts to their families.

Sitting in my car outside my aunt's house, I noticed Dawn peeking out the window so I headed in the house.

"Hey cousin Bolo," she said. She looked confused, contemplating if she wanted to meet me over at the sofa. "I just heard about what happened to your boy, Jay."

I motioned her to come sit next to me. "Baby, this is expected when people live this dangerous drug life." I said.

"What do you mean by that cousin Bolo?" Dawn said. She sat next to me folding her legs in the Indian style position. I began massaging the back of her left hand while she rested her head on my shoulder waiting for an explanation about the drug business.

"Well, since you're not educated on the dangerous business that I'm in, I'll tell you what you should know. You see, Dawn. This is a serious game where people are gonna either die, get locked up or make money then get the hell out," I said.

"But I don't want you to die, cousin Bolo" she coughed. Her voice weary. A teardrop slowly fell on the back of my hand. Her body tensed. I could feel the sadness coming off her body. Two more tears acknowledged their presence as they rested on my forearm.

"I'm not sweetheart. I assure you of that Dawn," I answered.

Her teary eyes gave way the tenderness of her heart. Her fingers tightened her grip. "But you just got shot last month," she said as her voice weakened.

"Dawn. I have enemies out there sweetie, and may never know who they are. Some surface, some don't."

"But everyone is afraid of you."

"So you'll be nineteen real soon," I kissed her forehead while drying her eyes and avoiding her last statement.

Dawn whispered, "Rhonda thought that she was pregnant. But don't worry cause it was a false alarm," said Dawn, laughing at the sight of me about to burst like a balloon.

"Hey nephew. I heard what happen to Jay." My aunt said as she walked into the house.

"Mom, cousin Bolo won't let me have a boyfriend." Dawn whined, as she rolled her eyes at me. "That's why whenever he fuck Brandy, I wanna watch." She said.

"You better watch your mouth!" I yelled.

Dawn quickly ran, hiding behind her mother. "Why watch porno's when I can watch the real thing," she grabbed her mother's arms. "I'll learn from you and Brandy."

"You deal with her. I'm out." Aunt Ann smiled, pushing Dawn into me.

Dawn and I discussed her wanting a boyfriend. Which I won't agree to until she attends college and concentrates on a degree. My Aunt Ann laughed her ass off as she listened to our conversation.

Chapter 6

Saturday morning at the Wilmington Cemetery on Thirty-first and Market Street, I stood at the gravestone of Joyce Dawn Jones, my mother, with three dozen freshly cut roses. I come here periodically throughout the years to spend some time with her and have our little talks. My mother is the love of my life. Every time I come here, no matter what season of the year it may be, a tear drop awakens the soil. Wind blows alert me of her presence.

I remember the conversation my mother and I had when my Auntie Ann took me to visit her at the hospital. We walked in her room while she was lying in the bed watching television. The Kool-Aid smile she had on her face when her little boy, her only child walked in, was priceless.

"Hi mommy." My smile was so warming when she smiled back at me. Her eyes lit up like the Christmas tree we decorated the month before Christmas.

She extended her arms then said, "Hey mommy's little boy. Come give mommy a big hug and kiss." I ran so fast and jumped in bed right into my mother's open arms.

"I love you, mommy."There was a metal thing on her finger, but I didn't care because I was so safe being in the comfort of her arms. We looked at one other and fish kissed.

"Mommy loves you too, Lance." She held me so tight. I felt her heart pumping next to mines. Her eyes glued on Auntie Ann, then Auntie Ann looked at her smiling.

"Hey girl," Auntie Ann said. She walked over to my mother and planted a small kiss on her forehead.

"Look at you girl, about to drop any minute."

"Next week Joyce, and I'm naming her Dawn. Which is your middle name." She was so tickled pink when my Auntie Ann said that. They both started laughing and rubbing on Auntie Ann's stomach.

I asked, Mommy, can I have this juice please?" She blew a kiss at me while reaching to her side table.

"Yes, Lance baby." She handed me the small plastic cup then looked back to Auntie Ann. "Ann, my time is near," she said.

"Joyce, I love you girl. Stay strong. I love Lance too, with all my heart."

My mother shed a tear while looking directly in my face. I knew she was so happy and loved me so much. Then she glanced at Auntie Ann and held her hands as another tear dropped. She asked, "Will you take care of Lance for me? Watch him grow up to be a man. You hear me? I love him so much."

Those words that she spoke. I positioned myself, then curled under my mother's arm. Somehow I felt sadness and the pain she was experiencing. I looked into her eyes and said, "Mommy, I love you so much." After giving her a kiss, I laid my head back on her chest. I was crying because I knew my mother was crying.

"I love you so much too, Mr. Lance Jones. Mommy will always love you, son." At that moment my mother fell asleep. Her heart wasn't reaching mines anymore. Auntie Ann kissed my mother's forehead once again, then she said, "Joyce and Lance, I love the both of you also."

"Auntie Ann, mommy sleep already." I said.

"Yes, Lance, mommy is asleep," she whispered, softly touching my mother's face.

"I love you, mommy." I planted a kiss on her lips.

"Rest in Peace, Joyce Dawn Jones. I love you, girl." Auntie Ann began crying profoundly, holding onto me tight as she could, then kissed my mother.

That was the last time I saw my mother alive. The last time she and I said we love each other. I cried as I looked at her picture. I will never forget that day. She once told me that cancer was eating her alive which I will learn about someday when I became much older. Joyce Dawn Jones passed away when I was six years old.

Looking back at the memories she and I shared, I bent down to kiss her gravestone. "I love you, mommy" I cried. Her picture as well, embraced her heart, then I placed the beautiful fresh roses against our memories.

Later that night at the Brandywine Regal Cinema on Naamans Road in Claymont. I accompanied Brandy and Dawn out to see a movie. "What are we here to watch, Dawn?" I asked.

"I have no idea cousin Bolo." She replied. Her eyes searching a group of boys walking from the video arcade.

"Brandy, do you have any idea what we're here to watch?" I asked, turning to face her.

She answered, "Not at all, Bolo."The sweet sound of her voice complimented her eyes sizing me from head to toe. "I came here for something else."

Once at the concession stand, Dawn begun smiling at the group of boys standing in line ordering food and winking their eyes at her. "What the hell are you looking at those pissy boys for?" I asked. Muttering directly to her face.

"Cousin Bolo, gosh" she turned away. Her girlish voice gave away her embarrassment.

"Gosh, my ass. What the hell y'all lookin at?" I asked, yelling at them.

They all backed away from the concession stand, raised eyebrows showed they recognized who I am. "Oh shit," one yelled, taking another step backwards while almost tripping on the others. "That's the dude that was on Channel Six last week. They labeled him as Delaware's Top Captain" he said. They walked so fast you would think they were holding a walk-a-thon at the Cinema.

Finding our way to the last row in the back of the theater. Brandy sat on my left side while Dawn on the other. "Cousin Bolo when is Jay's funeral?" Dawn asked, eating her butter popcorn than sipping on some soda.

"This Monday coming at the Cornerstone Fellowship Church on Lea Blvd, Dawn." I said. "The one in the back of the McDonalds on Market Street."

"That funeral is going to be jammed pack" said Brandy, placing her hand on my leg.

"My man Jay was well known, loved, and respected by many, Brandy and Dawn." I said. "But hated by so many that couldn't have what he had."

The theatre grew silent. The dark shadow of the movie attendant whisked by while checking to make sure everything was running ok before exiting.

"Cousin Bolo, you told me that just a few weeks ago." She leaned forward to nod her head at Brandy. "By the way, Brandy and I decided that we're gonna go to Jamaica to have some fun instead of Las Vegas," she said, smiling and continuing to nod her head.

"Girl, we are gonna have so much fun. I can't wait." Brandy's voice ricocheted, startling Dawn as she jumped out her seat.

"Bitch, like the fun you're about to have with my cousin Bolo" said Dawn, squirming in her seat, positioning herself for whatever was about to happen.

They stared at each other for a moment, silently speaking to each other, not noticing the movie had started. A kissing couple shared an intimate giggle. Brandy rose, quickly maintaining her composer while pulling up her ruffle black skirt. *I can't believe what is about to happen here*. Brandy bending down reaching into my pants, then pressing her walls slightly on my dick.

"BOLO, YES!" she shouted. Her warm pussy feeling the hardness of my dick while we experienced each other's climax.

Money morning came in the blink of an eye. Here I am, me and my organization standing at the front door of Cornerstone Fellowship Baptist Church. Dressed in all black, we stood ready to view my man, Jay's body. I noticed a tear fall from Dexter and Kev's eyes to the sound of, *It's so hard to say goodbye to yesterday*.

Walking up the aisle seemed like forever. People all dressed in black, a few crying, and some wiping their lonely tears away. Slowly, I paced to the casket with me in the middle, Kev and Dexter in front, Felix and Ty behind me. Many eyes are searching our presence as we begin viewing the body. Some are nodding their heads in assuage of the familiar faces. *Jay is asleep.* I kept telling myself, knowing reality hadn't set in.

I planted a kiss on both cheeks, than his forehead, on the coldness of his lifeless body dressed in black. "Jay was like family to them all. That one right there with the dark sunglasses on; he's been on Channel 6 News numerous times." A woman called out.

Slightly looking over my left shoulder while tilting my glasses below my eyes, searching for a ranting harsh voice. My eyes blazed to two black leather hats tilting, trying to cover their raging voices. "Girl hush, you're too loud." Her companion, a huge black woman quickly looked away from my dangerous stare.

"Oh my God, they call him Delaware's Top Captain," a child of about seven or eight yelled.

Finally, we all paid our respects to Jay's family and his girlfriend, Tamika. "I promise to you and your family Mrs. Watson that I'll finish the bastards who done this to him." I whispered softly, embracing his mother. She proclaimed a loud cry knowing that what I said, I meant by the seriousness in my tempestuous voice. That day was our last and final moment with our brother, our friend, our Family Jay.

Once outside, an all-black van slows down. Reactively, we all reach for our weapons as the van with no windows on the side sped away. "That might be the van my cousin Dawn was describing to me a few days ago. The one that was around her way shooting in the air." I said, as we watched them make a right turn on Market Street.

"Bolo, we'll definitely be on a lookout in case they try something else stupid," Kev said stepping out glancing to his right, than to his left making sure the coast was clear. "Damn, can't they at leave us alone during the time of our loss!" He yelled, distressed as a black, unmarked police cruiser approached.

Both detectives' eyes were directly on me. Harassment is their specialty. A marked Wilmington police cruiser cruised on pass while both occupants shamefully shook their heads. "You know the drill, Bolo. Get the fuck up against the car," shrilled voice, the driver quickly jumped from his vehicle.

"Y'all go ahead and get in the car. Let me deal with these clowns." I said, nodding my head, a gesture of dismissal. They all entered my car paying the ignorant detectives no mind.

"That's right muthafuckas, stand down" his partner Herald said, his voice watching my men.

Tough guys. One day both of them will bow down to me. Their wives will become my whores. Their generations will all sell my product on the streets of Wilmington. "What's the meaning of this?" I asked, placing both hands on the top of their car's dusty hood.

Frisking me, a voice answered, "Listen up, Bolo. Listen carefully. We need money and you're the only one that can provide what we need." Desperation saturated the morning air. The sun heavily raged at the top of its peak. Green leaves blew from a nearby tree teasing the wake of their cries.

"What could you muthafuckas do for me that neither my men nor myself can't do?" I asked sarcastically.

"Provide you with anything you like. We can find the things who whacked ya man, Jay" the driver said, grabbing my black 9mm Smith & Wesson from my waist, then rubbing his shaven bald white head.

They had grabbed my attention so tight, my heart pumped in more blood then it usually pumps. "How much?" I asked.

"Ten thousand a piece will begin a well perfect relationship between us," his partner nodded his head at the beauty of my weapon.

"When and where, muthafuckas?"

Placing my gun back on my waist, he said, "Next week, we'll throw ya up against the car, then tell you where to drop the money off. When you deliver the money, that's when we'll begin our search to provide you with all you need."

Damn, these guys are good, but very desperate. "Now get the hell outta here, you punk!" They both yelled when they pushed me back into my car.

Driving down Lea Blvd, to get to Governor Printz Blvd. Kev breaks the silence as usual. "What was that shit all about, Bolo?" he asked, turning the music completely mute.

"Stupid muthafucka wanted to know where Jay had his money that he made off me." I replied hastily.

Sophie called my cell phone minutes later, telling me that she saw the two detectives harassing me. She and the girls were chilling out for the rest of the day out of respect for Jay and his family so I asked could she and the girls meet me later on tonight for a dedication to Jay.

Dawn sensed something was wrong with me when I walked into the house alone. Her face sunk immediately. Her voice weakened when she said, "Hi cousin Bolo. How was the funeral?" she asked, her eyes wandering about.

"I just went to view his body Dawn, because I don't like funerals" I said, looking at her following me to the sofa.

"I understand what you're going through because I was going through the same thing when my home girl got hit by a car" she rested her head on my shoulder sighing.

Aunt Ann walked in from the kitchen. "Once Joyce passed away, Bolo. You saw her laying in that casket and you told me that you'll never attend a funeral again, unless it's viewing a body," she said as she sat to my left. "I promised Joyce that I would watch you grow up to be the man that she wanted you to be."

"Thank you Aunt Ann for keeping the promise that you made to my mother," I said as I tilted my head, a tear trickled down my cheeks, giving away the memory I had for my mother.

"Bolo you were only six years old when you said that, than two days later Dawn was born," Aunt Ann said, displaying a few tears that had soaked her brownish cheeks.

Dawn was so happy to hear that her mother named her after my mother's middle name. Despite the life I now live, I believe that my mother is my guardian angel and that she saved my life many times. "Brandy can't stop thinking about you cousin Bolo," Dawn whispered in my ear. A sign for my aunt to disappear.

"Oh gosh, let me get outta here. I know where this conversation is leading," Aunt Ann laughed, literally running upstairs.

Dawn said, "I told her that Brandy was sucking and fucking you at the movies. That's why she up and ran. I told her everything, even how I watched your dick move into her."

"You are so gross, Dawn." I shook my head, "You want to go to the 70's Player's Ball with me after you come from the Jamaica trip?" I asked.

"Yes, I'd love too," said Dawn.

My aunt happened to sneak back downstairs and crept back in on the conversation Dawn and I were having about the upcoming 70's Player's Ball. They both agreed on finding the items that are needed for Dawn's night out.

That night on the cold corner of Ninth and Clifford- Brown Walk. We all came together to commemorate our homeboy, Jay, and the memories that he left here on the Eastside of Wilmington. Kev, Ty, Mont, Felix and Dexter were all standing by with a bottle of Dom Perignon in hand. Stars are dangling in the skies. Full Moon hanging above and the wind blowing with a steady right here and there.

"Wait a minute!" Sophie yelled, Bianca and Crystal trailed behind her.

"Nice to have you ladies join us," I smiled, the reflection of the moon, lightening my appreciation.

"Thank you," they all responded in unison, taking a grip of a bottle of Dom Perignon each.

Sophie reached into her black purse, looking to see if anyone noticed her. "Rest in peace, Jay" she said, kissing the picture. Her eyes in the peripheral vision position. *I wonder why you didn't have anything like this for Miguel.*

"Rest in Peace, Jay!" I yelled furiously, as we all poured out some Dom Perignon. *Why the hell did she pull Miguel's picture out?*

Silence rushed through the coldness of the evening air. "Felix my man. The Eastside is all yours, you know the in's and out's. Your surroundings you're familiar with," I said placing my hand on his shoulder. "My lieutenant within the Eastside."

Everyone honored the new position that I had given to Felix as Lieutenant. We all understood that the business has to keep moving. I stepped up a notch in security, meaning posting two men at everyone's residence.

My place won't need any because very few know where I live such as my Aunt Ann, Dawn, and my real estate agent. Augustine cut off is a very pleasant, livable community where all houses range from half-million dollars on up. Fireplace, four bedrooms, hot tub, three-car garage, with a white BMW, black Mercedes, and Grand Cherokee. I can't complain.

"One more thing ladies and gentlemen, y'all know that the 70's Player's Ball is coming up soon. I'd like for everyone to attend if they don't have anything planned for that night."

"We're there, Bolo" Kev replied, answering for all the others as they nod their heads in agreement.

Sophie, Crystal and Bianca, we'll accompany you three shopping unless y'all wanted to do that girl, girl thing that you women do," I said as we all laughed out loud watching Crystal walk over to Bianca and Sophie.

"We'll do our girly-girl thing, Bolo," she said, throwing her arms around both their necks.

"Cool." I answered. "One of the guys here will provide you with ten thousand dollars a week. Since you ladies are waiting for my answer about joining my organization."

Women. What can they possibly do in my organization, how it will benefit me and my crew. Just as I opened my car door and was about to step in, Sophie's two-door black Mercedes Benz pulled up to a complete stop. She rolled her window down to say, "Our allowance per week. Thank you," she smiled. After tapping the hood of her car, she slowly drove away as they all waved at me.

Closing a business proposal I had with my banker at Wilmington Trust Bank. Constance is a very remarkable woman. She makes sure all of my accounts are updated as well as my real estate. Just outside, my cell phone began ringing. *Crystal, I wonder what she wants.*

"Hey Crystal." I said, my attention on some chick wearing black leather pants. Something my eyes can't resist.

"Hi Bolo" she said.

"Where are you baby?" I asked, shaking my head at the sight of those well-fitted leather pants deflecting in front of my very eyes.

"Looking at your lustful eyes staring at that bitch with the black leather pants on, bending over in front of you," she said, sounding betrayed. Her freezing tap on my shoulder gave way to the frost billowing from my mouth.

I quickly turned yelling, "Oh Shit!" her warm tongue slid right into my mouth as we began sharing a passionate kiss. "Let's take a walk? I asked.

"What about joining your organization, Bolo?" she asked placing her hand on her hips.

I replied, laughing, "I'll give Sophie my answer next weekend, than she'll let you and Bianca know what's up."

"You know I love to sleep butt naked," she grabbed my arm, turning me around to face her. "So I hope you catch me in my kitchen standing at the stove cooking. Now why don't you come over at your own risk," she stepped away from me. Her kiss blew at the tip of my lips, slowly inhaling memories of infatuation.

"See you, Crystal" I smiled, replaying the chemistry we both experienced three weeks ago.

I was standing at the corner of Twenty-fifth and Thatcher Street, hanging out with Kev and Ty when suddenly a black, unmarked detective car came screaming down the one-way street.

"So we meet once again, Captain Bolo!" The driver yelled while he threw the car in park. "Get the hell up against the car."

"Delaware's Top Captain" his partner yelled.

I gestured my men to back up a few yards not wanting these begging pigs to harass them. "You bastards," I said, my hands tossed on the hood of their car.

"We have a lead on who was driving that Impala that wacked ya man Jay. Twenty grand in the green dumpster in back of Rash' convenience store on Thirtieth and Market Street," he said pressing his hand on my back as his partner watched my men standby. "We'll drive pass and throw a cup out the window to let you know the time of delivery, which will be at nine o'clock p.m. sharp.

One they told me to get the hell out their faces, they hopped in the car. I knew that they became my inside connect into the Wilmington Police Department. They both threw their middle fingers high in the air.

"FUCK YOU BOTH!" I shouted.

Chapter 7

Armani's clothing store formally known as the Fashion Place, just on the corner of Eighth and Market Street in downtown Wilmington. Everyone is minding their business while having fun selecting their genuine taste in clothes. What made the owner change the name of the store when the only new items that they're displaying in Armani Wear.

"Ladies and gentlemen, help yourself to whatever you wish. Everything is on me," I said, stepping onto a wooden box to get fitted for an Armani suit.

"Bolo, check this out," said Felix, raising a wool brown Armani sweater.

"Cool, I like that. It's formal" I replied, lighting a vanilla flavored Black & Mild.

Sophie held a pair of black, tight fitted jeans smiling at me. "Can you imagine me taking these off, Bolo? You like them, Bolo?" she asked.

"That's definitely you girl," I watched her walk over to the sweater section.

"Bolo, where is the party?" Crystal asked. "And might I ask, who's having it?"

"Crystal, I believe Sophie can answer that," we all turned to Sophie walking towards the middle of the store.

"Bitch, my cousin Carmen and her husband, they asked me to invite some friends. So I want you guys to accompany me," she stopped and rolled her eyes while smiling. Her attitude is completely out of character.

Felix, Kev and Ty are all in the front of the store laughing in the corner pretending they don't hear Sophie is telling us all, especially her sarcasm. She was catching baby feelings over a stupid question. I wondered how much criticism Sophie could handle.

"Did you ladies make any attempt to shop for the items you need for this year's 70's Player Ball?" I asked, my arms extended horizontally. Everyone completely absorbed in what they're doing. The Chinese tailor hesitant about what move to make next while raising his eyebrows at me, feeling the voice of rage vibrating th cuffs he's measuring.

Choking from the warm air she breathe, "No, Bolo" Sophie answered, stepping away from me. *Damn! Why did you have to bring that shit in question?*

"I'll tell you why, it's because the three of you are so damn lazy. We can't even come to an agreement to do what the fuck I ask you three to do!" I yelled, "Then, a few days before the fuckin party, ya stickin asses want to do all this running around trying to find the perfect outfit!" I said, snapping. A customer hurled out the store.

"Bolo, it's my…"

"Sophie, you listen to me, you listen to me carefully, the three of you" I pointe to each one. "Look at me when I'm talking to you."

"Yes," the all answered, paying close attention to me, tears flushing their eyes.

"When I want something done. I expect for it to get done immediately. Not what I ask to be executed with procrastination. Not by my men, nor by the three of you."

Sophie, Bianca, and Crystal all tears in plain view wishing that this moment would soon disappear, shoulders dropped, afraid to inhale a breath or sound. "You three better all get with my men to find out what I like and don't like," I sai, a gesture of approval to my men.

Cautiously the tailor tilts his head up at me. "Mr. Jones, extend your arms out one more time please," he said.

"YOU WILL NOT DEFILE MY ORGANIZATION. YOU WANT TO JOIN MY CREW!" I shouted. "THIS AIN'T A FUCKING JOKE. IT'S A SERIOUS GAME THAT YOU WANT TO JOIN. MY FUCKIN' INVESTMENT!" I yelled louder.

Their tears quickly fell to the floor, disappearing into the well-manicured dark brown run. "Lazy asses, your fuckin lazy, the three of you. I'll have a word with you in private, Sophie." I motioned them away from me.

Double blinking in believing that my eyes aren't deceiving me. I watched a medium built, black man walked into the store, gun in hand pointed right at me. The sharp sound of his revolver whistling. His eyes ripped through my heart. *You make one more move*. He looked to his right, behind him, to his left with nothing but his eyes staring down the gun barrels of black 9mm Smith & Wessons. Quickly encircling the enemy, the tailor rushed behind me.

"Bolo, please" he said, fearfully shaking, grasping both my legs. "Bolo, please, please no trouble."

"Shhh!" I whispered, stepping down slowly from the wooden box. I siggest you turn your black ass around and walk back out that door." I said. "Before I give an order to blow your fuckin brains all over this store."

He shouted, "FUCK YOU, BOLO!" Then ran back out the store.

"Correct me if I'm wrong" I said. They all placed their weapons back in their coats. "But isn't that the nigga from Southbridge?" I asked.

"That's him Bolo," said Kev.

"I want the Southbridge. Can I have it?"

Sophie said, "Baby you can have whatever you want." She walked over and placed her arms around my waist.

"Just say the word," said Monte.

"Thank you ladies and gentlemen" I yelled, leaving seven thousand dollars to the owner's cashier.

"DELAWARE'S TOP CAPTAIN!!!" We all laughed, heading out the store leaving the owner on both his knees in the praying position.

Later that afternoon, Brandy and I went secretly to my place without my cousin Dawn tagging along. Brandy kicked off her shoes, started stripping down to her panties and bra, walked over to the CD player and begins signing along with Earth, Wind and Fire's *Reason*.

"Make yourself at home, Brandy" I said, opening a bottle of red Merlot.

"I'm already on it, Bolo" she replied, as she tossed her silver satin panties and bra at me. "Half hour, meet me in your bedroom" said Brandy as she patted her ass than vanished to her comfort zone.

My house phone was ringing off the hook but I paid it no mind and headed on up to my bedroom to wait for Brandy to arrive.

"Who was that on the phone?" asked Brandy as she walked into the bedroom, hair in two thick braids, chocolate skin tone naked as she climbed into the bed with me.

"I looked at the caller ID box and it was Dawn."

"She's not here, so why don't you handle your business, Bolo." She held my waist while coaching my manhood nicely into her tender, warm, wet pussy.

Brandy and I initiated the second round while grooving and grinding to the Motown sounds of the Miracles, *You really got a hold on me*. Brandy screamed out my name, BOLO! I grasped her waist, she exploded, I exploded, we both exploded enjoying the highest level of that two human beings can endure simultaneously.

Two hours later.

Dawn walked into my bedroom. "Both of y'all are so damn nasty, it's a shame." She said, shaking her head dishonoring the position that Brandy and I are in.

"Girl, what the hell are you doing here?"

Brandy interrupted, "It's okay Bolo, because the bitch missed the whole entire episode, especially the grand finale," she laughed, covering the both of us up.

"Cousin Bolo. I don't believe you fucked this bitch without my being present."

"Dawn, I'm sorry honey," I said. "This wasn't your party, it's ours."

"Whatcha lookin at bitch?" Dawn said, sucking air between her teeth, watching Brandy head out the bedroom. "Bitch."

"Aww, you missed all the excitement and positions," Brandy said while laughing, peeking back into the room.

"You!" Dawn yelled, turning to face me. "I knew you were up to something cousin Bolo. You weren't answering your cell or your house phone," she said, sitting down on the bed next to me.

Dawn and Brandy continued to curse each other out as they left my house together. Brandy bringing Dawn up to date on what happened between us this afternoon. I took a quick shower than called Sophie to let her know that I was coming over to talk to her about what happened at the clothing store today.

Finally I arrived at Sophie's house. "You made it. Come on it," Sophie said, holding the front door wide open for me.

"Thank you, Sophie," I smiled, placing my keys in my jacket pocket. *Next time let me use the damn door key that you gave me.*

She handed me a glass of wine. "Bolo, I apologize for not taking Bianca and Crystal out shopping to get outfits that we need for the 70's Player's Ball" she said, motioning me to have a seat. "I take full responsibility for all that happened, it's completely my fault and not Crystal's or Bianca's."

Her integrity I admire as well as taking all the blame for them. The question still remains embedded all over the city of Wilmington. *Why hadn't Sophie mentioned my former partner Miguel Lopez, who she was embracing in a portrait hanging on her living room wall? What's her intentions in really wanting to join my organization?*

"Sophie, you and your girls want to join my organization. I have no problem with that," I said. "But the three of you will follow my orders. I accept that your showing good faith, your integrity as well. I will not allow this to happen again or there will be consequences."

She positioned herself in the Indian style position while facing me. Her hair pulled back in a ponytail. She wore a pink flower nightgown pushed up above the waist line displaying her inner thighs, with no panties in sight. "Bolo, Kev and the rest of the guys explained to us what you expect and don't expect in your organization" she said, smiling at me and peeking between her legs. *It's yours whenever you want it baby.*

"Thank you Sophie," I said, watching her light a cherry flavored Black & Mild for me. "That was a quick and courageous response that all of you done at the clothing store downtown today. I admire such enthusiasm, action taken especially you, Bianca and Crystal who were on point with my men."

"You're welcome," she blushed. "You know that I have your favorite Louisiana cake. Would you like a piece?" Sophie asked.

"Yes please. And stop trying to butter me up."

"Bolo, I'm not buttering you up, smart ass," she stood, smacking my shoulder. "You want me to microwave it baby?"

"Please do, darling."

"Weeee!" She yelled, spinning, then jumping to run into the kitchen.

Joining my organization is a very serious and dangerous task. I was very impressed with the ladies' actions. It's what I expected of them when the gunman stormed into the clothing store. I watched Sophie come back smiling with a huge slice of cake for us both. "I'm back sweetie," she said, handing me the cake as she sat back down Indian style position. *You can have anything you want, Bolo.*

"Now, why were you ladies crying, Sophie?"

"Bolo. You literally, mentally kicked our asses verbally. And definitely gave us a piece of your mind."

"I hold no punches, and meant every word that blazed from my mouth."

"Bolo, we both seen what each other is capable of doing," Sophie said, swallowing the last piece of cake.

I asked, "Your point is what?"

Leaning back resting her head on her throw-pillow, displaying all that's between her thick thighs. Closing her eyes imagining me diving between them. "We both seen what my girl Bianca can do," she whispered, her hands behind her head. *Now please come eat this warm, wet pussy that's waiting for you.*

Curious, I placed my Black & Mild down, then finished the remainder of cake. "Yea I do," I replied. "What about Crystal?"

"Crystal, the bitch is dangerous, Bolo. No one seems to fuck with her anymore because they know that she's all about her business." *Now fuck all the questions. Come eat me, Bolo.*

I laid besides Sophie as we continued to talk about strictly business. Her pussy I sensed, was very wet and throbbing, wanting my attention so bad. So we just kissed and fell asleep to Jean Knight's, *Mr. Big Stuff.*

9 a.m, the next morning at The Post House restaurant on Lea Boulevard and Market Street, Dawn was sitting on my rest next to Aunt Ann. The three

of us ordered the same thing; hotcakes, scrambled eggs, bacon and orange juice on the side.

"Cousin Bolo, it's about time you made it to the house," Dawn said, sarcastically she turned to face me.

"Whatever, Dawn" I replied, slicing both our pancakes into bite sizes

"Mom can you believe he fucked Brandy on the sneak tip. That's why him and Brandy wouldn't answer their cell phones. Let alone the house phone," she said. Her fork dove into the hotcakes.

"First of all Miss Eighteen year old," Aunt Ann yelled, looking at Dawn. "You can't watch him lay up with every woman he gets involved with. It shouldn't have been a first," she added, rolling her eyes as she swayed her index finger.

Dawn quickly jerked back squinting her eyes, avoiding my aunt's saying finger working towards her mouth. "Mommy," she leaned back on me to protect her from her raving mother.

"Aunt Ann, your daughter should be a private investigator," I laughed, gesturing both hands to shield Dawn.

"She do act like one, nephew," Aunt Ann said, picking up her glass of juice while keeping her eyes on Dawn.

"Get off me fat ass" I teased Dawn, pushing her away from me.

"Lick this fat ass, cousin Bolo."

"When, smart ass?"

"It's nice and wet. Why not try it now?" asked Dawn, rolling her eyes at me.

"Y'all keep talking like that and you'll end up fucking cousins." Said Aunt Ann, shaking her head at us both.

"Hell no, that's nasty!" Dawn and I said at once while leaning back from each other listening to my Aunt laugh at us.

Aunt Ann knew where our conversation was going so she caught a ride home by one of her girlfriends that walked into the restaurant. My cell phone rang so I headed to the back to take the call. Kev was telling me that they were all over Southbridge including the girls who were screaming in the background. Once I left from having breakfast, I'd head in that direction, I informed them.

"Brandy and me are gonna strip for you cousin Bolo," said Dawn, not giving me a chance to hang up my phone.

"Brandy…yes. You…hell no."

"You know you wanna see my fat pussy," she said. "One day I'm gonna creep into your bed butt naked while you sleep, than start nibbling your lips."

What was going through this girl's mind I had the slightest idea. Maybe I should let her have a boyfriend. That would be the day I'll have to kill him. "You have a serious problem, Dawn." I said, shaking my head. My eyes shrieking past her while focusing on a beautiful light skin sista that walked in.

Laughing, her eyes followed mines. "Whatever," she said. "Let's see how much game you have big daddy. Then again, what can you do with a five-foot four baby butterball chick her size?"

Dawn began questioning me on my expertise in romance. We both watched the woman sit down next to me smiling. What she don't know is the more cushion for the pushing.

"Hello," she said. Nodding her head, a gesture for me to hand her the restaurant menu.

"Hi, I'm Bolo," I said, extending my hand out to her.

"The infamous Bolo. I've seen you so many times on television." Her eyebrows lifted high. "My name is Melissa, but you can call me Missy for short," she said, welcoming my hand as an invitation to carry on.

"Nice to meet you, Missy. This is my desperately seeking a boyfriend, cousin Dawn."

Rolling her eyes at me, Dawn said, "Hey, Missy. Don't listen to him."

"Hi, Dawn," Missy laughed. "I assume that you and Bolo are attending the 70's Player's Ball at Howard High School this year?" She asked Dawn.

Dawn put me on the spot before I could get a chance to say what I wanted to say. "Yes. Definitely, we'll be seeing more of you girl," she said, lashing her tongue out at me. Her eyes smiling to say that she got me back for what I've said about the desperate seeking woman that she is.

"Very confident. I take it that Dawn meant what she said, Bolo?" Missy asked, massaging my hand.

"Thank you, Dawn." I said.

Missy and Dawn high-five one another while rolling their eyes at me. So what, the only thing that I wanted was Missy's phone number and address which I succeeded. Dawn and I left Missy at the restaurant to finish her breakfast and went about our business. "Drive Dawn, please," I tossed her my car keys. "Don't look at me like that," I said.

"Cousin Bolo. You don't let anyone drive your car," she said.

"Please."

"Okay," she replied, hoping behind the steering wheel.

Southbridge is one of the housing projects that I want to take over. My organization will conquer any and everything that we want to accomplish. We will terminate anyone who stands in our way of success. Everyone is standing against their cars as Dawn and I pulled into Eden Park. "Hey guys, meet my, desperately seeking a boyfriend, cousin Dawn," I said, laughing at the sight of her rolling her eyes at me.

"Don't tell them that shit, Bolo," Dawn said, slamming my car door.

"Hey girl," Sophie, Bianca, and Crystal all embraced her while individually introducing themselves.

"Hey captain. The Southbridge housing projects is all yours whenever you give the word," said Kev, extending his open arms.

"I have very special plans for this filthy ass place over here, ladies and gentlemen." I said walking over to Dexter, until I stood beside him.

"Bolo. That nigga that came into the store. The one who pulled a gun out on you. We know where he lives," Felix said. Staring at Dawn's confused eyes, he quickly turned away from her.

I leaned to whisper into Felix's ear that I will give him a call to execute my command and any witnesses that are present at the time.

"I wanna go home, Cousin Bolo," said Dawn.

"What?"

"You heard me. I want to go home." Her eyes jolted at me. "And now," she said, flopping down in the passenger seat.

I told my crew that I'll see them later on that night and if not that we'll talk tomorrow. On the other hand, Dawn tended to get what she wants when she would catch her bitch ass attitudes. So I'll drop her off at home then head in my own direction. Make a few calls to some beautiful women and invite them into the Jacuzzi. Dawn slipped a CD, leaned back against the door then stared at me. "That's the Sophie you been fuckin. And when did someone pull a gun out on you, cousin Bolo?" She asked.

"It was a small situation, Dawn," I assured her.

"Small! What the hell you mean a small situation?" Her voice tainted, loudly spoken over the low sound of Jesse Powell's *You*. Her worried eyes dropped down to her lap, and then eased the next questions straight into my heart.

"What?" I broke the silence.

"You're gonna kill him or have him killed. You had Rick killed for threatening to kill mommy and me," she said, hands flailing, a gesture of *I know you're gonna kill him, Bolo*. "On top of that, he pushed me and slapped mommy." She added

Dawn already read between the lines whenever such tragedy happened. Now she's sounding like she has a relationship with this mothafucka that she don't even know. Let alone seen him. Her questions are the interrogation of those damn detectives that I have working for me and how they pissed me off, the way Dawn is now. "What do you expect? He pulled a fucking gun on me!" I yelled. "And I wasn't gonna let Rick continue to threaten the both of you. You're my family, damn it!" I looked over at her. Door ajar before the car came to a complete stop. She rolled her eyes at me and ran into the house.

Moments later I headed on upstairs to see what Dawn is up to, if she calmed down or still stuck on the controversy that she and I discussed in the car. The second I walked into her bedroom she immediately dropped her brown terrycloth robe to begin lotioning her body down.

"What are you doing in here?" she asked. Her girlish tone of voice echoed telling me that she's done with her interrogation about my killings, unless I tell her about them which is seldom.

"Came to see if you were okay before I left," I said, walking over to the bed to sit next to her.

"How can I be okay when you won't let me have a boyfriend and they're all scared of you?"

"Don't you throw that shit in my face, Dawn!" I hollered and echoed off the wall to startle her.

Shaking her head, "Gosh," she said. Looked away from me as if I were invisible.

"Gosh my ass. You're eighteen and about to attend college, Dawn. Men dog women. I dog women. You see me all the time, damn near every day." Her attention was now focused one me as she turned to face me.

She said, "Every woman that you come in contact with, you manipulate them just to get into their panties. Knowing that they want to give it all to you," she smiled. Reached for a piece of paper that was on her dresser and flashed it in my face. She knew that it has Missy's information written on it and that she was my next target.

"I can't help it," I grinned.

"Why don't we have sex now?" she asked, standing right over top of me.

"Girl you know we can't do that shit."

"Try me one time, Cousin Bolo," she grabbed my hand.

I looked up at her and said, "I can't Dawn."

"Yes you can," she pressed a button on the remote control. Feel how wet my pussy is." Barbara Mason, *Yes, I'm ready.* She pushed three of my fingers into her pussy moaning out my name. The next thing I knew I was standing up kissing my cousin and tasting her pussy juice from my fingers. I had to push away from her and said that she can have a boyfriend, but she refused to get one now.

"You're so fuckin nasty girl."

"You like it," she said, as she blew air between her teeth watching me leave. She smiled telling me that she wanted to experience what the other women were so crazy about. I can't believe me and my cousin Dawn became the kissing cousins that my Aunt Ann said we might become. She's so desperate to have a boyfriend, so eager to experience sex.

Later on that evening screeching up Thatcher Street, the unmarked detective car slows down while tossing a red Wendy's cup out the passenger side window. One hour before I make the twenty thousand dollar drop at the dumpster next to Rash's convenience store. First I'll make a quick stop at Trina's house to see how things are looking up on her end.

"Bolo, thank you for stopping pas. Twenty thousand as you requested," said Trina, looking back over her right shoulder to hand me a manila envelope. Her eyes surprise of the accomplishment that she's made since working with my men.

"Thank you sweetheart," I said. She bent forward into a fetal position holding on her stomach. "What's wrong, Trina?"

"I have cramps and pains in my stomach, Bolo." She replied, slowly sitting down. "That time of month, silly." Her laughing read my mind on the rough sex we both encountered last week.

One, two, three, four Wilmington Police cruisers heading into the Bucket housing projects. First car cruising down Twenty-Third Street. Second car coming down Locust Street while one is going up Thatcher Street and another up the one way street from Vandever Avenue. "What the fuck are they up too?" I asked.

"They were doing this all morning, Bolo" Trina said. Her hand held the police scanner. "You think that it's a raid?" she asked me. Voices sounded off that the Wilmington Police Department were making their presence known to the housing projects.

"No, Trina," I said. "They do this to see who's out selling drugs and which house they need to raid when they really do come."

She said, "I'm learning, Bolo."

We continued to watch every movement that the police were making. I made a few calls to Kev and Ty so they can inform the others of what's happening and to be on the look out. "Next weekend we're getting you a brand new car, Trina."

"WE ARE, BOLO?" she screamed

"Yeah. Look at that thing riding on a donut tire. Rusty and the interior is definitely shot."

"Thank you. Thank you, Bolo." She yelled, jumping up and down embracing me and not wanting to let go of me.

That night.

There I was, parked on the corner of 30th and Market Street in front of Kennedy Fried Chicken waiting for these dumb ass detectives to pick up the twenty thousand dollars they requested. Fifteen minutes later they pul up beside the dumpster. Passenger gets out to discover the brownish envelope.

"About time you dumb fucks," I mumbled. They watched me pull away as I gave them my middle finger. Now back to my Aunt Ann's house to check the outfit that they brought for my cousin Dawn for the 70's Player's Ball.

"You miss me cousin Bolo?" asked Dawn. Her voice fainted. "I want this dick," she said. Eyes focused on unzipping my zipper.

"Awww. You do baby?"

She answered. "Yes" tracing her lips with her tongue.

"Ya can't, nasty ass," I said, pushing her down on the bed, then walked to the door. She grabbed her silk body pillow and rolled her eyes at me while burying her face and mumbling a few nasty words.

Chapter 8

Saturday morning at the Philadelphia International Airport to pick up my cousin Dawn and her friend Brandy at Gate 7, flight 35 coming in from Montego Bay, Jamaica.

Crowded as usual, I headed on over to the Dunkin Donut shop to buy some donuts and a large orange juice. Something weird is happening as I notice three white men staring at me, all wearing black two-piece suits and dark sunglasses. One is actually standing at the donut shop staring at me, while another is looking up at the flight information board. Surprisingly there's another one just a few seats down from me pretending to be talking on a cell phone. Police, F.B.I., detectives or whoever they are. What a sloppy surveillance.

"Cousin Bolo!" Dawn yelled, dropping her bag, then running towards me.

"Hey baby, hi Brandy," I said, embracing them both. "How was Jamaica?" I asked.

"Bolo, thank you so much. Dawn and I had so much fun," said Brandy, tossing her bags at me smiling.

"I need ya'll to do something for me before we leave."

"What's that?" They both asked.

"Don't look yet," I said, handing them some money to buy a few sodas for the road.

Once I explained everything to Brandy and Dawn they were so excited to have a little fun. Not to mention the embarrassment they will inflict on the sloppy law enforcement. They both headed over to Dunkin Donuts to buy two extra large raspberry soft drinks with no ice. Dawn walked over to the flight information board. Brandy stayed by the Donut shop. Both in position, I gestured nodding my head so they could execute my command.

Seconds later they both bumped into the law enforcement officers while spilling their entire soft drinks on them. We all watched Brandy and Dawn run over to me smiling, as they both quickly reached my side. We grabbed the bags, looked at the three officers and began laughing, flashing our middle fingers at them. Everyone nearby all started laughing, watching us run into a crowd.

"Cousin Bolo. They better leave you the hell alone," said Dawn. She held her hand out while looking at my car keys. "Did y'all see their faces when we all flashed our middle fingers?" she asked. I caught my keys and jumped in the driver's seat laughing.

Once back on I-95 heading south we all begin talking about what they did in Jamaica to have fun. "Bolo, we took so many pictures of us in the lingerie that you bought us." Brandy said, changing the D as she reached over my shoulder to plant a kiss on my cheeks as well.

Dawn asked, "When can the three of us take a vacation together cousin Bolo?"

"Never," I answered.

"Why not, Bolo?" asked Brandy.

"Nah. Really. I would love for the both of you to go to Las Vegas with me next month."

They both screamed at the top of their lungs while jumping up and down in their seats. Dawn almost ran into the guardrail so I had to stop the car on the shoulder so that I could take over.

Back in Delaware at the house Dawn excused herself to the bathroom while Brandy and I stayed downstairs to chat about whatever.

"We're all going to Las Vegas next month?" Brandy asked me, smiling while sitting on my lap. Her arm swung around my neck pulling me closer to the air she breathes.

"Yes. We should all have a nice time there," I said. My arm slowly wrapped around her waistline.

Brandy's cell phone began vibrating so she jumped up the take the call while walking out the house with her car keys in her hand. Dawn is upstairs calling me to come up for whatever reason I don't know. "What the hell you want girl?" I asked. Her smiling eyes pierce through the mirror at me.

"You miss me while I was gone?" Dawn asked. Her steps glided her body melting into mines. Her lips caught the peeking of my tongue. Her embrace held firm.

"Yes," I moaned. My tongue fully submerged in her mouth.

"Then fuck me now."

"No," I answered. "It's bad enough we kissed, Dawn. We tasted your pussy off my fingers." Silence for a moment as we continued kissing, then came a break in silence.

She said, "But it's wet for you," her weak voice altering her hormones in a complete clicking of overdrive.

"Nope," I staggered a few feet back away from her. Stillness.

Back downstairs relaxing, minding my business as my Aunt Ann walked into the house watching Dawn come back from upstairs rolling her eyes at me.

"Hey mom," she said.

"Hey baby. Bolo. Brandy," Aunt Ann smiling at Dawn knowing her mind was far from her interrogative manner. "How was Jamaica?"

"Mom. It was so beautiful in Jamaica," Said Dawn.

"Yes it was Mrs. Ann," Brandy interrupted. "Bolo is taking Dawn and me to Las Vegas nest month," she said.

Aunt Ann dazed at what she was hearing and not hearing as Dawn and Brandy rammed her mind with all the excitement they had in Jamaica. Her perky eyes directly focused on me as her hands moved above her waistline. "Excuse me Bolo."

"Aunt Ann you can go too. But can you please make the reservations for us all at the Stratosphere Hotel and Casino," I said. Make sure that you book us for an evening show every night that we are in Las Vegas."

"Brandy."You and I will share a room together," said Dawn. "And mom, you too."

"Thank you Dawn, nephew, and Brandy. And ladies we will enjoy our ladies night out. Ladies, we'll have to do some serious shopping as in a shopping spree." Said Aunt Ann. The three of them begin jumping up and down while laughing and looking at me.

"How much will y'all need?"

"Definitely about twenty thousand dollars," said Dawn.

There was so much excitement in the room that my cell phone began ringing with a distinct tone. I motioned to my Aunt Ann to just use the credit card she has to get the funding she needed on their shopping spree. I took a drive over in the Riverside Projects to meet Kev, Ty and Monte at the abandoned building that was once the Wonder Bread factory on 30th Street and Todds Lane.

They all stood at the back door waiting for my arrival with eyes widely open with anticipation. *Click-click!*

"Where is this nigga they call, Black?" I asked.

"He's right over here, Bolo," Monte said, leading the way as he pulled his weapon from his waistline.

Turning around a brick wall I noticed a black male duct taped to a wooden chair, mouth included. His fear roamed the springtime air seeping through the molded cracks in the walls. Fluttered eyes as he watched Kev and Ty move swiftly behind him.

"Hey you, you remember me don't you or did you forget that you pulled a fucking gun on me at the clothing store?" I asked. His head tilted back a little while eyeing my black 9 mm Smith & Wesson.

"Hmmm," he mumbled, nodding his head in agreement with me.

"What? You have something you like to say to me?" I asked, "Somebody take that shit off his mouth please."

"Gotcha," Kev said. He reached to pull the duct tape off Black.

"Aaagghhhhh!" Black screamed.

"What the hell was you thinking about, Black, when you whipped that gun out on me?"

"Bolo, I'm sorry man," he said. His eyes rolled to his left then to his right to monitor Kev and Ty's every moment. "I tried to prove something to you so that I can join your organization." His hands trembling.

Laughing. " I respect that, Black. You're dangerous. You have potential, and I like that." I said, then asked, "So what's up with the Southbridge housing projects?"

"Bolo, its so much money over there." Fear, he smiled as if it were never introduced.

"Excuse me, Black," I said. A motion of my index finger silenced his breathing. "Someone untie him please." My expression approving what needs to be done. Black will be joining my organization, but first he has to be initiated. Everyone had to be welcomed to my initiation. Survival is the key to the organization. Black is loose, talking and walking with me,

"Like I was saying, Bolo," he jumped from the flicking of my lighter sparking my Black & Mild "It's mad money over there. But you have all the weight. We all can make so much money over in Southbridge," he said.

"Black, I'm down for whatever. We can do this then," I said turning my back towards him.

He yelled. "Yes. We can do this shit, Bolo!"

"C'mon, y'all and let's get the hell outta here. Take it easy, Black. But you'll have to be initiated first."

"When will that be Bolo?" He asked me.

"Now, Black," I replied. I began picking up my pace while nodding my head, alerting my men that I smelled death.

"Now?" Black asked. That was his last word before his lifeless corpse hit the cold cement.

"Nigga pulled a gun out on me and expected to live the rest of his days? He's fuckin crazy," I said.

"DEAD CRAZY!" Ty shouted.

We all hopped in our cars and went separate ways. I had to head on over to Crystal's houe before I turned in for the rest of the night. Since I have my own door key, I'll let myself in. She was standing there smiling as soon as I walked in the house.

"Look at you girl. Always smiling," I said. She followed me over to the couch as she sat down next to me.

"You make me smile, Bolo," she said. "Oh, we're all ready for the 70's Players Ball." Her eyes she rolled while turning away from me. *You're not kicking my ass anymore.*

"Crystal, that's good sweetheart. It's about time," I said.

"What about joining your organization, Bolo? Why are you holding back?" She asked. Her interrogation reminded me of my cousin Dawn questioning my having sex with her, which will never happen.

"Truthfully. I'm waiting for the right moment."

"Bolo," she said. "We all need our own money instead of accepting your money all the time." Her hand rested on my thigh as she handed me a glass of Dom Perignon.

"Crystal, I know that. Trust me when the time is right, you ladies will be making so much money."The champagne quickly rushed down my throat.

"My brother is so crazy about you, Bolo. He wants to join your organization."

"That's definitely impossible, Crystal." I leaned back to rest my head as she sat up to stare at me.

"Why not?"

"Your destiny is to join my organization," I said. The burning flame touched the tip of my Black & Mild. "If your brother made a mistake, than I would have to kill him. Now would you like that?" I asked her.

"Oh shit." Her voice weakens as she tilts her head down turning away from me.

"His fucking blood on your hands. I thought not." I grinned at the sight of her self-consciousness. "Men are the most snitches in all America Crystal, especially when it comes down to a murder or catching a fucking case that they can't handle."

"I understand, Bolo. Would you like anything to eat?" asked Crystal.

"Sure, why not you?" We both stood up. She smiled while watching me head towards the staircase.

Moments later, Crystal came walking in the bedroom butt naked, climbing on the bed then sat on my face as I began working my magic. Once she climaxed several times we both began calling out each other's name while making love. Relaxed, we enjoyed the sounds of Stacey Latisaw, *Let me be your Angel*.

Downstairs there was a knock. "Someone is at your door, Crystal," I said.

"Oh shit," she jumped up. "It's Bianca, Bolo" she said peeking out the window then at me.

"What the hell is she doin here?" I asked.

"Don't know. But I'll be right back," Crystal said. Quickly she threw her robe on and darted out the room.

Seconds later the door opened then closed. "*Hey Bianca*." I heard Crystal say.

"*Hey Bitch. Don't you think that Bolo's car should be in your garage instead of in your driveway?*" Bianca shouted. "*Where is he at anyway?*" she asked Crystal.

"*My bedroom.*" Crystal answered.

"You don't mind, do you?"

"Hell no girl, go ahead and ride that dick!" Crystal yelled, alarming me that Bianca was on her way up to the bedroom.

Bianca quickly made her way to Crystal's bedroom smiling and telling that Crystal is moving my car. Took off her clothes then jumped in bed with me as we made a few fireworks explode.

A few hours later, the three of us are in the living room drinking champagne and laughing at the Bugs Bunny Cartoons.

Back at home in the shower my mind is wandering back and forth to Crystal and Bianca, both laying there butt naked in bed with me. They both looked at each other then nodded their head. Crystal's riding me while Bianca's on my face.

House phone ringing. "Hello."

"It's me, Sophie," she said.

"Hey baby. You're back in town?" I asked.

"Yes, Bolo. My three asshole cousins aren't doing what their supposed to do and that's why I want to move my grandmother down here to Delaware," Sophie inhaled deeply through her nose.

"We'll talk about that tomorrow."

"Bolo. I want to move her into a nice senior citizens home so she can be around people her age, plus her kids won't be able to come live with her."

"You definitely have a point there, Sophie. Get some sleep and I'll make some quick calls before I go to sleep," I said.

I had to make a few calls to some very important people including a few of my men. Sophie, Bianca, and Crystal are all in cahoots together so I'll have to really make a move on them three before they can bring my organization to the ground.

Wednesday around one in the morning, dressed in all black, I round up my crew as we begin to make our move. Time for Sophie to reap what she's sewn. Bianca and Crystal as well. How can Sophie not mention the picture she's in with my ex crime partner. Now here I am standing in front of her looking at her naked body, hair rollers still in her hair. Blind folded not knowing that this will be her last moment alive.

"Bolo. What's the meaning of all this?" she asked. "And why the fuck am I standing here the hell butt ass naked, blindfolded?" she asked screaming. Her arms crossed resting on her breast covering her erected brown nipples.

"Today is the day, Sophie." I encircled her pondering my next move.

"Today is the day, huh?" she repeated. "It's about two in the fucking morning. Today isn't even near yet," her voice went beating to the nearby wall.

"I know, I know." I strolled behind her yanking both arms behind her back then tying them together.

"Didn't I give you a good fuck two days ago you bastard?"

"Shut the hell up girl. It's not about a good fuck!" I yelled, pushing her back against the steel walls. "Sophie, your trying to bring my organization down to the ground and I wont have this shit."

Crying, "I had no intention of destroying your organization, Bolo. None of us." Her cry alerting knocks on the door.

"You're a disgrace Sophie. You, Bianca and Crystal as well. Gentlemen, bring them in please!" I yelled.

The second the steel door opened, Bianca and Crystal came into play being pushed in by my men. Three naked women all are about to be executed because they know a little too much.

"What?" Sophie yelled. Her nipples lost their erection. "Bianca and Crystal!" she called.

"Sophie!" they both screamed out.

"Untie their stinkin asses." I motioned my men. Guns click ready.

"Oh my God, Bolo please don't kill us. We won't say anything about your organization, we promise." Said Sophie, begging as she embraces Crystal and Bianca.

We placed the three of them in a meat freezer as the temperature is a freezing below zero.

"Bolo you're really gonna kill us?" cried Sophie. "Can you pretend that we never met, please?"

"It's what the captain wants, you three know that he gets what the fuck her wants," Kev said.

Leaving them in the freezer was a good idea; at least their corpses wont decompose. Twenty minutes later we all went to check on the women whom were still alive, standing there shivering and crying. "Ladies we definitely have a problem here," I said.

"What- what's that, Bolo?" Bianca asked.

"Kev, Monte, Ty, Felix, and myself all decided that this freezing shit isn't working," I said, pushing Sophie next to Bianca and Crystal. "You're not dying, so were gonna help you by shooting you three to get this shit done and over with."

All screamed, " NOOO! NOOO! NOOO!" The sound of more guns clicking, more guns pointed at them.

"WE'RE JUST GONNA SHOOT YOU THREE INTO MY ORGANIZATION," I shouted, "SOPHIE, CRYSTAL, AND BIANCA… WELCOME INTO MY ORGANIZATION," I screamed at the top of my lungs while my men do the same.

"Damn you, Bolo," said Bianca rolling her eyes.

"How dare you, Bolo," Crystal cried happily.

Sophie said, "You had this whole thing planned."

"Come here my crybabies," I smiled. "Welcome to Delaware's Top Captain's organization."

Once I welcomed the ladies into my organization I had them put their clothes back on and for my men to escort the all home safely. They will all play a very important part in my organization whenever I decide to overthrow the housing projects in Southbridge, which will be soon.

Cruising down Market Street on Saturday afternoon before I head on home to shower for tonight's 70's Player's Ball extravaganza. I approached 28th Street watching two detectives frisk a few guys on the corner. "DON'T YOU MUTHAFUCKAS HAVE BETTER THINGS TO DO THAN TO HARASS PEOPLE," I shouted

"Delaware's Top Captain," one of them said.

"Asshole."

"Fuck you, Bolo" his partner glanced at me, then smiled.

"Bolo, don't pay them no attention!" a woman yelled.

I said, "I won't baby. They're the least of my worries."The light changed green as I sped away.

That night.

I walked into Howard High School at the 70's Player's Ball on 12th and Clifford Brown Walk. Everyone is dressed in 70's attire, plaid pants, afros, plaid shirts, thick high-heel shoes. 70's of the Motown sounds filling the air. "We finally meet again," I said, leaning forward to whisper into Missy's ear.

"Bolo. Hi baby," said Missy, surprisingly spinning around to embrace me. Her afro brushing my face. Her meaty insinuating curves felt the warmth of my hands.

"We've been missing one another. How are you doing? I asked.

"Fine. Now that you're here," she replied. "I've been very busy." Her arms slowly wrapped around my neck.

"Busy?"

She answered. "Yes, but I promise from now on I'll make it up to you in all the ways I can."

"Now, Missy. Don't make promises that you can't keep."

"Bolo. I tend to keep my promises whenever I make them," she said. Her tongue forced its way into my mouth. "Trust me on that sweetheart" she added.

"How long have you been here?" I asked.

"Only twenty minutes," she said.

"I see the both of you are becoming more acquainted with one another," Dawn said, smiling at the sight of Missy and I sharing a beautiful kiss.

"Hey, Dawn girl," Missy smiled. The sisterly hug they gave each other when they embraced

I walked away from Dawn and Missy leaving them both in conversation to spend some time together. Half an hour later there was a fight with a bunch of juvenile so I gathered my crew. Along with Missy, we all got the hell outta there.

Monday morning, I went to meet Constance in her office at the Wilmington Trust Bank. Constance opened the door for me saying nothing until the door closed behind us both. "Good Morning, Bolo." She said.

"Good morning Constance. How was your business trip?" I asked. My eyes glued on her tightly fitted brown skirt displaying her panty lines. Her hair dangling loosely down her back.

"Exciting. How was your 70's Player's Ball Saturday night?" She asked, smiling at me then following my eyes to her exposed cleavage.

"Phenomenon" I said, "Until these juveniles turned it out which they shouldn't have been there. But other than that…it was exclusive.

"Kids," she said. The motion of her hands instructed me to have a seat. Her eyes searching the cabinets behind her as she reached into it to pull out a folder with my name on it.

I said, "Thank you."

"The Devon high-rise would be very suitable and comfortable for

Sophie's grandmother to live," said Constance. "Whenver she moves her to Delaware."

"Constance, I told Sophie that I would get your approval to come meet with her. Then the both of you can discuss this business togheter.

"I would love to," she said, leaning forward to hand me some more papers.

"What are these?" I asked.

"I purchased two more houses as you requested, here in Wilmington. One is located at 2701 Thompson Place; the other is located at 709 South Harrison Street.

"Thank you very much sweetheart," I said. We both closed the folders that she placed in front of us while standing.

"Dinner at seven o' clock sharp tonight, Bolo." As we headed for the door, she tapped my shoulder while laughing.

"I'll definitely be there, Constance," I said. I motioned my hand, a gesture to blow a sweet kiss at her.

Chapter 9

Thunder roaring and quick flashes of lightening; it was the rain beating down heavily on my windowpane that awakened me on this soggy Tuesday morning. Someone's nibbling on my bottom lip as I begin to focus my eyes to welcome Brandy's warm body lying next to me. I was startled to see my cousin Dawn. I begin to comb her body to feel that she's butt naked. "Dawn! What the hell are you doing here in my bed?"

"Kissing you, what do you think I'm doing?" she asked. Climbing on top of me. Her body was heating element.

"We can't do this, Oh shit!" I yelled. My sound echoed pass her ears. I watched her stare at me moving down my body.

"Relax," she said. Her lips, her tongue, working my manhood in her mouth.

Seconds later she comes up to being riding me the way a two time champion jockey rides his horse. Both calling out each other's name. I grab her waist to toss her over on her back while moving down to suck her warm pussy.

"Yes, yes Bolo. Suck my pussy," she moans. Holding my head in place pressing, not wanting me to come up for air.

I moaned, "Yes, Dawn baby."

"Fuck me, fuck me, Bolo," she yelled. Her legs spread apart as she pulled me up experiencing my hard dick moving towards her pussy walls. Both climaxing and screaming each other's names.

Moments later I watched Dawn get up smiling while walking into my bathroom to shower as I went downstairs to do the same.

Later that afternoon, everyone was at the table when I walked into the dining room. Bianca, Sophie and Crystal all sitting on the same side of the table while Kev, Monte, Felix and Ty are sitting across from them. Two hundred and fifty kilos of pure, uncut cocaine ready to be packaged and distributed over into the City of Wilmington.

Three vicious women all dressed in black fatigues, ready for a dangerous task. Bianca's hair pulled back into a ponytail, the sight of her killing a woman at point blank range. Sophie's hair sported with a few corn rolls, the kidnapper of the Senator. Then there was Crystal, her hair styled in two huge braids down to her shoulders, who just last week beat a black couple to death with an aluminum baseball bat. "Hello ladies and gentlemen," I said.

"Hey Bolo," they all answered in unison.

"Crystal, Sophie and Bianca I want you to pay close attention and learn what you're about to see and do." I pulled a Black & Mild from my jacket as I began walking around the table. "Every time you come to this table you will have masks and gloves on with no exceptions, unless you're at the money table."Their eyes quickly focused on the Cherry wood table supporting over two million dollars.

Sophie asked, "Will we be rotating from table to table?"

"Yes, rotating is a must. It keeps your mind off certain situations as well as reducing stress." I said.

Kev stood up, than leaned over to give them all masks and gloves to protect themselves. Ty placed a weighing scale in front of each of them while Monte was handling them all a box of clear glassine bags. Felix walking around to each one while showing them how to open the package of uncut pure cocaine.

"How much are we dealing with, Bolo, if you don't mind me asking?" Crystal asked.

"All together ladies we have a total of two hundred and fifty Kilos of pure uncut cocaine," I replied, watching them all lean back with eyebrows raised.

"Damn!!!" they yelled, shaking their heads and smiling.

"Kev, will you please demonstrate to the ladies how to package, please?"

"Sure, Bolo," he said picking up the material he needs while standing up demonstrating to do what they all need to be taught.

"Guys, what do you all think about the ladies?" I asked.

"Bolo, I think they should have control of the Southbridge of the city," said Monte. His gaze to immediate action.

"Southbridge," Ty said. He nodded in agreement with what Monte has suggested.

"Ladies, the Southbridge housing projects are yours, if yall want it."

All answered, "Hell yea!"

"We can do this y'all," said Crystal. Her arms swung around Bianca and Sophie's shoulders.

I said, "Thank you three. You will have control of the Southside of Wilmington."

"Captain. I been ready," Sophie said. Her mind shotgun to the large amounts of money.

"Southbridge will be your territory. Your own rules, lookouts and your own junkies. But I must warn you, you will not allow this drug or this money to become your best friend," I said. "It will either have you behind bars or floating somewhere in the Delaware Canal or the Brandywine River." Their full-undivided attention all focused on me as I sat back down.

Felix stood. "Be careful of your surroundings ladies, because the junkies will go to the extreme to get a quick fix. Stay clean, have clean workers on your squad," he said, sitting back down.

"Welcome to the family Sophie, Crystal and Bianca. Your protection is your protection, therefore you protect each other," I said. "Don't let anything or any man come between the friendship and the relationship that you have with one another or you'll end up killing one another. We come," I paused, "and we go."

Once I mention to the girls that memorizing is very important in this business, the police, and enemies as well, they begin talking amongst each other. I explained to them not to take anyone to their place of residence or the F.B.I would be breaking down their doors. Felix and Kev began passing out 8x11 photos of different law enforcement agents to look out for.

Sophie said, "Bolo. We seen this one at the restaurant a few weeks ago," her hand held a photo of a white man walking out the police station with his wife and daughter.

"Yes, Sophie, that's absolutely right. Here you will notice their personal vehicles as well ladies," I said.

"Nice navigator," said Crystal.

Bianca said, "I like this Jaguar," her smile shined bright. "I want this Mercedes," Sophie said. I agreed to buy the cars that the ladies all picked out as long as they were all white vehicles. We all began drinking champagne then got to work on the kilos of cocaine.

Five o'clock that evening, Missy and I decided to have an early dinner at the Steak and Ale restaurant on Kirkwood Highway. "Bolo, did you enjoy yourself at the 70's Player's Ball?" Missy asked.

"Yes Missy. What about yourself?"

"I enjoyed every bit of it, especially with you being there, Bolo," she said. Her eyes on the waitress bringing us two menus and two glasses of red wine.

"You're beautiful, Missy."

"Thank you, Bolo. But what makes you think I'm beautiful?" She asked, her eyes widen, elope.

You asked me to save you a dance. I love your eyes and the way you kissed me the first time at the party," I said.

"So you like that?"

"I do," I answered. "You have a nice shape, a perfect butterball turkey."

"You know they come with a lot of juice," her mind took the conversation to another level.

"Really?" I leaned back waiting for her next move.

"Between me and you Bolo. I would love to wrap my lips around it, then suck it, until every drop of you covers my tongue and slowly moves down my throat," Her fingers traced her lips, ready for a quick action.

Missy leaned forward to rest her chin on both palms of her hands waiting for my next question. I sense that I came across a freaky woman, so I'll see how far she wants to take this. "Do you really think that you can handle all of this nine inches in your mouth, Missy?"

"Let's see and I'll tell you," she watched a couple get their dinner, then waited for our food to come.

"What are you about to do?"

"Shhh!" she whispered. She sat down next to me and started to work her magic. Missy asked for a doggy bad then asked me to drop her off back home.

Later on that night after dropping Missy off at home, I headed over to my aunt Ann's house to see what her and my cousin Dawn were both up to. Not a soul was out. This place is usually crawling with people. When I walked into the house to see them, they were both sitting in the living room quiet as a mouse. "What's up with Aunt Ann and Cousin Dawn?" I asked.

"Hey nephew," Aunt Ann said.

"Why is it so quiet out tonight and where is everyone?"

"Cousin Bolo, they were just shooting around here about ten minutes ago," said Dawn.

"Who was it this time?"

"That black van again. I'm scared," Dawn rested her head between my Aunt Ann's arm staring at me. They both watched me punch in numbers on my cell phone.

"Nephew, what are you about to do?"

"Aunt Ann, the both of you stay in the house, you hear me?"

"Yes," they both answered. Both sunk deeply into the comfort of one another while not speaking another word.

Once a shooting occurs in any area, the shooter or shooters will lay low somewhere nearby knowing that the police will be canvassing the area for any possible suspect. In most cases the suspect had already been described, so they will lay low until everything clears.

My cell rang, "Hello."

"Bolo, that black van we saw after Jay's viewing is over here on the corner of 12th and Clifford Brown Walk with about three or four niggas in it," said Kev.

"Kev, ten minutes ago they were shooting around my Aunt Ann's house again. In about five minutes I want everyone to fire at will. I'm on my way!" I yelled.

Dropping my cell phone I darted out the door cocking both my 9mm Smith & Wessons. Rain began pouring down heavily as I head up 10th Street covering my weapons from the upcoming traffic behind me, making sure I don't get a surprise visit by any Wilmington Police. Quickly I swing a right on Clifford Brown Walk heading towards 12th Street.

Seconds later, while approaching the middle of 11th and 12th Street, Kev and Ty recognize me and began firing at the black van headed in my direction.

Pop, pop, pop, pop, pop, pop, pop! The driver of the van slumped over the steering wheel while banging up a few parked cars before coming to a complete stop. Kev and Ty quickly ran up to the van, guns still raised to see if any occupants were alive.

"Let's go, let's go!" I yelled. We all ran to 14th and French where Kev's car was parked.

Cell phone ringing. "Hello, he's right here,"Ty said. His voice weakened as he looked back at me handing me his cell phone.

"Who the hell is it?" I asked.

"Sophie. She's crying, Bolo," he said.

"Sophie. Sophie, why are you the fuck crying?"

"Bo- Bolo, we need you to come over to 30th and Washington Street. NOW, IT'S BIANCA!" she shouted.

I motioned to Kev to put the pedal to the medal and head straight down 30th and Washington, which is where Bianca lives. Moments later, fearing the worst as we made a sharp right off Concord Avenue onto Washington Street, countless ambulances, detective cars, coroner's and damn near the whole Wilmington Police force has a road block from 2th Street all the way to 32nd street looking like Christmas in the month of March.

Parking the car, we all began to run the rest of the way, when suddenly Sophie spots us and began running to me crying. "Oh shit, what the fuck happened?!" I yelled.

"Bolo, Bolo, she's gone." Sophie cried out. Her voice trembling. Her body shaking uncontrollable.

"What the hell happened Sophie?" I asked. Kev walked over to Crystal bent over in a fetal position crying. "And what the hell you mean, she's gone?"

"She- she had a shootout with the police."

"For what?" My anger began to escalate.

"Don't know," she said. Ty came over to embrace Sophie, alerting me that a detective was coming up behind me.

"Mr. Lance Jones. May I have a word with you please?" he asked. His low crop hair recognizable. His deep voice touched the base of my eardrum. He was well-dressed in a two-piece grey suit.

I shouted, "WHAT THE FUCK DO Y'ALL WANT?"

His partner walked up beside him. His two-piece brown suit he wore neatly. His double holster supported two black .45 calibers resting, waiting to be fired. He said, "Bolo, Bianca was a suspect for the murder of Sharon Ross."

I shouted once again, "WHO THE FUCK IS SHARON ROSS?"

"She was the woman that Bianca shot in the head a few months ago at the Crystal Palace," his partner said.

"How the fuck you know?"

"Bolo. A witness identified her in a photo lineup," his eyes feared what was about to happen next.

"This conversation is over. Let's get out of here!" I yelled.

"Bolo," he called.

I stopped dead in my tracks and looked over my left shoulder, then walked back to the detective wearing the grey suit. Leaning forward to whisper into his ear, "I want you to find out where this bitch ass witness lives. Her family. I want their addresses."

Not one word came out his mouth.

Back home the next morning, I laid in my hot tub drinking Hennessey straight with no ice or chaser. Phone ringing off the hook. Jazz floating through the air. Eyes closed. "Damn Bianca" I mumbled, sinking into the water until it touched my chin.

"Hey you," Dawn said. She picked up my Hennessey bottle then shook her head at the amount that was left.

"What do you want?"

"Mommy and me had been calling your phones and got no answer. So she asked me to come over to make sure you were okay." She paused, "then we saw that your phone was at the house."

"Thank you," I said, staring at her stripping before my eyes.

"I heard what happened to Bianca on the news this morning," she said. "Plus the three dead men that were in that black van," she slowly stepped into the hot tub submerging in the water to her chin.

"Well they deserved it, Bianca didn't."

"Cousin Bolo, it's all over the news that Bianca was working under you," Dawn said. She reached to grab a nearby 1986 Jordan wine bottle. "Your face was all over the news claiming that you're the notorious Delaware's Top Captain and you have the City of Wilmington on lock down in cocaine, let alone small cities as far as Laurel, Delaware."

"Meaning what, Dawn? They can say what the hell they wanna say about me. Can't I have associates?" I asked.

"Yes. I know what you're going through, I know how you feel," her body completely emerged out the water. Dawn stood right in front of me while red wine is trickling and bouncing off her cleavage.

"What do you know about feelings, Dawn?" I asked.

She motioned me to stand up, "You have feelings, I have feelings," she said. Dawn sat down looking up at me. Her hands on mines as she slowly places the on her black, long, silky hair. Looking up at me one more time she moans, calling out my name as I did the same by moaning out her name.

Later on that afternoon at the Prices park basketball court, Sophie told my organization that Bianca's mother wanted her cremated. We will honor her mother's wishes. Bianca went out like a real soldier because she killed one police officer. Our enemy.

I sent Constance, Sophie and Crystal over to Bianca's house to send my condolences and to take care whatever expenses that they may have. She will always be remembered by us all.

One month later I asked Sophie's cousin Diamond to meet me at the Sears Tower in Chicago at the elevator's because I needed a vacation amongst other things. She walked up on me smiling. Her hair mushroom style, her body seductively heart shaped. Diamond's eyes met mines on her exposed cleavage. "Hello Diamond," I said.

"Hi, Bolo. Why are we meeting here and not in Delaware?" Diamond asked, her arms extended around my neck.

"I needed a vacation so I asked you to meet me here," her body of soft pillows waiting to be caressed.

She said, "Thank you for the invite. I've heard so much about you," her manicured finger touched the elevators up button. "Sophie asked me to join in with her and Crystal."

"Really."

"Yes. She said that you would like to talk to me one on one."

The elevator door opened as we both watched a couple and their child step off. We stepped on to wait until the door closes. Diamond looked at me as to say something before I interrupted her. "Press the top floor button please," I said. "How was your flight here?"

"Relaxing. My first time here in Chicago," she said. *You look so damn sexy Bolo.*

"You know this is a dangerous game, Diamond." The elevator door opened as a Chinese couple hesitated to step on, but backed away telling us that they're going to the ground floor.

"Yes. Bolo, I'm prepared."

"Diamond you will always be on point at all times. What I order you to do, you will do it within two weeks time."

"I understand your rules," she said.

We both stepped off the elevator then walked up two flights of steps to the rooftop into the brisk air. Her hair began blowing cautiously with the wind. We walked to the ledge. "Diamond, we do have fun in this game, so don't get it wrong.

"Yes, Bolo. Sophie told me how you and your boys kidnapped them and forced them into a freezer butt naked."

Laughing, "Did she? Well did she tell you that her crying ass pissed herself?"

We watched a helicopter land perfectly on a nearby building. Clouds rushed away making room for the peak of the sun.

"Oh my gosh, Bolo. She told me that too!" She turned her back towards me laughing. Hands covering her face.

Click-click. "Then how would you like a gun pointed to your fuckin head!" I yelled, pressing the gun against her temple.

"Bolo," she cried.

"Snitch ass, take off your fuckin clothes now!"

"Please, don't."

"Now, damn it!" I said. "Don't cry now, Diamond. Turn around." Her skin felt the white latex gloves against her neck.

"Oh my God," she pissed herself taking her panties off, standing butt naked.

"You wanna jump to your death or for me to blow your fuckin brains into midair?" I asked her. I pushed her by her neck as she began pissing more.

Crying. "Neither." Her eyes followed the helicopter slowly taking off.

"Pissy ass. Get the fuck dress and I'll see you back in Delaware tomorrow morning," I walked away.

"BOLO!" she shouted.

"WELCOME TO MY ORGANIZATION, DIAMOND. DELAWARE'S TOP CAPTAIN," I shouted.

Laughing and crying at the same time, "Bolo, Bolo!"

Smiling and looking back over my right shoulder, I said, "Saturday morning, Diamond."

When joining my organization you have to be initiated no matter what. I left instructions for Diamond to meet me at Sophie's house so I can hear her tell me everyone what happened in Chicago.

Back home at my cousin Dawn. Her face carried a weak sign of depression. "What's wrong, Dawn?" I asked.

She looked at me, "Cousin Bolo. I'm pregnant," she said.

"You call to make and appointment because you know we can't have no baby?"

"I'll call tomorrow," said Dawn.

Chapter 10

"Bolo, you need to get to Christiana Hospital, now," Aunt Ann's voice rattled. Her scream came roaring through my speakerphone.

"Calm down. Why are you crying?" I asked, reached for my house phone while searching the keypads on my cell phone.

"GET OUT HERE NOW!" she yelled. Startled. The cordless phone dropped to the door.

Racing out the house to my car. "What the hell is happening?" I mumbled, speeding out the driveway finding the shortest way to the hospital.

"Hello,"

"Hey, Sophie. Tell everyone that I have an emergency at Christiana Hospital, and that's where I'll be."

"Okay Captain, we'll be there," she said.

It seems like it was taking forever to get to Christiana Hospital. Backed up traffic jam, so I decided to ride the shoulder of I-95 all the way. Once at the information center, I patiently waited for the attendant to finish helping two other customers.

"Hi, may I help you please?" He asked, his hands hovering over the keyword.

"Yes," I said. "Can you please tell me what room Ann Brown is in?"

"Hold one minute, sir," he said. Leaning forward focusing his eyes on the monitor screen, he began shaking his head, a gesture of disapproval. He asked, "Is she a patient here?"

"I don't know. She called me from here," I answered. "What about Dawn Brown?"

"Let me see. Dawn Brown." He raised his left eyebrow. After tapping on the monitor four times, he said, "Ah ha."

"Oh, shit! She's here too?"

"Sir, she's in the intensive care unit in room four-twelve," he replied, dully. His voice faded as I began running.

Intercom announced code blues in room four-twelve, the room my cousin Dawn had been admitted to. Five staff members began rushing to room four-twelve with machines. I ran faster as Aunt Ann met me at the door. "Bolo," she pressed against my body throwing her arms around my neck crying.

"What the fuck is Dawn doing here in the Intensive Care Unit?" I asked. Seconds later the five staff members exit the room with all the machines they had taken in with them. *We almost lost her*, someone called.

Walking into the room is something I'd never thought I'd see. Dawn lying in bed motionless with a feeding tube running straight into her nostrils and many other tubes deeply sunk into her body. Her eyes were barely open. "Oh shit, this can't be happening," I yelled.

"Bolo, they beat my baby," Aunt Ann cried as she touched her daughter's hand lightly.

"WHO THE FUCK ARE THEY… WHO?!" I shouted. Fire blazed out of my eyes sticking to my Aunt Ann's head.

"Those two wanna be drug dealers who live across from Bancroft School," she said. "Bolo, they beat her because she wouldn't help them sell their drugs. She told me just before she slipped into that coma."

"They beat my cousin into this damn coma because she wouldn't sell their drugs," I said. Tears begin slowly moving down my cheeks. Anger quickly built inside of me. The enemies' families I will hunt down until they are found and into my hands.

"Bolo," Diamond placed her hand on my shoulder. White Diamond, her perfume was in the air.

"I want them muthafuckers kept alive until she comes out of this come, you hear me." I cried.

"We all hear you, Bolo," said Sophie. Her fingers catching the tears falling from my eyes. "You muthafuckas are gonna pay for this." Her scream echoed as she quickly ran out the room.

Crying, hoping that my cousin Dawn can hear me or send a sign that she's listening to what I'm saying. Her machines give signals that she's still alive and breathing. "Baby, you can't leave us now, Dawn. Please come back to us." I continued to cry out loud.

One week later, I was relaxing on the bed in my Cousin Dawn's bedroom reminiscing about the fun Dawn and I had together the summer at Great Adventures. We had so much fun there.

Diamond and Sophie walked in while I was laughing out loud to myself because Dawn pushed a woman into the water with the dolphins because the woman get smart with her then rolled her eyes.

"Hey, Bolo," said Diamond. Her hand rested on my left thigh as she sat next to me. Sophie smiled and waved at me while planting a kiss on my cheeks, then sat down on my right side. Dazing into the ceiling, I noticed Kev, Constance and Crystal walk into the room wearing downcast faces.

Kev said, " We all just came from spending some time with Dawn."

Constance sat at the head of the bed looking down at me while rubbing my forehead. "The doctors said that it's a possibility that she'll come out of the coma," she said. Her fingers stopped a teardrop from touching my ear.

"Damn it," Kev dashed back out the room.

"We have to- to find them before the Wilmington Police does," I said. More tears began flowing when Crystal told me that the two that beat Dawn into the coma were nowhere to be found. They all left my presence knowing that I needed some more time alone.

"Bolo. Bolo," someone called.

"Missy, I'm sorry sweetheart," my hand motioned her to sit next to me.

"Bolo. I just came from the hospital. Your Aunt Ann stayed out there, so I gave her some money for some food in case she got hungry. I'll be going bac out there tonight to be with them both," said Missy. She patted her hands on her thighs as she began crying.

"How is my Aunt Ann holding up, Missy?"

"She's furious, Bolo," she said. "Did they find the two guys that did it?"

"Not yet, Missy. Because I will find them first." My voice vibrated sensing raging anger. Missy leaned back to lay beside me. She held my hand to comfort the anger and emotions that I was feeling inside.

"Bolo. Dawn is like a sister to me and I love her so much. We're always having fun together," she said.

"She told me how ya ass fell down in the snow wearing those damn high heel shoes."

Laughing. "Oh my gosh, Bolo. I busted my ass that day," she paused. Tears filled her eyes. "I believe Dawn can hear us Bolo, so I'll tell her that you'll be out there tonight," said Missy. She jumped from the ringing of the house phone.

"Who could this be," I said, motioning Missy to hand me the white cordless phone.

Missy said, "It's Christiana Hospital." Her eyes were glued on the illuminated caller I.D. She watched closely as I slowly hit the talk button then placed the phone to my ear.

"Hello"

"Hey nephew," said Aunt Ann. Her crying touched the base of Missy's ears as she quickly sat up in the bed. Her stare caught my body go limp.

SHE FLAT-LINED!" I shouted.

Chapter 11

Leroy's Bar and Lounge. One of the many places I like to come before I turn in on Friday nights. Here I can relax while enjoying a Hennessey setup, which consist of a hint of Hennessey, hand full of lemons with orange juice on the side as a chaser. Crowded as usual. "Step-up, Bolo?" Roxy the barmaid asked.

"Yes, please," I smiled. Tevin Campbell *Tell Me* began floating into the air. A black, petite woman with a Toni Braxton hairstyle sat next to me.

"Excuse me," she said. "Wasn't your face on the channel Six News about two weeks ago?"

"You can say pretty lady. But don't you believe a damn word they say about me," I said. Roxy stared at me nodding her head. I motioned to bring another glass.

"They said so much about you," she said.

I interrupted. "And your name is?" I asked. My hand slightly under her breast.

"Penny, my name is Penny," she replied. Her girlish tone gave way that she was around twenty-nine years old.

"I'm Bolo, as if you didn't know that already. Nice to meet you, Penny."

There were two women sitting across from me rolling their eyes. I smiled at them then back to focusing on what Penny has to offer me. "First time seeing you here in Leroy's, Penny. What brings you out tonight, if you don't mind me asking?" I asked. I watched her eyes move to the two women then back to me smiling.

"Bolo. I'm from Atlanta, Georgia. I need to be in other surroundings," Penny said. She leaned to the side while placing a lemon in my mouth. "They must hate you Bolo, because I'm here talking to you."

"It happens all the time."

Roxy came over to refill my lemon cup smiling and shaking her head. Penny paid the two women no mind as well as Roxy. Her full undivided attention was all on me. "What made you come to Delaware?" I asked.

"My job. I'm the new executive assistant at AstraZeneca on Concord Pike," she said. She placed another lemon in my mouth, looked over at the women then rolled her eyes.

"Congratulations on your new promotion."

"Bolo," she said, reaching to squeeze my hand. "I don't have anyone to show me around. Would you like to do the honors?"

"Sure. I would love too, Penny." I said.

Ten minutes later, Penny and I headed on out so that she could show me here she lived. Before we left the bar Penny stopped at the door to motion her lips to call both women a bitch. Once she showed me where she lived, I left her place to answer a call from Missy wanting me to stop pass her place.

Later that night Missy woke me up telling me that she couldn't sleep so she and I started talking about whatever it was that was stopping her from sleeping. "What's on your mind, Missy?"

"Dawn. You, Bolo," she said, sitting up in the bed. "Dawn told me that you weren't nothing to be fucked with and people don't want to cross you in any way."

"Well, Missy, I'm not gonna let anyone take advantage of me, nor ruin my family," I said, resting my head on her bare thighs. "I love my family with all my heart."

"The police and F.B.I say that you're untouchable."

"Missy, I own stocks and bonds, CD's as well. My investments is where most of my money comes from."

"Bolo, every time someone gets murdered, Channel Six news is always exploiting you by showing your face and calling you the most dangerous man in the history of the state of Delaware," said Missy. Her hand held a remote control. Jazz floated through the air. "You're labeled as Delaware's Top Captain."

"I mind my own business," I said, moving my hand to massage her inner thighs. "Did the Mayor of Wilmington ever mention the three million dollars that I donated to this city?"

"Hell no, Bolo."

"You know how they found out, Missy?"

"Tell me baby," she said softly, bending forward to nibble on my ear.

"Missy, he was fucking his secretary, then she got pregnant and spilled the beans on his ass. My money is what made Rodney Square what it is today."

She laid flat on her back. "You're sweet and kind, Bolo, so many people respect you." Missy pulled me on top of her as we looked each other eye-to-eye.

"People will tak about their mother in a bad way if they have to."

They will, won't they?" she whispered. "Make love to me Bolo."

Missy and I fell asleep after giving each other the satisfaction and pleasure we'd both been looking for. That next morning the detectives asked me to meet them down at the Brandywine Park to tell me that they have a few addresses to where the witness Carmen Walker has been living. She was the woman who witnessed Bianca murdering a woman at the Crystal Palace.

Wednesday morning I rounded up my organization for business as we all headed on over to Speakman's park on 28th and Pine Street. A few kids running around in the park chasing their dog. A golden retriever. Everyone is talking amongst each other ready to accomplish our main goal. The Riverside housing project. "Hey guys!" I yelled. "Let's all do this for my cousin Dawn whom is not resting in a better place. She's definitely being take care of." Everyone's eyes all focused on me.

"Yea, yes, all right!" They all begin screaming and high-fiving each other.

"Next month is summer so I'm turning this shit up a few notches," I said. Diamond leaned forward off her car. "Diamond, tell me what I need to hear baby."

"Bolo. I have perimeters locked from Vandever Avenue and Bowers Street all the way up to Todds Lane," said Diamond. She checked the clip of her 9mm Smith & Wesson and leaned back on her Lexus.

"Crystal. What's happening with you sweetheart?" I asked.

"Bolo," she said, " I have perimeters locked from Vandever Avenue all the way up to Thirtieth Street on Govenor Printz." Her chrome .357 rested on the driver's seat of her Jaguar.

"Sophie," I walked over to her as she places her 9mm Smith & Wesson on the hood of her Mercedes Benz.

"Yes, Bolo," She smiled, "I have all perimeters locked from Vandever Avenue and Claymont Street all the way up to Todds Lane." Her eyes glared, ready for action.

I walked over to face Dexter. "Riverside is all yours, Dexter," I said.

"Yes, sir, Captain. My responsibility," he said. He stood tall. He stared back at me with dangerous eyes.

"Monte, Kev, Ty and Felix," they all leaned forward off their cars. "Are you guys ready?" I asked.

"As in yesterday, Captain," they replied, grunted, all checking the clip to their weapons.

"All your lookouts know that pay day will be in one hour," I said. "So, since we have a total of eight vehicles, I want them all parked in the shape of an 'L'."

Diamond walked over to me to light my Black & Mild, then walked back to her car.

Silence. "Well, here's how its gonna be. I need four cars parked on Twenty-seventh and Claymont facing Vandever Avenue. Then I want the other four cars parked on Twenty-seventh Street facing Govenor Print," I said.

Cars begin slowing down admiring all the expensive vehicles that were at the park as if a car show was happening. Everyone is ready, locked and loaded.

Sophie asked. "Bolo, who are you riding with?" Her driver side door swung open displaying her weapons on the door. I answered with a smile, "Dexter will be driving me over in my Navigator."

All white vehicles in route to the Riverside Housing Projects to claim what's mine. On Twenty-Sixth Street making a left on to Governor Printz

Blvd, no police in sight as planned.

Turning right on to Claymont Street as we take our position in the 'L' shape as ordered. So- called penny pushing drug dealers ceased all transactions. Passerby stand afar shaking their heads. People began peeking out their windows. Sparking another Black & Mild in my mouth, I emerged from the passenger side of my Navigator. "Listen up!" I yelled. Everyone's eyes focused on me. A grayish color pit-bull stopped in its tracks, laying down while waiting for my next move.

"OH SHIT, THAT'S BOLO. DELAWARE'S TOP CAPTAIN," someone called from a distance. Sophie, Diamond and Crystal all stood at the corner, side by side, holding their weapons downward towards the ground. Not a worry in the world knowing that all perimeters are secured of any law enforcements.

The bonafide lookouts all on point. One false slip up can cost them the five thousand dollars they were promised and most importantly, cost me and my organization some jail time behind bars.

I moved to the front of my Navigator. "You all know my man, Dexter. So from now on, he'll be in control of this raggedy shit over here," I said. Dexter moved to my side. Gun in hand. "Anyone has a problem with these crazy ass females, trust me, you wouldn't want to cross them."

Dexter stepped away from me. "You all know how I handle my business here in Riverside," he said. His .40 caliber gun raised toward the moving clouds.

"You're crazy too, Dexter!" a man said. He stood by a green electric box nodding his head.

"This session is over. You'll see more of me around her," I said. I hopped back into the Navigator while waiting for Dexter to finish his speech. Diamond, Sophie and Crystal stood by his side.

Later that night, Penny and I decided to have dinner at Red Lobster. Once the hostess asked us how many were in our party, my cell phone rang to alert me that I had to be somewhere important, so I took Penny home then drove as fast as I could to 35th Street in Eastlawn.

This is not what I expected to see. Kev, Dexter, Monte and Felix all with a malicious look on their faces, standing in the living room with their guns in hand. Nice Corinthian leather furniture matching the cream-colored entertainment system, fifty-seven inch color screen television resting in the corner. Walls professionally covered with diamond shaped mirrors. "What's the meaning of this, Kev?" I asked. "And where is Ty?"

"Bolo, he had to rush his grandmother to the hospital," he said. He motioned to follow him, the others as well.

Walking into the basement surrounded by the coldness of the concrete, dirty walls, the aroma from the smell of crack cocaine stilled the air. There they were as I took a few more steps closer, three black men all tied together side by side sitting on a run-down, torn, green couch. Crack pipes and about a pound of crack cocaine lay on a glass table with small amounts of money in plastic bags. Oh shit!" I yelled. "Do they know why they're here and why they're tied up?"

"We saved the introduction for you, Bolo," said Monte. Their eyes grew wider at the sound of our guns clicking. They were all getting high off the crack cocaine. Once had residue under his nostrils. A sign he was a snorter.

"Thank you, gentlemen." I stood over top of them. "Well, well. Look at what we have here. Do you have any idea why you're here?" I asked.

"Nah, man, your boys just ran up in here and tied us up," said the one in the middle. His hair was nappy and his voice rattled.

"I'll tell you why my men kidnapped your punk asses," I said as my gun waved, aiming at each one of their heads. "Let me bring something back into memory."They watched me sit down across from them. "Correct me if I'm wrong, will you?You three were in that dark green Impala that's parked outside several months ago. Out in the Arbor Place apartment, right?"

The bug eyed one immediately said, "Yeah man. I have a cousin that lives out there."

I quickly rose to my feet to ask, "Who in the hell was driving that piece of shit when my man Jay got killed?"

They all begin to blame each other and cursing one another out. I started to walk back up the steps, instead I stopped to say, "Y'all fucked up big time. This is the last minute of your lives." I took one more step and looked back at my men.

Pop, pop, pop, pop, pop, pop, pop, pop. That was the only sound I heard that night.

I came home to get away from all the drama that was happening. Then, called Penny to let her know that I couldn't make it to her place and she understood. I was preparing for a beautiful day tomorrow where there will be lots of excitement and many tears.

That next day I took a ride over to my Aunt Ann's house to see if she needed anything. When I arrived she was in my cousin Dawn's bedroom looking at her pictures crying. "Aunt Ann," I said. "Everyone is downstairs waiting." She looked at me with blood shot eyes.

"Bolo, can you believe my baby flat lined?" she said. Her eyes followed the gold framed picture to the dresser.

Minutes later we headed downstairs to see everyone standing and staring at the front door not saying a word. The front door quickly flung open. *SURPRISE, DAWN,* everyone shouted. "Oh my gosh. Look at everyone!" she yelled. Her eyes shined. Both hands covered her face as tears flushed down her cheeks. Missy stood behind her smiling.

"WELCOME BACK HOME, DAWN," everone shouted once again.

Dawn's eyes beamed past my organization. Passed Constance and Brandy as well. Her stare panicked to me and her mother. Aunt Ann held her close. I embraced her with a kiss on her forehead. "Cousin Bolo," she cried. Dawn held me tight.

"Why are you crying?" I asked, not wanting to ask that question knowing what may happen next.

She said, "They beat me into a coma because I wouldn't sell their drugs for them," her head buried deep into my chest as she sobs uncontrollably.

Stillness quickly sets. I leaned back a little to wipe her tears away. She wiped mines. Everyone stopped what they were doing to hear me say, "Baby it's okay. Cousin Bolo will kidnap their whole entire family very soon.

Constance came in from the kitchen rolling a four-foot pink and white cake that said, *Welcome Home Dawn. Happy Birthday.*

Dawn had once flat lined when she stopped breathing all because a faulty tube that had to be replaced. The music blasted, Peaches and Herb's *Reunited.*

Kev shouted, "THAN LET'S GET THIS MUTHAFUCKIN PARTY STARTED!"

Of course cousin Dawn didn't forget the sex we had experienced together so I ignored her and asked her when she would like to pick up her new BMW. We were all having a good time together. Dawn and I are dancing when she looked over my shoulder. "Cousin Bolo, look," she said. Her left arm raised, index finger pointing to two detectives standing at the front.

"It's okay fellas," I said. My men took a few steps backwards. "What the fuck do you want?" Both detectives followed me into the kitchen.

"Delaware's Top Captain," said Detective Johnson

"Shut the hell up you silly bastard," I leaned on the black two-door refrigerator.

"The so-called thugs who knocked your cousin Dawn into a coma are back in town," Detective Johnson said. His partner looked, smiling.

"How much assholes?"

"Twenty-five grand a piece," his partner said.

Detective Johnson interrupted. "One hundred grand to make them both disappear," he said. His partner grunted than placed his hand on his service issued revolver.

Astonished, I asked, "Two hundred grand, you'll bring them both to me?"

They both answered, "Say no more." The door closed as they made their way around the back of the house.

Back to all the excitement that's going on. Dawn walks up to me with both hands on her hips. "Cousin Bolo, what the hell did they want?" she asked.

"Nothing Dawn." I kissed her forehead not telling her that the two thugs that beat her into a coma are back in town. I asked Kev to call who he needed to call to find Dawn's attackers.

Chapter 12

June 27, 2002. Summer cookout at the Christina River Park, 98°clear and sunny skies. We all come together a few times each month during the summer to have fun and play games. My organization along with some of my mother's relatives whom I don't really give a damn about. Aunt Ann is on the grill flipping burgers and singing along with Dionne Warwick's *Walk on by*. Kids are playing baseball while some are doing cartwheels. Cousin Dawn and Brandy are both walking towards me. "Hey Cousin Bolo," said Dawn. She's wearing pink tight shorts with matching tennis shoes, and a white shirt. Her jet black hair hanging loose to her waistline.

"Hey Dawn," I said "Where have you two been?" Missy came running along beside her before Dawn answered my question.

"Hi, Bolo."

"Hey Brandy and Missy. Dawn answer my question," I tilted my head slightly to the right waiting for her answer.

"Back at the house," she said. Her eyes bulged at Brandy and Missy. They all threw their hands behind their backs like a child hiding something from its parents.

"You better not have been with none of those pissy ass boys, girl.

Dawn, Brandy and Missy all begin circling me, poking and laughing at me."This pussy is all yours cousin Bolo, and you know it," Dawn said.

Laughing. "Nasty ass," I said. You ladies enjoy yourselves." The second I walked away, the three of them started laughing harder than before. They laughed so hard at me that I literally ran over to my Aunt Ann.

"Hey nephew," she said. "Would you like a sandwich?" She place a cheeseburger on a bun, grabbed ketchup, mustard, lettuce and tomato and handed it to me. Her eyes gazed over to Dawn, Brandy and Missy while shaking her head at them.

"Thank you, Aunt Ann" I deep sigh relieved the tension I was wearing all over me.

"You're welcome," she rolled her eyes. "They better leave you the hell alone," she said. We both watched Kev, Ty, Felix, Monte and Dexter walk up to them. Everyone looks over at me and Aunt Ann smiling.

"Yall better leave my nephew alone," she said, waving a one-foot metal fork at them. They starte walking on the other side of the park. Sophie headed in my direction. She's wearing blue right fitted shorts, and a fish net shirt with a blue bra to match. Something serious is on her mind.

She yelled, "Bolo, may I speak with you for a moment please?" asked Sophie. She kept glancing back at the water. "Excuse me, Aunt Ann."

"Yeah, what's up?" I asked. I wrapped my arm around her waist as we began walking. Her heart was pumping at an irregular rate. I felt her blood begin boiling for action.

"Remember the two speed boats that we saw that night we were out here alone?"

"Yeah, why?"

She stopped concerned, looking once again out into the water. "Baby, they're out here today," she said. "And I don't like the way they keep riding pass here slowing down to look at us."

"How long does it take them to ride back through here after they leave?"

"About fifteen minutes, Bolo," said Sophie. She watched all the kids playing baseball, some chasing after an all-white pit bull while some are just walking around eating a sandwich. Shaking her head, she wondered what would happen to those kids if gunfire erupted.

"Listen to me. Here is what I need you to do," I said, placing both hands on her shoulders. "I need you to alert everyone of what's happening. Tell my Aunt Ann and Cousin Dawn to have all the kids get on that bus and get them the hell out of here. Now." We both watched the two white speed boats ride slowly pass us once again. All occupants nodding their heads and smiling.

Moments later the bus pulled out with the kids. Everyone is on point for whatever tragedy may be afflicted upon us. Sophie, Kev, Ty and Crystal are standing back by the concrete gazebo on guard while having fun in the mist.

Diamond, Felix and Dexter all sitting down at separate picnic benches alone on guard. Speedboat passes by. Everyone reached for their weapon when suddenly they accelerated and sped away. Dawn walked over to me smiling, looking back at Missy and Brandy to make sure they're not following her. "Hey girl." I said.

"Hey, cousin Bolo, nice barbecue since all the kids are gone," Dawn said. Sitting down next to me. Her eyebrows raised at the sight of organization spread about.

I distracted her. "You need new tires on your BMW," I said. The daze she was in quickly vanished. She answered, "I know, I have an appointment at Pep Boys on Concord Pike tomorrow." Her eyes went from a daze to a deep tamper on both speedboats. "Why do those guys on those speed boats keep staring at us when they pass by?" A question I was hoping she wouldn't ask.

"Dawn. I informed everyone because I don't like what I see."

"Cousin Bolo, that's why you had all the kids get on the bus to take them away from here?" she asked.

"Yes, Dawn," I said.

Brandy and Missy came over to get Dawn and take her over to my Aunt Ann. They're all talking about my organization on guard. I can tell because they're searching each one at their standing post. When Constance saw that Dawn, Missy and Brandy has come over to where she was standing when she was talking to my Aunt Ann, she began walking over to me smiling. *You're definitely free to talk to me now.*

"Hey sweetie," she said. "Nice cookout." She sensed that I was worrying about something but couldn't pin point what it is so she kissed both my cheeks.

"Thank you. Trust me, there's many more to come this summer." I said.

To get me to laugh, Constance went into her purse to show me a few pictures of herself when she was much younger. I laughed so damn hard I couldn't hear someone yelling until I looked up to see Diamond raising her gun.

"BOLO! BOLO!" she yelled.

Boom! Hearing a shot rang out, I shouted, "EVERYONE GET DOWN. GET DOWN NOW!" Pushing Constance flat to the ground was not in mind at all. All the contents that was in her purse fell out. I begin moving towards the water while looking at the rest opening fire on both speedboats.

"Cousin Bolo! Cousin Bolo!" Dawn cried out, embracing her mother. Both standing, crying as everything starts to get worst.

Sophie, Crystal and Diamond all ran towards the speedboats.

Explosion erupts. One of the boats burst into a ball of flames. "GET DOWN. GETTHE HELL DOWN, NOW!" I shouted. Rolling to the ground then coming to land on one knee with my runs raised. Dawn and my aunt dove to the ground. People crying, yelling and screaming.

Boom! An explosion view of the second speedboat hitting the side guardrail. Ball of flames beneath the Fourth Street Bridge stopping all moving traffic.

Moments Later.

Once at Aunt Ann's house we all gathered together to talk about what happened at the Christina River Park. Dawn and Constance are both ringing trays of Cranberry juice and ice to us all. Crystal, Diamond and Sophie are checking the clips on their 9mm Smith & Wesson weapons. The men are smiling at a job well done, definitely because no one got hurt on our end.

"Did anyone know those fools?" I asked. They all took a sip of cranberry juice, looked at me and said no. "We dropped them muthafuckas like sitting ducks."

Everyone laughed as we continued to talk about how much fun we had at the cookout today. Missy got up and had some business to attend, but before she left she motioned with her lips to come to her place later on.

Constance stood up, "Well guys, I love y'all," she said. Everyone tackled her with a brotherly and sisterly hug. "I'll call tomorrow from my parent's house."

Later that night I went on over to Missy's place to spend the rest of the evening with her. I was laying flat on back, head propped up on one of Missy's satin, burgundy pillows minding my business watching Lethal Weapon Two when suddenly, the television went off then the music scored a perfect smooth sound. Strawberry scented candles illuminated around the bed. There she was, taking Lilliputian steps in tune with Keith Sweat's *Right and Wrong Way* playing in the background. Slowly removing her bra, she stoppe to wiggle her matching satin, gold panties to her ankles. She definitely has the walk. Her hair pulled back into a ponytail and her pearly white teeth showing when she smiled.

"Thank you for coming over, Bolo," Missy said. My erection caught her eyes. "I've been thinking about you all day," she said. Her tongue came tracing her cherry lips as she begins climbing onto the bed.

"Have you?" I asked. *Please can we get this over with.*

"Yes, you know I have Bolo. Oh yes, yes," she moaned. The lips of her warm, wet pussy glided easily over my erection gently tapping the base of her walls.

"Oh yes, Missy," I moaned. My fingers sunk deeply into her waist. *Damn girl, keep it wrapped around my dick.*

"Ah, ah, ah, Bolo. I love- love you," she cried. Missy pressed her body against mines. We both kissed as she laid on her back pulling me on top of her.

Panting and moaning Missy and I begin grinding harder and harder until we both climaxed then fell asleep.

The next morning I went to my place to take a shower and made a few calls. Headed on down to the Eastlake housing projects on and between Twenty-Six and Twenty-Third Streets on Locust. Taking a stroll along side Prices swimming pool I see a few hunnies that I would love to holler at and maybe get their phone number.

Both hands on the fence, I watched the lifeguard blow her whistle for someone to get out the pool so she could speak to them. Glancing slightly back over my shoulder, I notice a black unmarked squad car pull up behind me with two plain clothes detectives inside.

"Delaware's Top Captain," Detective Johnson called. I heard the car doors opening and closing. Sighing, I could sense their closeness.

"That's what they call him," his partner said. His voice harshly keen is my ear. My body jerked backwards resting on the hood of their car.

"What the fuck do you clowns want?" I asked. My legs spread and my arms extended.

Kev and Ty came from out of nowhere ready to blaze both detectives for roughing me up against their car. I shook my head motioning them both to stand down. Gun fire would have erupted had both or even one detective saw them.

Detective Johnson's partner began frisking me. He said, "We convinced our boss that you had nothing to do with the death of the speed boats occupants. Luckily we were the first on the scene," he then grabbed my left arm, spinning me around to face them both.

"Let's see, Bolo," Detective Johnson stood in front of me. "Your Aunt Ann and Constance's license will definitely place them at the crime scene along with this film, which I believe to be, if developed, has the time and date on all the pictures." He said, placing all three items in my pocket easily.

Back sitting in the car, Detective Johnson leans out the passenger door while resting his chin on both arms smiling. "That will cost you a cool fifty grand, Bolo."

"When?" I asked.

"Tonight at Rash's dumpster, nine o'clock sharp." Seconds later I walk to the car leaning forward, staring at the both of them laughing in my face.

"Gentlemen," I said. "I'm your fuckin boss…remember that. I control your weak ass minds."

"FUCK YOU, BOLO," they shouted at me as they sped away.

After spending some time down in the projects with Kev and my crew, I went over to my Aunt Ann's house to give her the license that the detectives found at the Christina River Park. Constance was sitting next to my aunt when I walked into the house. They were both listening to smooth jazz and drinking Merlot red wine.

"Hey nephew," said Aunt Ann.

"Hi, Bolo," Constance said.

"Hello Ladies," I said. I came in further than sat between them.

Aunt Ann handed me a glass of wine. Constance stood up to say, "Sorry, but I have to leave." She kissed my aunt's forehead.

"Wait a minute sweetheart. I have something for you."

"Oh my gosh, thank you Bolo," Constance looked amazed at her license when I extended it to her.

Dawn came in right after Constance left the house, talking about the occupants of those speed boats. They were all stick-up men. Once they held a family hostage, later that evening they killed the parents in front of their eight and nine year old children.

"They got what came to them," I said. Lost for words when Brandy walked in wearing tight, white shorts and pink fishnet shirt with a white bra on. Her hair hung low down to her shoulders and pink polished toe-nails.

"Hey girl…Mrs. Ann, hi Bolo," she said walking over to Dawn and embraced her like a sister.

Brandy, Dawn and me continued to talk about the upcoming events for this summer and the both of them hanging out at my place for a few hours. Aunt Ann was a little tipsy so she went on upstairs to get some rest after drinking half a bottle of Merlot.

One hour later Kev asked me to meet him at the corner of 26th and Pine Street. He said that he has a very important message for me from someone who has been dealing with me for quite some time. When I arrived he handed me a dark blue piece of paper with Amillio's name and phone number on it to give him a call. Amillio is my New York drug connection, someone whom I buy my kilos of cocaine from.

"Business, Bolo," he said. He glanced back at the sound of both car alarms activating for security. "Amillio wants to know if you wanted to get your hands into the heroin business."

At the basketball court, Ty, Dexter and Monte were playing a game of three-on-three. The winners get paid one hundred thousand dollars and a beautiful money green Bentley someone put up. "I'll have a talk with Amillio bout this heroin, which I don't really want to deal with," I said. "Not unless you guys want to handle that shit."

"Hell, no!" They all yelled.

I scored two-points with the basketball then let them all continue their game. They told me that they all wanted to take a trip to Las Vegas, so I made a call to Constance so she can set everything up for us.

Chapter 13

2512 North Madison Street. Carmen and I met at her graduation at the Delaware State University when she ask me to join her at an all-night skating party in Elsmere Skating Rink. Her invitations for next weekend said to meet her family at dinner, which couldn't have come fast enough.

Her mother, an administrator at the PNC Bank on Union Street. Carmen's father is the founder and owner of Walker Construction Company on Naaman's Road in Claymont. Her brother attends Temple University in Philadelphia majoring in Computer Technology, has been for the last two years.

Later that evening we all sat down at their expensive China glass dining table for eight to have dinner. In the corner sat matching china cabinet displaying all crystal dishes.

"Mr. Lance, would you like some sweet potatoes?" Mrs. Walker asked. Her aging gray hair loosely touching the tip of her shoulders. Dark complexion with bright white teeth made her smile gleam.

"Yes, ma'am. I would love to have some, thank you," I said. She handed me a blue bowl with sweet potatoes with marshmallows on top.

Mr. Walker lowered his gold-framed glasses below his eyelids watching as his wife carefully hands me the bowl. His hair sported gray sideburns. "Son, would you like a glass of wine?" he asked. Tapping his fork on a bottle of Merlot red wine.

"Sure, sir," I said. Tony, Carmen's brother excused himself from the table because he had to retrieve a present for his parent's anniversary.

Carmen invited me to her bedroom after dinner to listen to soft music and relax. Her canopy bed dressed in hot pink linen trimmed with white protruding roses. Heart shaped pink and white pillows rested at the head of the bed.

She changed from her two-piece brown suit to a black Victoria's Secret one piece night gown. Her sandy brown hair blended with her caramel complexion skin tone. She laid flat on her back with her silky legs hanging off the bed. "Have a seat next to me, Bolo" said Carmen. She patted to the spot where she wanted me to sit. "Why don't you get more comfortable if you know what I mean," her eyes undressed me from head to toe.

"Carmen, I have to use the bathroom first, sweetheart," I said. Backing out the bedroom watching her smile at me.

On my way to the bathroom I noticed some music coming from another room so I stopped past on my way to the bathroom and noticed Tony sitting down at his computer bobbing his head to the music. "Hey, Tony," I stuck my head inside.

"*Hey Bolo, what's up?*" I replied sarcastically. Tony's brain made a lovely screen saver for his desktop computer.

Back in Carmen's bedroom, I watched her body slowly disappear under the covers. Her smile begged me to jump in with her. "Come on and get in sexy," she said. "And why do you have black leather gloves on?"

"Let's play a game baby. You have to guess who Bianca is, if not, you die. If you remember who she is then you definitely die bitch." I held my black 9 mm Smith & Wesson with a silencer attached to it.

"Um-Um," she mumbled. Her body exposed her refusing to feel the cold, black steel submerged down her throat.

"Shhh! Bianca is the woman who you picked out in a photo lineup, you know, Carmen," I said. "The one that shot Sharon Ross in the head that night at the Crystal Palace." Her eyes bulged in fear. The aroma from her feces started to give me a headache, so I covered Carmen's face with a pillow then blew her brains to smithereens.

Back downstairs, Carmen's parents Mr. and Mrs. Walker were both reading the News Journal while relaxing and enjoying each other's company.

"Goodnight, Lance" they both muttered. Their eyes focused on my weapon.

"Go to hell," I whispered. One bullet lodged into Mr. Walker's chest, then another bullet deep-root into Mrs. Walker's throat. Her head rested on his right shoulder. Their eyes watching me as if I did something wrong. I wiped off everything that my hand touched and got the hell away from there.

10:00 a.m. the next morning while driving down Fourth Street, four deep in my Navigator, Sophie was behind me in her white 500 Mercedes Benz with Crystal and Diamond inside. We made a sharp right onto Madison Street heading towards Sixth Street. Monte began pushing a female away from him as he acknowledged our presence.

"I see you guys finally made it over here," he said. He opened the driver side door for me.

"What's up my nigga?" I asked. We high-fived then watched the ladies get out the car and walk up to us. People begin gathering from afar. Kids playing basketball with one another.

"DAMN, THAT'S BOLO. DELAWARE'S TOP CAPTAIN," someone shouted.

"Hey Monte," said Sophie, admiring the sun ray beaming down from the morning skies.

Everyone embraced Monte as they all begin talking about the cook-out that we're having the next weekend at Prices Park. Two men are sitting together talking. One pulled out a thick, yellowish rubber band while the other is helping to tie it around his friends arm. "Yo, Monte, what the fuck are those two niggas doin over there?"

He answered. "Bolo, those two dumb asses are over there about the shoot-up." His eyes snarled directly at them.

"Not around those kids playing in that fuckin park!" I yelled, shaking my head at him. He sensed the anger erupting in my voice. Diamond, Sophie and Crystal are all watching my posture wanting to reach from my gun and blast their asses right out the park. Those innocent kids are holding me back.

"I'll handle that, Bolo," Monte said, grabbing a two-foot pipe.

"You're damn right you better handle that shit," I said.

"I'm with 'em," Ty trailed behind Monte.

Monte and Ty approached the two drug addicts while talking to them and looking in my direction. They quickly tossed their works into a black bag.

"Bolo, we apologized, seriously!"They yelled. I nodded my head at them both to get away from the park as they walked away.

A few minutes later we're all talking amongst each other as two Wilmington Police cars pass by. The officers shake their heads at the sight of us all pouring out Dom Perignon in memory of Jay and Bianca.

"Hey Bolo," a female girlish voice called from behind me.

From the expressions on the ladies faces it wasn't looking good on my side. My boys stepped aside smiling. I quickly turned to see a beautiful black sista walking across the street. Her hair styled in corn rolls with blonde stripes touching the tips of her elbows. Brown spandex gave her a heart shaped ass a woman would cry to have.

"Hey girl, what's up?" I asked.

"Nothing much, Bolo," she said smiling. She kept walking like she wanted no parts of what Sophie, Diamond and Crystal were thinking about.

"Stinkin bitch," Diamond said, rolling her eyes at the chick then at me.

"Too bad she cant have him," Sophie said, grunting while placing her hands on her hips.

"Damn!" I yelled. "Can't I have friends?"

Crystal said, "Bolo, your meaning of friends is fucking her to the extreme whenever and where ever."

The three of them circled around me. Laughing and poking my body with their index fingers. Monte, Kev, Dexter and Felix stepped forward. "You see, my true niggas are on point," I laughed. A tug on my shoulders pulled me away from the circle the ladies had me in.

All laughing, not paying attention to our surroundings. Sophie's eyes beamed down to Fourth Street not letting up. She said, "Captain baby, we picked the right day to come over this muthafucka."

"Damn, what the fuck do they want?," I mumbled. Everyone watched the black jump out van pull up. Five men in all black began screaming and yelling at us to all get down on the ground Weapons drawn on my crew.

"GET THE FUCK ON THE GROUND...NOW," they all shouted. I nodded to my crew and we all fell to our knees, hands behind our heads.

"Gentlemen, I'll take over from here," said a familiar voice. "Who's the boss now muthafucker?" Detective Johnson laughed.

"You stupid ass bastard!" I yelled, tilted my head back to motion my crew to get up. Seconds later we all jumped in our cars and sped away.

Later on that afternoon Sophie, Crystal and Diamond are all at the table counting and wrapping stacks of money. Kev, Ty, Monte and the rest are packaging the last of the five kilos that are left on the table. I examined both tables while making sure everyone was accomplishing their goals in what they have been taught. Everyone acknowledged my presence by nodding their head at me. I motioned my hand for all to call me then left the house to head over to my Aunt Ann's place.

Dawn, Brandy and Aunt Ann were all sitting down eating cake when I walked in the house. Wedging myself between Brandy and Dawn, they immediately planted a kiss on my cheeks while smiling. "Hey guys," I said.

"Hey, cousin Bolo," said Dawn.

"Hey nephew," Aunt Ann said. She laughed at Dawn and Brandy stuffing cake in my mouth.

"Hello, sweetie," Brandy kissed me, placing soggy cake in my mouth from hers.

"You know they had your face on the eleven o'clock news, Channel Six again, Cousin Bolo," Dawn said. She placed her saucer on the glass cocktail table. Her legs folded Indian style.

"Really," I said. "What the hell were they saying about me this time?"

Brandy interrupted. "They officially ruled you out as killing the six people in that speedboat incident," she held my hand tight as she could as if she was afraid of something.

"Wow! I didn't know that they still considered me as a suspect."

Aunt Ann stood up. "You're still considered Delaware's Top Captain," she said as she walked away, wagging her finger at me.

Once Aunt Ann left the room, it gave them both open air to say what they wanted to talk about and what was on their minds. "Cousin Bolo, please don't let us down this time," Dawn reached into a Victoria's Secret bag. "Because you said that Brandy and me can model our lingerie for you," she said.

Shaking my head, "Y'all better put one hell of a show on for me too," I said. We all looked at Aunt Ann stop at the front shaking her head then walked out the house.

I had to take a call from Penny telling me that she loved the diamond tennis bracelet that I brought her last week for her birthday. Hanging up with Penny to answer an out-of-state call. "Hello, who' this?" I asked.

"Amillio," he said.

"Nice of you to call me," I said.

"Bolo, ya man tell you about my proposal?"

"Yes," I said "I was considering it through."

Amillio asked, "What do you think about it?"

"Why don't I make a visit to New York next week and you can walk me through this shit which I have no knowledge of."

He laughed. "That will be nice Delaware's Top Captain."

Aunt Ann cancelled her plans for tonight to have a small get together at the house with a few of her girlfriends.

Brandy and Dawn called to tell me that they were coming over to model their lingerie they brought from Victoria's Secret. Setting the tone and mode right, I decided to lay a plush red carpet out from the door to my four-person burgundy marble Jacuzzi. A few bottles of Dom Perignon submerged in ice resting on the ledge. Chocolate scented candles dispersing aroma into the embracing air. Lights changed to red as the Motown sounds of Stacey Latisaw's *Let me be your Angel* began floating. I sparked up a cherry flavored Black & Mild and began relaxing.

Dawn and Brandy stepped onto the red carpet. They were smiling with their hands placed on their hips. Jet black hair hung below their waistline. Brandy showing off her multi-color panty and bra set with a white fishnet overlay. Dawn sporting her Victoria's Secret satin laced gold panty and bra set with a black fishnet overlay.

"Hey, Bolo," said Brandy. She looked at Dawn, rolled her eyes, then strutted down the red carpet towards me. Her hair swinging behind her.

"Cousin Bolo," Dawn whispers. One step forward. She spun around landing side by side with Brandy.

"You ladies look marvelous," I said, motioning them both to join me in the Jacuzzi.

As I began pouring champagne for the both of them, they slowly removed one piece of lingerie at a time, starting with stepping out of their panties. Their thoughts came about as they stood completely butt naked facing me. Once everyone was quite tipsy, Brandy began slowly sucking my dick as Dawn watched, nibbling on my ear getting me more aroused.

"Ladies, I have to be in Baltimore in a few hours," I said. We all begin drying ourselves off after a nice hot shower. "Will you please lock up for me?"

They both laughed and said, "Yes, most great one."

Once in Baltimore, I had a meeting which went well with my bankers. I convinced them that my money (30 million) will help them avoid bankruptcy and do them justice as long as I get my twenty five percent.

Back on I-95, I head north to avoid all possible traffic jams. Police as well. Dawn called to confirm that she and Brandy had left my place and made sure that all doors were secured and locked. My cell phone began ringing distinctively. Vibrating then singing, vibrating back to singing. Missy's face was appearing on my screen alerting me that she was calling in. "Hello?" I asked.

"Bolo, this guy has been following me from work lately," said Missy. Her voice trembling.

"What do you mean lately?" I asked. "Who is it" I accelerated from 55 M.P.H to 70 M.P.H flowing with the traffic while placing her on my speaker car phone.

"He's been stalking me for about a month now," she said. "My ex-boyfriend Jahleel."

"A whole month, Missy?" I asked, barely holding my composure not wanting to frighten her. "I could have taken care of that problem then."

Silence. I watched from my rearview mirror as patrol car lights flashed behind me. I slowly pulled over into the right lane as he flew pass me.

"I'm scared Bolo, that he might hurt me," Missy said. Her voice weakened. I could hear the fear pounding from her heart.

"Missy, I'll be over to your place in about one hour."

She asked, "Why so long sweetie?"

Because I'm, well I just left Baltimore," I said.

"Bolo, please hurry honey."

"Click over Missy, and call this number."

Missy placed me on hold with not a word mentioned of who she was calling. Kev picked up on the second ring so I blurted into the phone to say, "Kev, it's me, Bolo. I have a serious problem man.

"What's that, Bolo?" he asked.

"I need you and someone to head over to Missy's house, like yesterday. Stay with her until I get there. I'm about forty-five minutes from Wilmington.

"I'M ON IT NOW, BOLO!" he yelled. The phone line went dead so I had Missy to call 911 in case a patrol car was somewhere in the area. The dispatcher asked Missy where she lived while keeping her calm.

"I live at 634 Baynard Blvd, ma'am. Bolo, someone is breaking in my house," her scream almost made me rear end another car.

"Ma'am, I have a car on the way!" the operator yelled.

"MISSY, IT'S GONNA BE OKAY, KEV IS ON HIS WAY ALSO," I said.

"Yes, thank you. *Gagging* Bo-Bo-Lo," her voice suddenly disappeared.

"MISSY- MISSY!" I shouted. The phone line suddenly went dead. I called Detective Johnson to get in touch with a Delaware State Trooper to meet me and guide me the rest of the way to Missy's house. Of course his opportunistic ass asked for twenty-five grand which I agreed upon.

Thirty minutes later the State Trooper got me through the road block they had set up on Baynard Blvd. An ambulance, detectives and fire engine were in front of the house. A coroner pulls in front of my white Navigator.

I jumped out to begin running toward the house to see Kev with a sad face, head downward to the ground. "Bolo, Bolo," he said, "She's gone man. She's gone. The police arrived before we did."

"Baby, I'm sorry," Sophie said. Tears flowed from her eyes as she wrapped her arms around my waist.

Fifteen minutes sooner and I could have saved Missy from her attacker. I had my doubts about her ex-boyfriend Jahleel and his jealous ways. Now he has to pay the price. "How?" I asked, as tears constantly flowed from my eyes.

"Whoever killed her, Bolo," said Sophie, "They slashed her throat and cut the phone lines from the wall the police said."

"Her ex-boyfriend Jahleel killed her. We were talking on the phone and she was telling me all about him," I cried. Sophie then held me close to her chest as she wiped my eyes. "I will have his life and whoever's in his presence at that time. You hear me?"

"Yes," she answered. Her eyes swelled from the heavy crying.

We begin walking towards my Navigator. Pedestrians from all over watching us shamelessly shaking their heads. The coroners are hoisting Missy's body lying on the stretcher, into their vehicle. Sophie yelled, "Damn you, Jahleel!" as she opened the passenger side door.

"You knew about this, Sophie?" I asked.

"Y-y-yes, Bolo," she replied. Her words barely blew with the air she was breathing. Her eyes sticking to the dashboard.

"AND YOU SAID NOTHING TO BRING THIS TO MY FUCKIN' ATTENTION," I shouted directly at her. "KNOWING THAT SHE'S FAMILY TO US ALL!"

"Bolo," she choked.

"DON'T YOU FUCKIN BOLO ME, SHE WAS FAMILY." My voice lowered. "Damn. What the hell am I gonna tell Dawn?"

Sophie looked at me. "Bolo, I'm sorry" she said.

"Leave me alone, Sophie."

"Yes, Bolo."

Sophie left my presence covering her face and wiping the tears away from her eyes while clutching her stomach. Kev rushed to her to help her get into his car. They both drove away not even glancing in my direction.

Dawn and Aunt Ann were both sitting on the couch watching the television when I walked into the house. They were both in their night clothes finishing up on their last spoon of ice cream. They smiled as I sat between them.

"Hey Dawn. Why are you up so late?" I asked. "Hey Aunt Ann."

Can't sleep for some reason, Cousin Bolo," she said. They both planted a kiss on my cheeks.

"Dawn. When was the last time you talked to Missy?"

"About three hours ago," she said. "She wanted me to come over to spend the night with her…plus she wanted a gun."

"Gun?" Aunt Ann and I asked.

"Yes," she replied softly. *Please don't drill me with any questions Cousin Bolo and mom.*

"So you knew about her ex-boyfriend Jahleel stalking her?"

"We were gonna tell you about him, Cousin Bolo," said Dawn. She folded her hands together and placed them between her legs.

"Come here baby."

She buried her head into my chest screaming. "NO-NO-Nooooooo!"

"He killed Missy about a half hour ago while she was talking on the phone with me, Kev and the police," I cried with her. Aunt Ann embraced us both.

"I'm so sorry," said Aunt Ann.

"You see why the both of you shouldn't hold anything back from me?"

Dawn leaned back, "Yes, you could have saved her Cousin Bolo," she said. Her eyeliner ran below her chin.

"That means you too Aunt Ann. Meaning I had to terminate Rick's life." Tears began flowing out my Aunt's eyes. She said not one word.

Chapter 14

Brandywine Park. Detective Johnson and his partner were both standing side by side under the I-95 underpass, well dressed and smoking cigarettes when I pulled up. The temperature was 98 degrees outside. Water seemed to glide a top the hood of their black, unmarked squad cars. A figment of my imagination.

I took an extra precautions to use a few more minutes to enjoy the coldness inside my car. A white couple jogged with their black and white pit bull following alongside them.

"Gentlemen," I said as I stepped out of my car then closed the door.

"Anyone follow ya out here?" Detective Johnson asked. He flicked his cigarette to the ground, stomping it out.

"Nah what's up?

His partner spoke, "We're about to do a massive drug raid over in the Bucket projects this coming Wednesday," he said.

They motioned me to stand down by the water while they enlightened me about the upcoming raid.

"Damn," I grunted lightly. I walked down by the river as instructed to do "So tell me what I need to hear."

"Sal," detective whispered. I knew it was Detective Johnson, so I chose the next question carefully.

"What about Sal?"

"He's all talk about Kev and Ty. We know where your money house is at in the projects and where your package house is. Also, where you package your drugs," he said. He threw a rock into the water while making it skip three times.

"How did all of this shit come about?" I asked. As they applauded me throwing a rock into the water making it skip three times.

"Sal told Kev and Ty that he got stuck up for half a kilo of your shit. Which he lied about," Detective Johnson said. They both stood by my side. His partner kindly lit my cherry Black & Mild.

"Bolo, he got arrested trying to sneak into Colony North development by our men who drives the burgundy Crown Victoria," his partner said.

"Thank you," I said.

"You're untouchable Bolo and the want to build a case against you starting with Sal and this massive rain this Wednesday," detective said. He turned around to wave at the Park Ranger. He continued to say, "you need to move all your shit before Wednesday."

"Gentlemen, I thank you for your time," I said as I opened the driver's side door to bend down and turn on the ignition. "You will find fifty thousand dollars in this bad. Have fun with it."

I jumped in my car pulling away leaving them both shaking their heads smiling at me. Kev happened to call my cell phone so I asked him to call everyone and tell my organization to meet me at the waterfront in one hour sharp.

Instead of going home I went to my Aunt Ann's house to make a few important calls before I headed on down to the waterfront. Constance's voice was somewhat disturbed when she picked up the phone. It trembled. "Hey Constance," I said.

"Hi Bolo, how's your day going?" she asked.

"Promising. How about yours?"

"Bolo, I have this jack ass co-worker who keeps pestering me. He thinks that I like him." She whined. "Baby he keeps asking me to go out on a date with him."

"How is that coming about when you have your own office?"

"Every time my door is ajar he peeks through from time to time and now he's really plucking my damn nerves." Her voice began trailing through outer space as she continued to talk about her situation. I could tell that she shed a tear or two.

"I'll have a talk with him, Constance."

"NO!" she yelled. "I'll have a talk with him on a professional level. Then if he doesn't approve of what I say to him; that's when I'll have you step in honey. Her laughing alerted me that she was back in the mode of things.

"Are you truthfully sure because I can handle that today?"

"Bolo, sweetie, I know you don't have any problems taking care of business. I'll handle him professionally," said Constance.

"I am a professional Constance," I said.

"Hush your mouth, Bolo," she laughs. "You take a lot of things professionally for me already."

"I'll see you when you get off of work. My professional and personal head hunter."

"Yo – I'm gonna get your ass when I see you tonight, Bolo…see you." Constance laughed louder than hung the phone up.

Kev called me to say that everyone was down at the waterfront waiting for my arrival. I left my Aunt Ann's house and ran into an old friend of mines, Leon, who just came back into town wanting to join organization. Everyone was altogether when I arrived at the waterfront. Diamond stepped from the crown then walked toward my car as it came to complete stop. She opened my car door for me. Kev came to light my Black & Mild.

"Ladies, gentlemen," I nodded. "Thank you all for meeting me here."

They all yelled, "No problem, Bolo!"

"You all are probably wondering why I called everyone down here all of a sudden," I said.

"Capt, when you call on a spur of a moment meeting like this, we know that there's something very important to you as well as our safety," Sophie said. She started walking along side of me. Everyone else joined also.

I stopped. "Someone is a snitch," I said. "I will not allow that in our family at all."

They all stood motionless at the sound of my yelling. I placed my hands behind my back while staring each individual directly in their eyes.

Diamond said, "I wouldn't do no shit like that, Bolo!"

"Me neither," said Sophie.

"Shit...we're all loyal to you. We make more than enough money in this wealthy organization you have," Kev said.

"Thank you all for your loyalty, honesty, and respect because it's none of you," I said. They all sighed a sign of relief.

"Bolo, what's up?" Kev asked.

"Yeah Capt., what's happening," Ty asked. He pierced over Diamond's shoulder. She looked back then smacked him upside his head, smiling.

"Kev and Ty step forward, please." I looked down at the ground where I wanted them to stand. Raising my eyebrows, I sparked up another Black & Mild.

They both asked, "What's going on, Bolo?"

Crystal's in the background shaking her head. We all turned to watch a small blue canoe with two white females inside. They smiled and waved at us.

Kev and Ty are so damn nervous that they want to know what's going on. "Of course, no one can answer this question but me alone. They're standing before me today because Sal, that's working under them is a cold-blooded snitch."

Everyone began shouting what they had on their mind. Ty and Kev are dumbfounded to not know what's going on. I started to explain to them that Sal had gotten arrested and not robbed as he claimed her was. "Somewhere he has a half a kilo of cocaine that belongs to me."

"That muthafucker," Ty said.

"Calm down, it's not your fault that we have a corrupt spark plug in the engine!" I yelled. "The plan is for ATF to raid the money and stash houses in the bucket. You two know what ya'll have to do immediately cause it's going down this Wednesday."

"Capt., he's trying to bring down the family. I'm going to kill his ass," Diamond said. Her gun downward toward the ground ready for action.

Swaying my right hand, "No-no- no," I shouted. "He's gonna continue to work the fields. He won't know what happened. We will all make him out to be a liar," my voice lowered.

When the meeting adjourned, everyone was surprised when I suggested that Sal stays aboard my organization. He will have his time to shine one day.

That night I patiently waited for Diamond, Sophie and Crystal to meet me at the Thunder Guards Motorcycle Club. I was sitting in my Aunt Ann's two door, black 500 Mercedes Benz when Diamond's white Jaguar parked right in front of me. Three glamorous divas dressed in tight daisy dukes shorts, stepped out the car as if they were attending the tightest shorts contest. They all leaned against the car searching up and down Governor Printz Boulevard searching for the arrival of my white Navigator.

Sophie asked, "Girl, why in the hell did you bring us to this dirty ass place? The Thunder Guards of all places?"

"Shut the fuck up, Sophie and come on," Diamond replied sarcastically. She walked into the middle of the street then walked back to her car. "For you information, bitch, I asked Bolo to meet us here tonight."

Crystal yelled, "Y'all two bitched need to shut the fuck up and wait for Bolo."

They all leaned back on the car watching the champagne colored BMW from New York park in front of Diamond's car. This dark-skinned brother emerged then smiled at them. He was medium-built, bald fade, about 5'7" tall. His bling around his neck and wrist shined like a twinkling star. He looked at the girls then said, "Hey ma." He stood right in front of the three while fiddling with his hands.

"WHO THE FUCK ARE YOU?" Diamond shouted. She rolled her eyes at him. I eased myself below the dashboard cocking my 9mm glock in case he tried something he wasn't supposed to.

"Double-R" he said.

"Girl, he's that nigga from the projects over in Salem, New Jersey. They said that he got it going on over there," said Crystal. Her smile sharpened his next question. "I have a man."

"What about you, ma?" His eyes trailing Sophie's brown tight shorts.

"Nigga fuck you, you just tried to get with my girls," said Sophie. Just because you control Salem projects over here you aint shit here in Delaware."

He walked away looking back. "Fuck you bitches then."

Sophie ran around to the passenger's side door and pulled her 9mm Smith & Wesson out. Crystal chased behind her reaching to lower the gun to the ground. "Did y'all hear what that nigga just called us?" Sophie asked. Her rage came in an instant. She shook her head placing the weapon back in the car.

"Sophie chill," said Diamond. "You know what Capt would say, "HANDLEYA FUCKIN BUSINESS," they all shouted all at once.

Pulling away from my parking space, I slowed down to stop in the middle of the street while on my cellphone. "Handle ya fuckin' business," I said.

"Bolo, Bolo, Bolo!" They all yelled, standing in the middle of the street laughing and waving at me.

Each lady called me one after another the next morning laughing and talking about the kid Double-R from Salem, New Jersey. How they want to kidnap his ass then torture him for calling them all a bitch. So like I always told them, my organization *to handle your business.*

Constance was standing at the door of her office when I walked off the elevator. Her hands on her hips with a smile. She was wearing an all-black two-piece business suit. She traced her cherry red lips with her tongue. "Hello Mr. Lance "Bolo" Jones," she said. "You're on time."

"Hey sexy," I said. I smiled at her slightly brushing my lips against hers.

She said, "thank you for a wonderful time when you came over late last night. Your houses are making tremendous progress." Her hands motioned me to sit in her office chair.

"Will you give me an update on them please?" I asked.

"Well, all four houses are bringing in a total of twenty-two hundred dollars a month and with all the other access you have totaling what the bankers in Baltimore owes you, will be an exact eighty thousand dollars." She walked over to sit down on my lap. Tapping the desk with a gold point colored pen, she began playing with my earlobe.

"Okay. You find the house that you would like to own yet?" I asked. My arm gently wrapped around her waist. The fondling of her fingers to my ear aroused my manhood.

"Bolo, I must warn you baby," Constance said easing away from my earlobe. "It's in the Bear area and it costs four hundred and fifty thousand dollars."

"So what, you deserve it. When can we go out to see it?"

"This evening around five thirty," she said.

We ended the meeting on that note. I went my way heading to my Aunt Ann's house to see how everyone was doing. She was in the kitchen making dinner. Pork chops, macaroni & cheese, broccoli and my favorite blueberry muffins. Dawn was nowhere in sight at the time. "Hey nephew," said Aunt Ann. She gave me a sample of her delicious macaroni & cheese.

"Mmmm, very tasty," I said. We embraced, pecked one another on the cheek to show love. "Where's Dawn and why are you smiling?"

Dawn interrupted as she walked into the kitchen. "So what", she said.

"One day I'm gonna call her and Brandy to my place so they can model for me," I said while extending my arms out to embrace her.

Aunt Ann rolled her eyes. "Look at her now, nephew, all smiles."

We both helped her lay the food out on the dinner table. Aunt Ann shook her head wondering about her precious innocent daughter. She doesn't have any idea what Dawn and I are really into and if she did, it would break her heart.

We're at the dinner table blessing the food. Something we haven't done in a while. When I was a child, my mother always taught me to say grace before I begin eating.

"Amen," we said. The smiles on our faces showed the unconditional love that we had for each other.

"Here my precious children," said Aunt Ann. She reached across the table placing two pork chops on each of our plates.

"Mom, you need to stop that," Dawn laughed, shaking her head. She reached for the broccoli almost knocking her wine glass over.

"What?" Aunt Ann replied smirking.

"Calling Cousin Bolo your child."

"He is my child and I know that Joyce wouldn't mind me calling him my child," Aunt Ann said. Highly pleased with the lovely words that gallivant from her lips. Their faces distilling at the sight of teardrops flushing my cheeks.

"Damn, I miss my mom" I mumbled as I lowered my chin to my chest. The five words that departed from my mouth made a stream of tears flow like tearing in the wind, out of Dawn and Aunt Ann's eyes.

Wiping our tears away, Dawn ended up breaking the silence by talking about hanging out in Baltimore. She said, "yes, cousin Bolo. Me, mommy and Constance. Brandy will be coming with us if she gets back in time."

"Y'all better be careful down there…it's crazy," I said.

"Cousin Bolo, look who's talking. You know we have crazy family down there," said Dawn. "But not as crazy as you are."

"I'm not crazy, it's just that I'm very protective over my family and the ones I love."

"Awww, you love me and mommy?" She began teasing me as we all began clearing the table.

I stayed a little longer to clean up the kitchen while the ladies got pretty for an evening down in Baltimore. Just as I finished the drying the last skillet, I received a call from Kev telling me that Ty has been arrested, for what reason he doesn't know. He had some business to handle for me so I headed over to Ty's girlfriend Cheryl's house.

Cheryl was wiping her eyes when she answered the door. I knew she was crying and it wasn't because Ty was locked up. They were having some serious problems in their relationship that was far beyond saving. Her hair was neatly wrapped around pink jumbo rollers. Dressed in a pink one-piece cotton nightgown that was above her knees. She was prepared for bed but had some worries she had to get off her chest. "Come in Bolo," she said as her eyes sharpened. Her chocolate skin tone a man would not and could not turn away.

In the drug game, women they come and they go. Some we may fall in love with for a few months or so and some only one night stands. "Cheryl, why didn't you tell me that Ty was hitting on you knowing I don't allow that in my organization?" I asked.

"I – I was scared, Bolo," she answered. "He might kill me, especially when he placed is gun to my temple." Cheryl wanted to embrace me and pour her whole heart to me. Shaking my head, I grabbed her chin to examine the purplish bruise that was on her cheeks.

"He will stay in jail until he learns his lesson," I said gritting my teeth. "Does he give you any money, Cheryl?"

"Only when he wants me to go grocery shopping and when he wants some pussy," she said. We both sat down on the couch at the same time. Her legs slightly parted. She was hairless showing nothing but pussy lips.

Lost in my train of thought, I had to refocus on the television changing channels up and down. She told me that Ty had allowed all of her bills to escalate over fifty thousand dollars. She cried, "Bolo, I'm so sick of his ass, seriously." Cheryl was so distraught that she leaned back, propping herself up in front of me not knowing that she's displaying all that she's working with between her legs.

"Don't worry," I said. "I'll have my Aunt Ann and Cousin Dawn come over tomorrow and write you a check, Cheryl. Plus give you an extra twenty grand for yourself."

"Thank you so much, Bolo," she continued to cry. Noticing my eyes peeking between her legs. Come fuck me, Bolo, it's all yours baby. Embracing Cheryl, she fell asleep so I covered her up with a blanket and let myself out the house.

I parked and walked up Fifth and Franklin Street visiting my main man, Jahleel, whom I've never seen or met before. He answered the door in his Polo pajamas puffing on a marijuana cigarette. Ignorant as he seemed to be, he blew the smoke right in my face. From the description that Detective Johnson had provided to me, I immediately recognized Jahleel. He was light skin complexion, bald headed, 5'8", with a medium build. He yelled, "Who the fuck are you nigga?" He motioned me to close the door and follow him in the living room.

I grabbed my black 9mm Smith & Wesson with a silencer attached from my waistline. I raise it to his chest and whispered, "This is for Missy, mutha-fucka!" His chest opened, spitting out blood. His eyes closed as his body jerked back into the wall then sliding to the floor.

A woman called out, "baby what's happening in here?" She asked while walking into the room silently abridging her scream. Hypnotized by the sight of my silencer pointing directly between her eyes. Her skin tone chocolate, bugged eyes and black shoulder length hair; she was wearing only her satin pink panties and bra.

"SHUT THE FUCK UP BITCH," I shouted. There was two distinguishable voices singing along with the Miracles *You Really Got a Hold on Me.* A yellowish fluid began seeping through her panties down her inner thighs.

Shaking her head, "please- please don't kill me." She begged for her life. A squirt of her tears rushed her cheeks, eyes rolled back into her head. Her lifeless body slumped over Jahleel.

"What the fuck is going on down here?" A male voice called. He was a white man in brown boxer shorts, tall, blonde, and muscular. I raised my weapon.

"SHIT!" I shouted.

"What the…" was the last words he said before his body tumbled to the end of the steps.

The woman's voice stopped singing. She asked, "Baby are you okay down there?" Her voice became clearer. "Oh my God!" She stood at the top of the steps. She was white and naked.

"You too," I said. "Shut the fuck up and come here" with a gester of my gun. She began walking down the steps.

"Oh, God, please don't kill me," she cried.

"You should've stayed wherever you were bitch, now join 'em." Her body landed right on top of the white man's boy. They belonged together, dead.

Chapter 15

Dawn and I cruised around the city on Thursday night talking about any and everything that comes to mind. I've very hesitant about telling her that our two enemies who beat her into a coma are back in town. I just don't know where they could be.

Market Street is always an attraction for Dawn because damn near everyone knows her. We even stopped a few times to holler at some of her girlfriends. Moments later, we approached a brown brick warehouse building on Twenty-sixth and Market Street. It felt like winter when she and I walked inside.

Dawn's dressed in all black, her hair neatly pulled back into a ponytail. Her expression wondering why we were inside of this old warehouse. She asked, "What are we doing in this old, dirty, run down warehouse?"

"Don't worry sweetheart, you'll see."

"Cousin Bolo, don't tell me that you're about by this place."

"No," I said. "But something's on your mind that you need to tell me."

We stopped at a steel rusted double door.

"Cousin Bolo, I'm pregnant" said Dawn. "The doctor said that I'm one month pregnant."

I said, "You know that you can't have this baby."

"I know, that's why I have an appointment for an abortion in two weeks."

"Dawn I really need you to handle something for me." I handed her a pair of black leather gloves. "What you're about to see will be very upsetting and very disturbing , but you must not break down, you hear me."

Confused , not saying a word, she just nodded her head agreeing to what I said to her. I quickly pushed the steel double doors open as Dawn and I took a few steps forward. "Oh my God!" she yelled. Her jaws damn near dropped to the cold, concrete floor.

"This is what the both of us have been waiting for sweetie," I smiled. Her heart I seen literally see popping out of her cotton, black shirt.

There they were, our enemies, hanging from the ceiling by a five-inch tight rope butt-ass naked. The two men, the so-called wanna be drug dealers whom beat my cousin Dawn into an unbearable come that almost ended her life. They were shivering from the coldness of the warehouse. "WHO THE FUCK ARE THEY? I DARE YOU TO START FUCKING CRYING, BECAUSE I'M NOT TRYING TO LEAVE ANY FUCKING EVIDENCE BEHIND. NOW WHO THE HELL ARE THEY?" I shouted.

Sobbing, she said, "T-T-They're the two who beat me into a coma Cousin Bolo."

"Now put this body suit on."

"What are we gonna do to them?" Dawn asked, looking at our enemies as they try to wiggle themselves free. Her body suit made her look like a child with her mother's clothes on.

"You're gonna kill 'em with no objections," I said.

"Kill' em?" She asked, taking two steps away from me. *You must be outta ya mind if you think I'm gonna kill somebody.*

"Look at me. In my eyes damn it!" I yelled. Her jaws rested in the palm of my right hand. Her glassy eyes staring straight at me. "These punk ass niggas almost took your life away from your mother and me. They didn't hesitate not once when they beat your ass into a coma and on top of that you're a female."

Her vivid courage kicked in rapidly. She yanked her face from the palm of my hands then said, "Cousin Bolo, they almost killed me. They beat me into a coma for a whole month." Her eyebrows raised, as her eyes blazed with fire wanting to immediately destroy her enemies.

"NOW WE'RE GETTING SOMEWHERE", I shouted. We both walked over to them. Feces and urine aroma gave way that they were there for a few days or so. Both malnourished.

Minutes later, I handed Dawn two syringes filled with 50cc's of pure, uncut cocaine. I then held my gun to one of their temples daring him to make one move. "That's it baby, let 'em suffer, let 'em die slow." I lowered my weapon then stepped aside.

"You two muthafuckas like to beat on women, do you?" asked Dawn. She motioned me to remove the duct tape from their mouths by running across her mouth with her hand.

The pain from ripping off the take made their bodies jerk, eyes tightly closed then quickly opened back up. "We didn't mean to do it, Dawn and Bolo," one said. His voice sluggish from the effectiveness of the cocaine.

"WHAT NIGGAS," I said. "YOU TWO BEAT MY COUSIN INTO A FUCKING COMA BECAUSE SHE WOULDN'T SELL YOUR DAMN DRUGS!" I shouted. I drew my second gun on them wanting to blaze them both. Dawn ran over to grasp a four-foot long, silver samurai sword.

"You bastards," she yelled loudly. Her arms extended the samurai sword high towards the ceiling.

"Whoa – whoa. What the hell are you about to do?"

She stopped dead in her tracks. "You always told me to handle my business, Cousin Bolo. Now step back, please," Dawn said, then charged at her enemies beheading them both with one powerful swing.

They both screamed for mercy while Dawn was in motion. Not one did she hesitate about cutting off their heads. She's my hero.

Dawn sprinted upstairs to shower once we arrived at the house. Her job well done, a professional. Maybe I'll take her on a few murder beefs with me. Sal, I'll have her kill his snitching as for me…maybe.

Brandy and my Aunt Ann walked into the house carrying shopping bags from Macy's Strawbridge's. Bright smiles as usual. "Hey nephew," said Aunt Ann.

"Hi sexy," Brandy kissed my cheeks.

"Hello ladies. Where have you two been?" I asked knowing they been to the Christiana Mall.

"To the mall," they both answered. Brandy sat down next to me and Aunt Ann sat across from us smiling.

Dawn came running down the stairs to see who I was talking to. She was wearing a pink, full-length, satin nightgown. Her hair was tied up with a brown, terry cloth towel. "Did y'all buy the shoes that I wanted?" she asked.

"Yes bitch, we have the shoes you asked for," said Brandy, tossing the blue box over to Dawn.

"Thank you" Dawn said, holding her stomach and covering her mouth "Oh shit, I have to puke." She jumped up then ran into the kitchen.

"Oh, oh, someone must be pregnant," said Aunt Ann.

Brandy blurted, "trust me, MRs. Ann, that girl don't get any dick so we can cross that one out."

"I don't know Brandy," said Aunt Ann. "She could be sneaking around to get some."

"I'll kick her ass if she's pregnant," I said

Dawn walked back into the living room rolling her eyes at us. "Mom, I'm not pregnant either," she said. "As tight as my pussy is, pregnancy is the last thing on my mind." She looked at me once again rolling her eyes.

"Hmm, mmm," I mumbled.

"Besides, my man won't approve of that shit anyway," she kissed my forehead.

"Ewww girl, brush your damn teeth, kissing on me."

"Bolo, (kissing my forehead) I'll kiss you again."

"Nasty ass, ya breath stinks, Dawn."

Dawn began walking up the stairs while Brandy followed behind her. They started arguing about something, which I enjoy hearing those two go at it from time to time.

Sunday morning, Diamond stopped me in the middle of the street. Market Street between Twenty-third and Twenty-fourth backing up all the traffic. "Bolo, you know that nigga Double-R that we had a shout out with at the Thunder Guards," she asked.

"Yeah, what's up with him, Diamond?"

"He's in Gander Hill, Bolo."

"Does he have a bail?"

"You said that he operates the projects over in Salem, New Jersey right?"

"Yup"

"Bail him out Diamond, then you tell the others to handle their business," I said. People began tooting their horns. We pay them no mind as Diamond give them all both her middle fingers.

She said, "I know just the right person to bail his ass out."

"Cool, I want his life, ya hear me?"

"Yes sir," she replied, blowing a kiss at me then pulled away.

Cal's barbershop on Thirty-first Street and Market Street was the only barbershop that opens on Sundays with the exception of the Wilmington's mayor whom I had to rough up a few times to get his cooperation. It would have been his family next but he finally gave in to me.

Cal was cutting someone's hair when I walked inside. My cousin Art was just standing there flicking channels on the television remote while talking to Cal and the customer. They all looked at me coming inside then closing the door behind me. "Hey cousin Bolo," said Art. He shook the excess hair off the black apron he held.

"What's up Art and Cal?" I asked. I held my car remote high to activate my car alarm. The customer nodded his head at me watching as I placed my 9mm on the top of the counter. *Please get me away from this crazy nigga.*

"Sorry to hear what happened to your man Ty," Cal said. He smiled down at the expression his customer made when he saw my gun.

"Ty was into so much shit y'all that I didn't even know about. So ain't no telling who killed his ass," I said "Whoever done it, they will pay the price."

"You mean enemies?" Art asked. He watched me jump into the barber's chair. The customer paid for his service then hurried out the door.

"Exactly," I answered.

Cal asked, "You heard what happened to those niggas that was going around the city robbing people?" He began sanitizing his barber equipment. "Well that abandoned warehouse on Twenty-sixth and Market Street, how they found them boys arms chopped off and both their heads decapitated."

He didn't give me a chance to answer, but it was music to my ears. That there was the work of my Cousin Dawn.

"Come to think of it Art and Cal, they were the ones who beat Cousin Dawn into a coma."

"I remember that, Bolo. The police have witnesses that they saw them arguing with a few guys from the Westside." Cal yelled. A customer came in shaking his head then immediately walked out, not saying a word. We both laughed at Art because he said that the customer noticed me in the chair.

"Damn, it's like that?"

"Yeah, Bolo it's like that," said Art. "Bald head."

"Please, I have a special date tonight," I leaned back as he began shaving the little bit of hair that I had left on my head.

Crystal, Diamond and Sophie had to execute Ty by tying him down to his bed then pouring gasoline on him and setting his ass on fire. That was after I finally bailed him out, then he went to the two detectives that work for me and told them about my business. Dirty rat he was.

That night, Ty's girlfriend Cheryl asked me to meet her at the Courtyard at the Marriott here in Wilmington, Delaware. When I waked into room one thousand seven, she was standing at the window with two champagne glasses in one hand and a bottle of Dom Perignon in the other.

Her jet black hair styled with two shoulder-length cornrows. She was wearing navy blue laced panties and bra, with matching high heels and full brown chocolate lips. "Thank you for coming, Bolo," she said. We met at the head of he bed. It was dressed in black satin linen, two dozen red roses lying on two fluffed pillows. There were scented candles all around the room including around the Jacuzzi. A bed of strawberries floated atop the water surrounded by pink suds. Keith Sweat's *Nobody* began filling the air.

"Cheryl, are you sure that you want to go through with this?" I asked. "Because we can set it up for another day."

She stood face to face, "Bolo, I know that Ty is dead now and yes I do grieve." Her hands began to pull down my jean shorts. "How can you love a man that continues to beat on his woman like she's nothing?" she asked. *Now please give me what I want.*

Cheryl placed her right index finger against my lips motioning me not to say another word. We both looked downward to watch the stiff erection of my manhood. Kissing, she gently lays me flat on the bed to begin working her magic. It was a beautiful thing that Cheryl and I experienced together.

That next morning, Cheryl and I continued to finish where we left off. She went her way and I went mines. I was hungry so I headed to the Posthouse on Market Street. As I was driving past the cemetery I noticed Sophie standing at my ex-crime partner Miguel Lopez's gravesite. I wonder why she hasn't mentioned his name to me yet. Is she out to get revenge? Does she have any idea that I killed him?

Someday. I will bury her ass next to him. Then she can grieve all she wants to.

Chapter 16

Sal answered the door singing Tupac's *Me Against the World.* He smiled, motioning me to follow him into the living room where he was playing PlayStation. There were Corona beer bottles all over the black glass, oval shaped table and a few lines of cocaine he tried to cover up from me. I had no idea that he was getting high.

"Have a seat, Bolo." He held the television remote then turned the TV off.

"How's your days down in the Bucket?" I asked.

He leaned forward to sit straight up. "Lovely, Bolo," he said. "The guys are treating me like family. Money is good, bills are being paid." Sal then paused, "all of the above."

"The reason I came here Sal, is because I have a proposition for you that you may like as well as have you making more money." I leaned forward so we were now eye-to-eye.

His eyes glowed. "Word," he nodded his head rubbing both hands together.

"Listen," I said. "My man Ty is dead Sal, so I want to offer you the position next to Kev, if you like."

"Hell yeah, Bolo!" He yelled. He jumped up so fast, he almost landed on me when he sat back down.

"Calm down, calm down. This position involves working with my connect, handling my money and drugs."

"I'm listening," Sal's ears radared to high level.

I said, "Kev will teach you the rest of what you'll have to accomplish in each and every task."

"Yeah Bolo, cause I know it already," said Sal. He picked up another Corona then popped it open. "I'm a helluva observer."

One helluva snitch you are. Anyway Sal, you'll need your own car which I'll get for you this coing weekend and your own house as well," I said. *You better hope that I don't attach a bomb to the car.* "My bankers and real estate agent will also contact you this Tuesday."

Sal excused himself, walked into the kitchen then a few seconds later returned with another six-pack of Coronas. I can tell that he gave himself a quick fix because of the white powdery residue lying beneath his nostrils.

At five-nine, two hundred and fifty pounds, a big boned black man of his size; it'd take about three slugs to knock him off his feet. He sat back down next to me, popped open another bottle then guzzled it straight down without stopping.

I asked, "Will you take all responsibilities that come with the territories?"

He said, "You can trust me Bolo, I can definitely handle it." His eyes glanced into the ceiling.

"Okay, okay, I'll have Kev to hit you off with ten thousand dollars for starters."

"Thanks Bolo, because I could really use the money." Sal said excitedly. *That is my cocaine habit.*

"Well, I better get on my way," I stood up. "My man Sal, thank you for accepting this new position." His left shoulder felt the strength of my right hand.

Standing up, "I won't let you down, Bolo," he said. His deep voice roared like a lion.

"I'll have Kev call you and explain to you all that I expect in my organization. Delaware's Top Captain."

"Cool, Bolo," he walked in back of me as I headed to the front door. "I'll give him a call as soon as you leave."

"But Sal, I just want to know one more thing, my man," I said facing a giant two times my size.

Looking down at me, he asked, "What's that Bolo?"

"How is it that you got stuck up for a half a kilo of my cocaine when you offered vital information to the detectives who work for me?" I asked. "My organization you muthafucka." I stepped back about four feet cocking my 9 mm weapon.

"Bolo, please let me explain to you," he cried. The cocaine high he had burst from his body and ran.

"MUTHAFUCKER, YOU TOLD THEM EVERYTHING ABOUT MY ORGANIZATION," I shouted as rage began building inside me. "THEY REPORT TO ME. WHY THE HELL DO YOU THINK THAT WHEN THEY RAIDED THE BUCKET THEY FOUND NOTHING."

"Bolo, man" his voice rattled, body trembled. "I – I."

"Kiss your ass goodbye nigga! I yelled. My weapon raised. His heart pumping.

Boom! Boom! Boom!

Sal's body leaped into the cherry wood china closet that was resting against the wall. It fell, landing on top of his body My exit was quick and easy.

The news of Sal's death had awakened the city because his body was discovered a few hours later by his mother, the mayor's ex-wife and Sal's fiancée coming back from grocery shopping. The Channel 6 News broadcasted it damn near all morning long. They said that recently he's been spotted in the Bucket Housing Projects several time selling drugs under the infamous "Delaware's Top Captain," a.k.a Lance 'Bolo' Jones.

House phone ringing, "Hello," I said.

"Hey Capt.," said Kev. He was choking

"What's wrong, Kev?"

"Sal," he answered.

"What about Sal?"

He said, "That black, fat, rat, snitch is surely dead, all over the news."

"Let the mothafucka rest in peace, Kev" I replied grumpily.

Laughing. "Peace," he said. The phone line went dead.

Cheryl called as soon as I hung up with Kev. She was excited about how beautiful the house was that I bought her. Dinner was served next Saturday at her place, which I couldn't wait to initiate the whole entire house.

On Thatcher Street driving towards Twenty-sixth Street, I noticed the jump out team has several people on the ground spread eagle. I slowed down to see if any of my men were involved. Not one. I swung a left onto Twenty-sixth Street then another left on Locust Street parking my Navigator in front of the Price's swimming pool to admire two fine females take a deep dive into ten feet. They both climbed out at the same time.

Hot sunrays beaming down, water slowly trickled off their breasts and ass onto the scorching hot ground.

"Hey Bolo," they both waved smiling at me.

"Hello ladies," I replied. They watched me walk up to the fence. "Both of you are very sexy. May I ask, what's your names, if you don't mind me asking?"

The Chinese female spoke first. "My name is Kimberly, you can call me Kim for short."

"My name is Naomi," the dark-skinned sister said. They both approached the fence.

"Nice to meet you ladies," I smiled. "How come I haven't seen you ladies around before?"

Naomi said, "That's because we both live in Dover, Bolo."

"Let's see," said Kimberly, her Siamese cat eyes pierced through my white tank top. "Your real name is Lance 'Bolo' Jones, slash Delaware's Top Captain." She smiled at the sight of my chest jumping up and down. Kimberly had on a hunter green two-piece bikini swimsuit. Her jet-black hair hung loosely to her elbows.

"Damn media," my eyes focused on the water dripping between Kimberly's cleavage.

Laughing, Naomi said, "You're exactly right, handsome." She pushed Kim to the side. Naomi is sporting an all red two-piece bikini swimsuit. Her shoulder length, sandy brown hair blended with her silky skin tone. Shiny, full brown lips reached out to me. They were glossy.

I asked, "Where are your boyfriends?

"I'm all single, Bolo," said Kimberly.

"Kimberly, you tell me that as beautiful as you are, that you don't have a man?"

"Bolo, men are so afraid to talk to me because I'm beautiful." She spun around flinging her hair from front to back.

Naomi has a man but said that she is willing to play house with me and whatever comes along with it. After we exchanged information I asked the ladies to accept my invitation to have dinner with me next week at my penthouse.

Leon was standing outside G&P Pizza shop on Twenty-eighth and Market Street when I pulled up. He smiled when I motioned him to jump into my Navigator. He couldn't stop smiling.

You're on time, Leon," I said.

You told me to meet you here at one o'clock, Bolo," he said. He finally stopped smiling to pay very close attention to what I had to say to him.

"Call Kev," I said and handed him five thousand dollars with a white piece of paper. "Here's your cell phone and Kev will take you to get any car you want as long as it's white. Leon, welcome to my organization, Delaware's Top Captain."

Not getting excited is what I expect. He said, "Thank you, Bolo. I'll call Kev right away." Leon got out at the top of Twenty-sixth and Market Street then immediately called Kev. Leon was definitely about his business.

At Southbridge Housing Projects- Sophie, Diamond and Crystal have control of my organization. They improved their game by selling fifteen kilos of cocaine to a whopping forty kilos every two week. Their main clients in the New Jersey and Maryland. So I headed over to spend some time with all of them. When I approached Eden Park they were leaning against Sophie's white Mercedes Benz.

"Hey Bolo," they all spoke at once. Leaned forward to acknowledge my presence. Diamond walked around to the driver's side to open my door.

"Thank you," I said. "Hello ladies."

"You're welcome, love," said Diamond standing side by side with Crystal and Sophie.

I asked, "What's been happening out here?" I watched Crystal spark up a cherry flavored Black & Mild and hand it to me.

"MONEY, MONEY, MONEY," Sophie shouted. She started jumping up and down like a child with her hands behind her back waiting for ice cream.

"Bolo, what about that fat- rat snitch, Sal. He deserved what he got, didn't he?" said Diamond.

Before I answered, Crystal interrupted. "His girlfriend (fiancée) almost committed suicide when she walked into the house and saw Sal with three slugs in him and laying in a pool of blood."

Sophie turned to Crystal, "That's because the bitch was on drugs and now she can't get any more freebies." She laughed out loud.

I looked at Diamond, she looked at me. We wondered when Crystal and Sophie were going to give me a chance to talk so we just laughed along with them. I said, "They took her ass to the state hospital on DuPont Highway where she belongs." My eyes followed two Wilmington Police cruisers. "How long have they been lurking around here?"

"First time, Bolo," Sophie said nodding her head while walking in front of her car.

Before I left the girls, we talked then reminisced about how they were initiated into my organization. How I left Diamond butt naked on top of the Sears Tower in Chicago. She was so embarrassed when I mentioned it to the girls that she pissed herself. She had it coming for laughing at Sophie and Crystal for when they pissed themselves in the ice cold freezer I placed them in. Bianca was there too. May she rest in peace.

As daylight fades away, the streets lose momentum and drug dealers stray the corners patiently waiting for their next customer. I slow down watching the fiend drop to her knees for her next hit. She dominated oral sex. Sorry ass wanna-be drug pusher. *I'll deal with him another day.* I stopped past my Aunt Ann's house to see if they needed anything before I turned in for the rest of the night.

Dawn's best friend, Rhonda, was found dead in her mother's bedroom of a possible overdose of some type of drug. I never knew Rhonda was using drugs. She hated the sight of seeing drugs anywhere. She was pregnant so I know definitely that that wasn't the reason to commit suicide. Dawn, on the other hand won't take it lightly tomorrow at the funeral.

Brandy and Dawn were watching cartoons when I walked into the house. They were laughing at Spike, the vicious dog, chasing after Tom and Jerry. "Hello ladies," I smiled and kissed them both on their cheeks.

"Hey Cousin Bolo," Dawn said. She reached up and planted a kiss on my cheeks.

Brandy said, "Hi Bolo." Her girlish voice sharpened my ears. Her chocolate colored lips touched my bottom lip.

"Where's your mother?"

Aunt Ann heard me, "I'M DOWN IN THE BASEMENT, NEPHEW. HOOKING UP THIS COMPUTER I BOUGHT TODAY!" she shouted.

"OKAY, I'LL SEE YOU WHEN YOU COME BACK UP," I shouted back then looked at the sudden sad face Dawn was carrying.

Dawn said, "Cousin Bolo, I don't believe that Rhonda was using any drugs."

"What makes you say that sweetheart?" I asked. Brandy turned the television off.

"She met this guy name Marcus," said Dawn. "Word on the street is that he was definitely a heavy drug user." I witness a single tear slowly move down Dawn's cheeks. She quickly wiped it away.

"I'll check into it baby," I said, sitting in between them both. "I'll find out what this nigger really knows about Rhonda's death, cause I keep hearing the same damn thing, Brandy and Dawn.

"Please do, Bolo," Brandy rested her head on my shoulder.

Dawn said, "Thank you cousin," her head came crashing under my armpit. Both began crying and tightened their grip around my arms for security. I felt their pain. I shed tears with them.

Aunt Ann had come up from the basement. She served us a pitcher of nice, cold orange juice. "Hey nephew," she said watching me nod my head to comfort both ladies.

I asked Dawn, "When do you start your college courses?"

"This September," she answered, facing her mother to wipe away her tears.

Brandy said, "Girl I wish that I could go there with you, but I don't have that kind of money." Her girlish voice lead her to place her hands in between her thighs. She was sad.

"I know girl, we could go shopping and be the best looking bitches in there!" Dawn yelled. She then noticed the sadness Brandy was experiencing.

"Yes, you do Brandy," I smiled.

"Huh?" she replied, gracefully sitting up.

"You head me," I said. "You have the money to attend college with Dawn and I'll give you girls the same money to go shopping."

"THANK YOU! THANK YOU!" They shouted. Their embrace became wet with tears.

"Auntie, Auntie!" I yelled, loudly at the top of my lungs trying to wiggle my way out from in between them.

Laughing. "Nephew, I'm staying out of this one," she said. "You're the one who keeps spoiling their asses, look at 'em." She stood up shaking her head walking away. Dawn and Brandy continue to cry.

I promised Brandy and Dawn that I would definitely look into the death of their best friend, Rhonda. Truly indeed I want to have a talk with this Marcus character that everyone is talking about. So I gave Detective Johnson and his partner a call to meet me in a scheduled area in the city.

They pulled up alongside of me in the middle of the old Merchant Square shopping center on Governor Printz Boulevard. Both our cars were facing different directions.

"Guys, I have a problem," I said. "Rhonda Lewis, she used to date this gentleman name Marcus, don't know his last name. But I need you two to find him. Find out what he has to do with Rhond's death. You said that the police has evidence?" I tossed them two manila envelopes.

His partner smiled. "We'll work on it all night, Bolo."

"For one hundred grand. You damn right you will." I sparked a Black &

Mild. They both sparked cigarettes then blew the smoke like a chimney.

"Damn, you have that shit like running water, don't you?" His partner asked. He leaned across Johnson as if he hasn't seen me before. *Oh, I forgot you run the whole damn city of Wilmington in the drug trade.*

"ALL EIGHTY MILLION DOLLARS OF IT, ASSHOLE," I shouted arrogantly.

Detective Johnson said, "Maybe we should stick him up," he laughed throwing his cigarette butt out the window. Then gritted while watching me pull away.

I yelled, "You do that muthafucka!" I threw my car in reverse and once we were face-to-face again, I paused, "I'll kill your entire fucking family" clenching my teeth. I then spat on their car and sped away.

Home, Constance called me as I stepped out the shower. She was laughing about something or at someone. "Hello," I said.

"Hey Bolo, I'm sorry sweetheart," she said.

"Why are you laughing so hard, Constance?"

"Looking at this video of you when we were walking together in the rain. Then you fell in the muddy hole trying to save me from falling." *And you really busted your fat ass that day.*

"Oh that funny," I asked laughing along with her.

"I'm gonna miss you Bolo, when I leave for my seven day business trip," said Constance. Her voice dejected quickly.

"Baby, when you come back from your business meeting. I promise to take you out to the movies and dinner. You and I will spend the whole entire day together. Then – ," I said, " I'll pamper you at my place with a manicure, pedicure and anything you want me to do to you, okay?"

"Yes," she cried. "I love you Bolo, good night."

Constance had become so emotional she propelled the words *I love you* from her mouth, not knowing what she said. I'll confirm what she told me when she returns from her business trip. I'll ask her at dinner.

Rhonda's funeral was so packed that it was a long line outside the church when I drove up. I parked right in front of the door. Everyone began staring at me as I got out of my white Navigator. Someone whispered, "*Oh shit, Rhonda knew Bolo, 'Delaware's Top Captain'.*" While another whispered, "*Rhonda was Bolo's cousin Dawn's best friend. Damn, I feel sorry for whoever has something to do with her overdose.*"

I walked into the church to see Dawn, Brandy and my crew all sitting around Mrs. Lewis, Rhonda's mother.

"*Oh, it's definitely gonna be trouble now because Rhonda knew Bolo and he's gonna find out what happened to that innocent girl.*" A woman nodded her head at me as I glanced over at her. She literally read my mind.

Rhonda looked asleep in the pearly white casket she was laying in. She was dressed in an all-black, satin, laced dress. Her hair neatly rested on her shoulders. Her dark red lipstick matched the dozen red roses wedged between her hard, cold hands. I cautiously viewed her body, shaking my head. People crying out Rhonda's name as they watched me bend over to kiss her forehead. I turned to face her mother. "Ma'am," I said. "I'm truly sorry for your loss."

"Bolo, my baby never done drugs in all her life. Why would she start now?" said Mrs. Lewis. Her tears longing for answers of her daughter's death.

Whispering in her ear, "I'll see what I can find out," I said.

"Mrs. Lewis, Rhonda was like a sister to us all. I miss her so much," said Dawn with tears running down her cheeks.

As Mrs. Lewis and Dawn were embracing, Kev tapped me on the shoulder to tell me that Detective Johnson and his partner just walked into the church. So I excused myself then began walking towards them with a dirty look on my face, wondering why they were at the funeral while Rhonda's family was grieving. Before I said a word, Detective Johnson motioned me not to say a word knowing that I was about to explode at any given second. He lowered his dark sunglasses below his eyelids.

"We found her boyfriend Marcus' fingerprints on the syringe that was left in Rhonda's arm."

"Now we're getting somewhere," I said.

"What about Mrs. Lewis, Bolo?" his partner asked.

As the three of us began walking to the front door, everyone's eyes were focused on us. "*I wouldn't be surprised if that young man has theWilmington Police Department on his payroll as much money as they say he's worth,*" this woman loudly said. She was quite old in age.

They both agreed not to tell Mrs. Lewis that her daughter had been murdered by her boyfriend. They jumped in the car knowing to bring this Marcus character to me or finish what needs to be done and to anyone in his presence.

Later that afternoon, I ran into Mercedes whom I haven't seen in a few months. We took a quiet walk at the Brandywine Park. We laughed and had a few good moments with each other. Today was her birthday so I took her to the Jeep dealership onThirtieth and Governor Printz to buy her the black Jeep Grand Cherokee that she always wanted.

The end of the day, Brandy and Dawn came over to my house to remind me of what they were working with and of course what I was missing. After relaxing in my Jacuzzi and drinking champagne, we headed to bed. Dawn and Brandy positioned themselves in the doggy-style position. They allowed me one minute to be inside them; from Dawn to Brandy, Brandy to Dawn to see which one I could climax in. Of course it was Dawn. Later that night Brandy wanted me to do the same to her so I did just as I was told to do.

International House of Pancake on Route 13 is where the three of us ended up the following morning. We ran into my crew there so everyone agreed that we'd get a suite at the Taj Mahal in Atlantic City the following month.

Chapter 17

Monday afternoon hanging outside the fence at Price's swimming pool talking to the Delaware's Park and Recreation officials about having a pool party this Saturday. The temperature reached ninety-nine degrees.

I had convinces them that there wouldn't be any trouble at this coming event on Saturday. They finally all agreed to let me have the party after I offered them all three thousand a piece. There was a police chase coming down Twenty-Third Street, which they apprehended their suspect by throwing their nightstick at him.

Cell phone ringing. "Hello?"

"Hey, good looking. How are you doing?" Kimberly asked. Her voice sounded as if she were standing right behind me. Naomi screamed and shouted *hello Bolo* in the background.

"Kimberly, where are you ladies?"

"Why don't you take a look at the corner of Twenty-six and Locust Street," she replied, laughing softly.

Taking a quick glance to my right to notice a burgundy ultra, stretch limousine parked at the corner of Twenty-sixth and Locust Street. The chauffeur began flashing his lights.

Laughing, I asked, "Oh my gosh. Are you two spying on me?"

"Yes," Naomi said. "I must admit that you do look fine, Bolo, standing there with your nice blue jeans and brown tank top."

"Then why don't you two walk your asses down here to me," I said motioning them to get out the limo.

"Bolo," said Kimberly. "Don't faint out here in this hot weather when you see us."

"I'm waiting Kimberly and Naomi," I started to close my phone when I heard Kimberly tell Naomi to come on.

Tom, my chauffer got out to open the door, then took a few steps backwards looking down as Kimberly emerged first, then Naomi. Kimberly was wearing white pumps, tight white shorts, a pink bra and fishnet shirt. Her black silky hair fell below her waistline. Naomi stepping out wearing red shorts with matching pumps, white bra and fishnet shirt. Her shoulder length, sandy brown hair hung loose.

They begn walking slowly towards me with all smiles on their faces. You would have thought they were professional models living a magazine world the way they both strutted down the hot, concrete sidewalk.

"Ouchhh!" I yelled watching them stroll down to me.

"Shut up, Bolo," said Naomi, hands placed on her hips.

"Why should I when I like what I'm adoring?" I asked. "Welcome back to Wilmington."

They both said, "Thank you."

We embraced then I motioned my chauffeur to come down to pick up the women. I gave them five thousand a piece for a shopping spree to wherever they wish to shop. "I need you both to be ready by seven o'clock this evening because he has to have you at my penthouse at exactly eight p.m. sharp. Please be on time."

They jumped back into the limo waving at me while slowly pulling away. Kev came out from the driveway smiling and nodding his head. He asked, "Who were they, Bolo?"

High fiving. "What's up Kev?" I asked. "Remember the two chicks that I was telling you about, the babes that I met at the swimming pool?"

"Right, right. Kimberly and Naomi," Kev continued nodding his head at the limo turning down Twenty-third Street."

"It's me and the ladies tonight."

"Get your groove on Bolo," he said. "Sophie and the girls are checking to see what's up with the suite at the Taj Mahal in Atlantic City."

"Cool, Kev, that's what's up. You set that meeting up for next month?"

"Yes, sir," he said. We both watched Leon smack one of his protégé's in the face.

Next month, the men in my organization had set up a meeting with one of the most notorious drug lords from New York City. Amillio, whom I spoke with over the phone but never met in person. Addicts and buyers coming in from out of state had been asking about who has the best heroin around, so my men ask me to put some product out in circulation to see what they can achieve.

Brandy, Aunt Ann and Dawn were hauling groceries into the house when I pulled into the driveway. Dawn stopped, then rolled her eyes at me. She said, "Can you help us or what Cousin Bolo?"

"Keep those beady eyes to yourself, smart ass," I snatched both bags from her.

"Thank you, Bolo," said Brandy. She looked at Dawn and rolled her eyes at her.

"Nephew, are you coming to the cookout?" Aunt Ann asked.

"I'll be here, auntie," I said. Brandy then grabed my hand to follow her back outside to get some more bags.

"Don't worry about Dawn, Bolo, cause the bitch is just coming off her period, so you know how bitchy we women can get at this point in time," said Brandy. She spun around to kiss me.

Back in the house, Dawn apologized the way she sounded off at me. Aunt Ann brought in glasses of orange juice as we all sat down to talk.

"Cousin Bolo, we're going out tonight. Would you like to come with us?"

"Nah, not tonight Dawn. You ladies have fun tonight," I said.

"You must have a date tonight."

"Yes, I do Dawn," I said. We talked for the next few hours, then I headed on out to the stores, came back to spend some more time at the cookout and off again to get ready for a lovely evening with Naomi and Kimberly.

Eight o'clock that evening, Naomi and Kimberly walked into my penthouse at Parkview dressed alike wearing a one piece, above the knee, black sparkling dress. Both had on matching high heels with their hair hanging loosely. They stopped in the middle of the living room, admiring the all crystal dining room table with two dozen yellow roses resting on top. The lights were dimmed and jazz played softly in the background. "Good evening," I smiled.

"Good evening, Bolo" they both replied happily, smiling as they watched me stand to acknowledge their presence.

"You're both beautiful," I motioned them to come closer.

"Same to you handsome," said Kimberly. Her eyes on Naomi answering her cell phone.

"Yes, no, please don't say that. I'll be there, Kimberly and I ," Naomi shook her head weaily.

"What's wrong, girl?" asked Kimberly.

Teardrops fell from Naomi's eyes. "Bolo, I'm so sorry, but we have to go."

"Okay, Naomi, I'll have the limo waiting at the entrance for you both," I said. They ran out the door. Kimberly and Naomi are two fine looking chicks, but I sensed a little danger in them both and I would love to have them both join my organization.

Wednesday morning at Constance's office, she handed me some deeds to some property that I requested some time ago. "Thank you Constance," I said. She motioned me to have a seat across from her.

"Bolo," she said, "you have in front of you full deeds to the mansion that you requested in New Mexico, and that you requested down in Tampa, Florida."

"How was your meeting?" I asked.

"Well, my parents were so excited that you sent them there with me, they want to buy a timeshare for themselves."

"Constance, take the money from my account and tell them both that I said *Happy Anniversary*." I handed her the deeds back for safekeeping.

"Oh my gosh, Bolo. They're gonna be so happy when I tell them the good news," she jumped up then walked to the window.

I asked, "Will you be joining us at the Taj Mahal next month in Atlantic

City?" I met her at the window as we stared into Rodney Square.

"Most definitely I will," Constance said wrapping her arms around my waist then planting a kiss on my cheek. We kissed for a few minutes then said our goodbyes until later.

Happy hour at 1334 French Street. There were people everywhere when I walked into the building, music playing loud as hell. A few black sistas and white chicks running around half ass naked, drinking martinis. This wasn't my kind of party. It looked to me like it was maybe a lingerie party or a fashion show. I was there for one reason only... business that needed to be dealt with. "HEY BOLO," someone shouted out my name.

"Who the hell..." I turned around. "Mercedes what are you doing here?"

Before she could answer my question, a dark-skinned man walked up and grabbed her by the waist. "Who's this?" he asked. His breath smelled full of alcohol, eyes were of someone who was smoking Crack Cocaine.

"Baby, this is Bolo," said Mercedes.

He started walking away. "Oh whatever have fun," he spun around while looking back at us not knowin who I was.

"Who the fuck is he?" I asked yelling over the loud music.

"My boyfriend, Bolo," she said, looking away from me. "His name is Marcus, he used to date your cousin's Dawn's best friend Rhonda."

I was about to backlash her stinking ass until this fat ass white, blonde headed chick asked me to dance with her. Mercedes felt the rage in my voice but quickly said me to help myself with something to eat. On the other hand, the blonde pulled me into the middle of the floor to dance. "You know anything, goes in here tonight sexy," she bent forward to whisper into my ear.

"Yeah, yeah," I mumbled watching Mercedes dance with Marcus.

"Are you listening to me?"

"I'm sorry sweetie, what were you saying?"

She faced me, " I said that anything goes tonight."

"Meaning?" I asked curiously.

"Just look around and you'll see what I mean," she said. A gesture of motioning her hand over the crowd. A man holding a woman's head as she performed oral sex. In the corner there was a woman laying down as a white man enjoyed performing oral sex on her.

"DAMN!" I shouted. Damn near everyone that was in the house was in some type of sexual activity. Mercedes and Marcus has disappeared that fast from dancing.

"Come 'mere handsome," she motioned me to follow her to a closet near the kitchen. "We can slip in here and lock the door behind us."

Once in the dark closet she began touching my chest to find my face. "What's up?" I asked. My hand searched the split of her breasts.

"Would would you like me to do?"

"Anything you like baby," I said.

Pulling my shorts down, she began to perform oral sex on me until I climaxed in her mouth, then bent over so I could fuck her the way that she wanted me to fuck her.

Two hours later, the party ended as I was upstairs using the bathroom. Closer and closer voices became, a woman's voice...Mercedes. She asked, "Baby, can we take a shower?"

A man replied politely, "not yet Mercedes," he said. "After we do a few lines then make love." It was Marcus. They walked past the bathroom laughing as she happily agreed with him.

Moments later, I began hearing the both of them moaning out each other's names, telling one another to suck this and suck that. I assumed they were in the sixty-nine position giving each other oral sex.

Silence. Marcus yelled out, "Ride this dick, Mercedes."

She responded with a loud scream. "Yes, Marcus! I will baby."

By the time I got to the bedroom door, Mercedes was climbing onto Marcus as he grasped her waist tightly. "Damn," I mumbled remembering how Mercedes use to climb on top of me then ride me like her personal pet Jaguar running through the jungle.

Wild sex had ended as they began engaging in a few lines of Cocaine lined up on the black bed stand. Marcus held a syringe in his hand while subduing the remainder of the air that was visible. Mercedes nervously looked on as if it was her first time.

Click – click. I burst into the room; 9mm raised pointing directly at Marcus' chest. "NO NEWS IS GOOD NEWS, MUTHAFUCKER," I shouted. They both jumped. The syringe fell between them.

"OH SHIT. WHAT THE FUCK," Marcus shouted.

"Bolo, what's the meaning of this?" asked Mercedes, not worrying about the syringe. She covered the both of them with a filthy, multi-colored quilt.

"Why don't you tell her, Marcus," I stepped closer making sure they don't make any false moves.

"Oh shit, they call you 'Delaware's Top Captain'," said Marcus. His voice trembled. "You're- you're fucking dangerous man. Please don't kill me."

"You like syringes muthafucka?" I asked. He watched me reach for my other 9mm then pulled it out. "You shoot up too Mercedes?"

She said, "I- I didn't want to Bolo. He said that I better at least try it once or…"

I interrupted. "So he could kill you the way he killed Rhonda."

"I – I," Marcus stuttered.

"Shhh, nigga, they found your fingerprints on the syringe that you left in her."

"YOU MUTHAFUCKER," Mercedes shouted. She smacked Marcus twice in the face.

Mercedes was troubled that Marcus wanted her to shoot Cocaine into her veins Bad enough he gotten her hooked on cocaine, so I had her shoot a few cc's into his veins so that she could see what would happen to her if he had injected her. She started screaming at the top of her lungs when I put two slugs into his chest.

She begged me not to kill her because she was one month pregnant with my baby and said that she would have no problem getting an abortion. "You're damn right, you're gonna get one," I said. "Now get the syringe out of Marcus' arm because your fingerprints are all over it."

"Okay," she said as she reached to remove the needle.

"Go to sleep baby," I whispered. My fingers ran through her brown, shoulder length hair. Her head fell into Marcus lap as I placed a single bullet into her neck. She looked as if she was performing oral sex on a bloody dead man.

That night I headed on over to Constance's house. After I took a shower, I laid up in her pussy for the rest of the night. We even fucked outside in the backyard under the full moon and twinkling stars.

Saturday morning, I began making last minute preparations for this evening's pool party at Price's swimming pool. Today, the temperature reached it's ten-year high, one hundred and one degrees. The Channel 6 meteorologist said to drink plenty of water. By nightfall it should reach a low of ninety-six degrees. Kev and the other guys are out of town on business so the girls and me are going to have fun together tonight.

Diamond, Sophie and Crystal all dove into the pool at the same time. They were all wearing two-piece swimsuits. Sophie had on a red one, Diamond had on a navy blue and Crystal was wearing a hot pink one. They could pass for swimsuit models. Many were here in couples, while others mingles to see what they could get in to. "What's up, Bolo?" Crystal asked. She started splashing water on me. The DJ cranked the music as loud as it could go.

Splash. "Y'all look so damn good too!" I yelled, smiling at the sight of water splashing their faces.

"I'M GONNA KICK YOUR ASS, BOLO!" shouted Sophie. They all started to swim for me. Diamond caught me and jumped on my back.

"Damn you're heavy girl."

"Just carry me knucklehead," said Diamond smacking me upside my head. Crystal and Sophie followed through by pushing my head forward one at a time.

Several hours into having fun, the swimming pool had reached its seven hundred count capacity. There were people everywhere. Women flashing their breasts.

"OH SHIT, LOOK AT THIS NIGGA Y'ALL," Sophie shouted out while pointing at a man they call Double-R.

Softly speaking, Diamond said, "That's the pussy that called us bitches."

"Yeah Bolo, that sucka is from Salem, New Jersey," said Crystal. She gritted her teeth and rolled her eyes at him.

"Handle your business," I said. "Get rid of him. He's on my soil now."

Sophie looked at me then motioned Diamond and Crystal to follow her as the three of them made their way to the exit of the swimming pool. No telling what those three are up to these days. Double-R was flirting with two Spanish chicks when I looked over at the diving board. I sat up on the ledge thinking about what Sophie and the girls are up to. They once told me that they followed Double-R over to New Jersey to check out how he was operating. Maybe that's where they're headed while Double-R is at the pool having fun.

"Hey sexy lady. What's your name?" I asked, watching this black sista wearing an all-black swimsuit pass me slowly.

She asked, "Are you talking to me, Bolo?" She stopped, grasping the ledge beside me. Her body screamed for immediate attention. Water came rolling off her body as she stepped out he stood over top of me. With her full blown lips, everything about her was calling my name.

"You know me?"

"You didn't answer my question, Bolo," she said. "Yes, I know you. Delaware's Top Captain. I believe everyone knows you, handsome. I'm Teresa." She extended her hand out to me as she sat down on my left side.

"Hi Teresa," I said.

"What do you want with me, Bolo?" asked Teresa. *You better say what I want you to say too.*

Shoulder to shoulder, I said, "Honestly Teresa, I would like to take you out to dinner. Fuck you like you never been fucked before," her skin felt like silk.

Teresa held my hand. "At least you're honest with me. The question is, Bolo. Are you gonna be able to handle all this chocolate stuff?" She continued holding my hand while moving up and down.

All I could say was, “Try me.”

“Since the party is over, why don’t you meet me at my red BMW right there,” Teresa pointed outside the gate at a red BMW sitting on 23rd and Church Street. She stood up, then bent over touching her toes giggling at me.

“I’ll be there in ten minutes, lovely Teresa,” I watched her stop to talk to some woman. Double-R started walking in front of me towards the men’s locker room.

Soon as I walked into the locker room, the attendant motioned me over to his booth where I recognized my belongings. “Hey Bolo, what’s up man?” he asked.

“Nothing much, Jack. How are you?”

“Tryin to join your organization,” his smile sincere. He handed me my belongings.

“We’ll talk about that tomorrow,” I said.

Someone shouted. “That’s the guy they call Delaware’s Top Captain, right?!”

“He ain’t to be fucked with Double-R,” a voice came screaming from behind me. At that time another attendant was announcing that the men’s locker room was now closing. Everyone begin making their entrance when suddenly three mask men stared into my eyes. I smelled death. My heart pounded.

They were all dressed in black with black bandana’s covering their faces.

“What the fuck!” yelled Double-R. He was directly behind me.

Boom! Boom! Boom! Boom! Boom!

Gunfire sounded off. Shell casings flew in all directions.

People yelling and screaming, “Get down, get down.”

“Oh shit!,” I smiled, nodding my head at Sophie, Diamond and Crystal.

They looked at me then whispered that they’ll talk to me later. They disappeared. *Call the ambulance somebody, my sister been shot.* A man cried out. He was embracing a woman.

Seconds later ambulances and police squad cars train across the grass to get to the scene. *Teresa, lil' sis, please don't die on me, please.* He cried once again.

Damn, that was the chic I was supposed to meet at her car. I mumbled. I heard someone say Double-R was dead.

Chapter 18

Parkview Penthouse. Kimberly and I were both on the balcony drinking Dom Perignon, glancing at the stars and admiring the City of Wilmington, Delaware's skyline. Looking down at the I-95 traffic flowing steadily. The sounds of Smokey Robinson's *Cruisin'* began floating into the midnight air. She began singing along while staring at me smiling, knowing what was going through my mind. Kimberly has on an all while silk robe. She opened it up to let it fall to the floor. She was wearing only a white pair of fishnet panties. Her jet black, long hair rested upon her breasts.

Kimberly took a few steps away from me then asked, "You ever fuck a Chinese woman, Bolo?" She began staring at me while wiggling her panties down to her ankles. *I hope that you say no because I will be your first.*

"No," I answered. "But I'm quite sure you'll be my first."

"Then follow me," she said. Her eyes searched my body from head to toe telling me to remove my robe. I followed behind her to the bed.

"Kimberly," I whispered.

She climbed on the bed then laid on her back with legs spread wide open. "Shhh!!! I'm all yours, Bolo." Her arms welcomed me to do whatever business I needed to tend to.

As I began diving in for the gold, she spread her pussy lips apart feeling the warmth of my tongue. "Yes Kimberly," I softly moaned. Her body tensed as my tongue moved deeper and deeper between her wet clit.

"Oh, Bolo, yes baby," she moaned. "Lick this good pussy, oh yes." Kimberly began looking on as she massaged my ears. Something that she loved to do to concentrate on climaxing multiple times.

"Hmm, hmm," I continue moaning, feeling her warm fluids rush onto my tongue and down my throat. My dick is so hard that it needs some serious attention.

"Bolo, Bolo, yes baby! I'm cummin', I'm cummin'!" she yelled out. Her hands held my head as she pressed, not wanting me to come up for air. Three times she climaxed. My face covered with body fluids as she pulled me up. We begin kissing, then Kimberly laid me on my back.

"Kimberly." I watched her tongue move about my abs while working her way down to my stiffness. She began teasing the head in a circular motion then suddenly swallowing it while until I climaxed. She never came up for air. I felt the tip of my dick deep throat her. Once I laid her back down on her back, we kissed as she pulled me on top of her.

"Fuck me," she screamed, feeling all nine inches of me against her pussy walls.

That next morning Kimberly and I were at it again. This time on the balcony as the morning sun came rising. We took a shower then I went off to a business meeting. Kimberly stayed at the Penthouse.

Tension climbed the walls when I walked into the house to see everyone's eyes turned directly to me. They're wondering why I suddenly called an important meeting. They were all sitting up as I surveyed the entire room to see who was present and who was not.

"DISLOYALTY IS AMONGST OUR FAMILY!" I shouted. Everyone jumped. "WE WILL GET TO THE BOTTOM OF THIS TONIGHT." They all rambled about.

Their fear canvassing the silent sound of my footsteps as I began encircling the table. Eyes are watching me. Sophie taps the table with her well-manicured, brown fingernails. She began biting her lower lip. Nervously Kev asked, "Capt., what's up?" He knew I was about to explode any second.

"The ladies that's in my fucking organization have a problem keeping track of my fucking money," I said. "$2.5 million dollars worth." They all watched me slip on my black leather gloves.

"Bolo, baby," said Sophie. She stopped biting her lip then rested her hands on the table from tapping.

"CAPTAIN TO YOU, YOU HEAR ME!," I shouted at her. Sophie's head jerked back from me pulling her ponytail.

"Yes, Captain," she replied her eyes rolled back at me begging me not to pull another inch.

"I told you, you and you time and time again to be careful with your surroundings!" I yelled looking at Diamond, Crystal and Sophie shaking their heads in agreement with me.

Dexter said, "Shit Captain, we learned our lesson." He motioned a gesture to Kev and Leon.

"Where's my money Crystal, Sophie, Diamond?" I asked moving between Diamond and Crystal. They watched me place my black 9mm Smith & Wesson on the table.

Diamond stuttered, "c – c- captain."

"Captain, my ass. Scared asses, it's not about you three." We all began laughing. All three women started smacking me upside my head then each planted a kiss on cheek.

I retrieved my other gun then placed it on the table along with my leather gloves. I sat between Diamond and Crystal.

"Captain, what's going on?" Kev asked. He started polishing his .357 Magnum.

"Just take a good look around and notice who's not present with us today," I said. We all searched the room nodding our heads. "You should all be aware of your surroundings when I call a sudden meeting for the family."

Crystal shouted, "Oh shit cap't, Felix isn't present with us today."

I asked, "Anyone knows why he isn't present with us today?"They shook their heads. Dexter pulled his lighter out to light my Black & Mild.

"No, not really. He was told Cap't," they responded. Everyone reached for their weapon knowing that what I was about to say meant death.

"Do I not take care of you all well. Shit, I'll do anything for you that y'all ask, plus I've given everyone a half a million dollars apiece for a bonus."

Monte leaned back then began taking his cornrows out. "Damn, right Cap't," he said.

"I called this meeting because Felix felt as though I wasn't paying him enough. So he decided to skip town with $2.5 million of my money," I said.

Slowly leaning back nodding my head.

Click – Click. They all raised their weapons above their shoulders ready for action, ready to bring Felix to his knees. Taking money from the organization is like taking food from our tables to feed our family.

"He's a dead man," Crystal yelled. She stomped her feet on the floor lifting herself into the air. I had to calm everyone down. Without me closing the meeting properly they would've went straight on a rampage. Everyone seemed dumbfounded when I stated that I would deal with Felix sometime in the near future. What man on this Earth would stay in his hometown after stealing $2.5 million dollars? *I know that I wouldn't.*

Therefore if Felix doesn't resurface in the next three weeks or so; I will cause extreme pain to his subconscious by mincing his mother's arms, then his father's, sisters and brothers until he's dead and gone.

Diamond, Sophie and Crystal were all ready, locked and loaded. On the other hand, Kev, Monte, Leon and me just shook our heads knowing what the media is about to catch wind of.

Dawn was at the entertainment system when I walked into the house. She looked at me and just rolled her eyes. Her smile was touching. Aunt Ann was nowhere to be found. Dawn asked, "Where have you been Cousin Bolo?" as she wrestled with compact disc case.

"Just came back from a very important meeting."

"You and your meetings," she said. "May I ask what this one was about?" Dawn finally found a CD that she wanted to hear.

"Well," I said, "Felix ran off with $2.5 million dollars of my money."

She quickly jumped to her feet then sat next to me. "Oh my gosh, Cousin Bolo. What are you gonna do about that?" asked Dawn.

"No one knows but you and my crew Dawn, so don't tell anybody."

"You're about to get his family if you can't find him, right?" she asked. *Because that's how crazy your ass is when you really want to get to someone.*

"Then his family will be my family until their all dead and gone," I paused. "One by one."

"I believe you too, Cousin Bolo. I remember you telling me about how you killed Marcus, which he deserved, but why Mercedes."

"Dawn, she was a witness to me killing Marcus so I had to put her asleep," I leaned back resting my head. We watched Brandy walk into the house.

Brandy sat down at the other end of the couch after giving me a kiss. She smiled rolling her eyes at Dawn. We watched Dawn get up and walk into the kitchen returning with three glasses of ice-cold orange juice. Here comes Aunt Ann walking in the house. "Hey, Brandy and Dawn," she said. "Hey nephew," she took my glass then drank half my orange juice.

"Mrs. Ann, Brandy and I are spending the night at Bolo's penthouse," said Brandy. Her head bowed, "we're modeling for him again."

"Oh boy. Anyway, when are we going shopping for you ladies' college clothes?"

"Mom, cousin Bolo said that we could go next month or whenever you want to take us," said Dawn.

Aunt Ann smiled, "Then we'll go three weeks before you ladies attend college," she said.

Later that night, I had to make a quick stop before I headed over to Constance's place to see what she wanted. I met up with the Detectives first to thank them both on a job well done on the evidence the police has on me that Felix provided them.

Monica was about to go to bed before I came by so she invited me into house to have a talk with me. She was wearing a pink and black striped pajamas set. Her hair styled in two shoulder length ponytails. Monica was only four feet and six inches tall with all the right curves. Her eyes were poppy and very seductive. Expensive life style she always lived. The house was full of crystal chinaware. Finally, she motioned me to have a seat. She asked, "what brings you here tonight, Bolo?"

I answered, "Monica, I wanted to see how you were doing amongst other things."

She watched me crossing my legs, "what did my brother do this time?" She set the tone by playing jazz then sat down next to me.

"Where is he anyway?" I asked. Her question I didn't bother to answer.

"Bolo, he came in her yesterday acting all nervous and suspicious as if he done something seriously wrong," she said. Monica leaned her head back. "Felix is always up to something when he isn't with you." *I better not tell you that I saw him in a Detective's car.*

I began to fondle with one of her ponytails. "I once told Felix, Monica, that his family would be my family one by one if he ever fucking crossed me." I gently held the other ponytail. "He did just that," I said. Her lips I kissed. Streaks of blood poured from her throat as I ran across it from left to right.

Monica eyes were on me as if she tried to say, "Why you had to kill me. I done nothing to you." I closed her eyelids then made a call to 911 from the house phone to report that I heard someone screaming. That will definitely send a message to Felix's family. *I meant my family.*

Constance was already in the bed when I arrived at her place. She was butt naked laying on her back, legs slightly spread apart. Luther Vandross' *Here and Now* playing in the background. Her eyes followed every piece of clothing that I removed from my body.

I said nothing while wasting no time diving into her warm pussy. My tongue slowly moved deeper and deeper. Constance body began trembling minutes thereafter. We began making love. She cries out my name, "oh Bolo." Soon the words I love you screamed, but I paid her no mind and gave her all that I had to give her.

Next morning, we showered then had a scrumptious breakfast for the both of us. "Back to business," she said. "Bolo, I handled the problem professionally."

"Well congratulations, sweetheart," I said. "How did that happen?"

"It's not over yet, Bolo, because he has to come back to the office to pick up his things when they clear him," Constance said. She glanced into the wall mirror looking at me. Her hand moved from left to right as she was applying her lipstick to her lips.

I asked, "Would you like for me to be present, Constance?"

"No thank you sweetie, I can handle this one myself. Besides there will be others nearby," she said. *Gosh I hope he doesn't try anything foolish.*

"If you say so sweetheart." I watched her walk over to the black and glass cocktail table to pick up her watch.

"Bolo, when are Brandy and Dawn starting college?"

"Another two months," I said. "A few weeks after we all come back from Atlantic City's Taj Mahal, which is my birthday and only you, Aunt Ann, Brandy and Dawn know about it."

Her face glowed, "Oh yeah, your birthday is coming up soon." Her tongue traced the outline of her lipstick as she walked over to me. "I'll have to surprise you with a gift that you don't already have," she said. *You will definitely be surprised by what's coming your way, honey.*

Constance grabbed her car keys and mines then out the door we went. Our separate ways until later.

In route to the Westside of the city to holler at my man Monte. I made a right onto Fourth Street from Spruce while passing the Wilmington Police Station when suddenly about seven police cruisers and a brown unmarked detective squad encircled my car. Then they all sped away heading in my direction towards Fourth and Madison Street.

Monte spotted me coming up the street so he walked to the curb then waited until my car came to a complete stop. He smiled, "Hey, what's up Bolo?"

"Nothing much," we high-fived. "How's business over here?" I asked.

"Busy as usual," he replied his eyes careened to a white woman walking up to one of his workers.

"You know that we have that impending meeting next week on Miller Road."

"Yeah, I can't wait either," he said. Nodding his head to go ahead and make the drug sale. He said that he hadn't ran into Felix yet.

"Don't worry about him," I said. *His youngest sister won't make it to the airport tomorrow, that's my word.*

"Hey Monte," a girlish voice called. She was a redbone chick driving a cranberry red Jaguar. Her friend smiled at me as if she wanted to holler at me or something.

"Hey Rosland, what's up?" Monte asked. He walked to the car.

"Movies tonight?" she asked. Her girl whispered something into her ear then looked at me.

"Ten o'clock," said Monte.

"Monte," said Rosland. "My girl wants to know if your friend wants to come with us to the movies tonight."

"Oh shit girl, that's Bolo," she yelled, head bowed down. "Damn, I'm sorry, Bolo."

"That's okay, why don't you get out the car and come holla at me," I motioned her to step out. I held the door open for me.

She jumped so high that I thought she wanted me to carry her. She said, "Well since I know you Bolo, my name is Unique." She politely pulled her mini skirt down. Her panties were blue satin laced.

"Unique, it's a pleasure to meet you." I extended my hand out to her. "Let's walk and talk," I said.

Rosland shouted, "OKAY GIRLFRIEND!"

Laughing. "Don't mind her crazy ass Bolo," said Unique. "Trust me, I'm not that unique. My focus is completely on your sexy."

Unique and I exchanged information and went our separate ways. She's a redbone, 5'7", about one hundred and forty pounds. Her hair styled like Toni Braxton.

I left Monte to handle the rest of the business he needed to take care of. I called Kev to see I he wanted to go to the movies tonight but he had already made plans to celebrate the anniversary of his girlfriend's parents. Leon and Dexter were both out of town on a very important business meeting.

Trina was standing at the door when I pulled up in front of the house. She smiled while holding the door open for me. "Hey Bolo," she said

"You're forever smiling girl, for what...I don't know," laughing, I shook my head.

"You make me smile baby knowing that you'll be inside me before you step back out this house."

I stopped in front of her. "Confidence, I see," I said. We were face-to-face.

"You know the drill, smart ass," said Trina. She smacked my shoulder then shoved me gently into the house.

"I just got off the phone with Kev and he was telling me that I received more guns yesterday."

"Yes, I'll go get them for you," she began walking towards the basement.

"No, please, I'll check them out before I leave," I said as I sat down.

Face-to-face Trina sat me down. We kissed for quite a while. She had on a pink and red nightgown with flower designs. I could see that she wasn't wearing any panties. She whispered in my ear that I was easy access for me.

"Now tell me about his nigga that's been harassing you, Trina."

"Bolo, his name is Dirk and the bastard lives out in Kimberton Apartments, him and his bitch ass girlfriend," she started to cry resting her head on my chest.

I held her close to me. "Why are you crying, Trina?"

"Because, I'm really sick of him Bolo." I felt a teardrop on my arm.

"He keeps calling me all kinds of bitches and whores cause I won't give him my phone number," she said.

I felt the pain Trina was going through as she continued to tell me more. She was trembling uncontrollably. "Don't worry about it baby," I whispered into her ear.

"I – I wanna k – kill him s – so bad, Bolo."

"Then what the fuck is stopping you?"

She said, "I – I – I' scared."

"Where there's a will, there's a way if you know what I mean, Trina." Tightly I embraced her. Her soft breasts rested under my arms.

We talked some more about the business she needs to handle with that disrespectful, bad mouth Dirk. Afterwards, we completely lost focus. Trina sat up while wiggling her nightgown down to her knees. Kev walked in smiling at us. *Damn, we forgot to lock the door.* Her smile I followed out the living room. She excused herself.

Kev nodded his head. "What's up, Bolo?" he asked.

"Nothing but that money," I said. We high-fived then sat down.

"Did Trina tell you about that nigger Dirk?"

"Yeah, she and I are gonna pay him and his girlfriend a nice special visit someday."

"What about the new 9mm Smith & Wessons?"

By the time I could answer that question, Trina was fully dressed wearing blue jean shorts and a light blue t-shirt. She was wheeling several huge boxes behind her. We all opened a box at the same time to see nothing but brand new Smith & Wesson 9mms.

"Kev, I need you to call everyone to the table and have them exchange their weapons." I nodded my head motioning the two to grab a fresh gun and silencer. "I'll call my boy at the Phoenix Steel factor to get those used ones the fuck melted down," I said. We close the boxes then took aim at the door ready for action. The three of us took a silencer each. Kev left the house. I kissed Trina then told her to be ready to get down and dirty for a hit next week.

Monte called as soon as I walked into my Aunt Ann's house. She was standing with her hands on her hips. When she stands in that certain spot by the kitchen I know she's about to lecture me on something I've done. "What's wrong," I asked.

"Those two," said Aunt Ann. She swayed directly at Dawn and Brandy. They were sitting on the couch. "Stuck up under your ass, you keep spoiling them, you give them anything that they ask for.

I laughed, "They're not spoiled, Aunt Ann."

"Bolo, you bought them both houses months ago for college. Not once that I can think of, have then spent one night in them and you spent over a half million dollars on those houses that's going to waste." She walked over to both of them gritting her teeth. "You," she paused.

I interrupted, "you what?"

"Nephew, you bought them a Bentley and a Lamborghini."

Dawn shouted, "COUSIN BOLO, DON'T LISTEN TO MOMMY!" She ducked from her mother's hand almost hitting her head.

"You two are some spoiled ass brats," I grinned, staring at them both.

Brandy said, "You made us this way, Bolo." She lowered her head into her chest. She was picking at her clothes like a child.

The door opened and Monte stuck his head in. "Captain, you ready?" he asked.

"Here I come, Monte." The door closed behind him.

"Where are you going?" asked Dawn. Her and Brandy stood up.

"Have fun," said Brandy. "We love you." They both kissed my cheeks then rolled their eyes at Aunt Ann and ran upstairs.

Once at the Painter's Crossing Cinema in Pennsylvania, Unique and I really got to know one another. She's a very brilliant, who's also the owner of a hair salon in Philadelphia and about to start another one on downtown Fifth and Market Street in Wilmington. Finally the movie was over so we went to her place where she mentioned to me that the last time she had sex as a year ago.

Chapter 19

Constance came running into my Aunt Ann's house as if someone was chasing her. Her face was blackish blue in color. Streaks of black mascara ran down her cheeks. Her body trembling. I quickly snatched her to me to embrace her. "Calm down, calm down," I said "What the hell happened to your face, Constance?"

"I'm scared. I'm scared, Bolo. H – h – he punched me in my face," she cried out loud. Aunt Ann came running downstairs to see what all the commotion was about. Dawn came right behind her. She was in the shower. Her body dripping with water as she closed her robe.

I shouted, "WHO THE FUCK PUNCHED YOU IN THE FACE, CONSTANCE?"

Calming down, "Chris, Bolo, when he came to pick up his belongings from work today," she said. Dawn and Aunt Ann helped her sit down on the couch.

"I want his address and a picture of his ass. Do you hear me, Constance?" I raised my index finger into the air at her.

She looked at me with teary eyes. "Yes, I'll get it to you tomorrow, Bolo." She folded her hands to place them between her legs.

Aunt Ann shaking her head. "Come on Constance, and let's get you cleaned up," she said, grabbing Constance's hands. I watched the both of them make their way upstairs.

Dawn stared at me as I she saw a ghost standing behind me. *I know you're going to kill him.* Her words were too heavy to come out. Then she spoke, "His ass is in for it, isn't he, Cousin Bolo?" she asked, both eyebrows raised.

"You're damn right he's gonna pay the price, Dawn."

"Can I come with you when you decide to do his punk ass?" Dawn asked. She reached for her brown handbag and pulled a gun out.

I headed upstairs to see how Aunt Ann was coming along with Constance. She was sound asleep in Dawn's bedroom. I could tell Aunt Ann was crying because soon as I walked into the room she turned away from me. She kissed Constance on her badly bruised face shaking her head and walked out the room. For the rest of the day and throughout that night, I laid in bed with Constance then fell asleep.

That next morning I shot to Philadelphia Airport to pick up Sophie, Crystal and Diamond. They were in California handling some business for me. We really didn't had time to mingle with each other because I received a disturbing message from Penny to meet her at her office.

When I arrived at Penny's office at AstraZeneca she was pacing from the window to her desk. She was biting her fingernails. "Thank you for stopping pass, Bolo." She motioned me to have a seat. "You miss me?" she asked.

"Yes," I said, leaning back into the chair. "What's the matter?"

She stopped at the window. "Then why were you kissing some redbone bitch at the movies last night or the night before?" Her hand rested on a statue mold in the form of a woman holding her child.

"Penny, you're in no position to ask me this question." I then leaned forward waiting for the statue to come flying at me.

She yelled, "YOU FUCK HER THE WAY YOU FUCK ME?" She began pacing once more. Eyes were on me.

I said, "You're not the only one that I'm fucking sweetheart." She watched me stand up with fire in her eyes.

Penny threw the statue on the floor, shattering it in half. She shouted, "YOU BASTARD, GIVE ME MY HOUSE KEY AND GET THE FUCK OUT OF MY OFFICE. BEFORE I SMACK THE LIVING SHIT OUT OF YOU!" She stood in my face then backed away about two feet. Her eyes flushed with tears.

I reached in my pocket to pull out a silver colored key. "Here, take your shitty ass key because you're not worth shit. You're a piece of pussy to me, Penny!" I yelled, dangling the key with my thumb and index finger.

Hand extended. Her eyes grew bigger. She shouted, "YOU SORRY

MUTHA..." she raised her hand. Penny wanted to smack me, instead she poked my forehead with her finger. She was left-handed.

Raging, I shouted, "DON'T YOU EVER LAY ANOTHER FUCKIN FINGER ON ME, PENNY." I held her wrist tightly in front of her face. "I'LL CHOPYOUR STINKIN BODY INTO SMALL PIECES. THEN FLY YA ASS BACKTO ATLANTA FIRST CLASS WHERE YA ASS ORIGINALLY CAME FROM."

"Yes Bolo," she answered. "I'm sorry, please don't hurt me/"

"Penny, I could've called you a whore, a bitch and much more but you're none of that. You have class, and you have real potential," I said. "See you, Penny." I whispered pushing her hand out the way. I kissed her lips then turned to walk out the door.

Penny cried, "I'M SORRY BOLO," she shouted. Her voice echoed vibrating the surrounding windows.

Patients' visiting hours at Christiana Hospital. I made a rapid stop at the gift shop to pick up some balloons and a pink teddy bear with a red heart, then headed on to the elevator for the fifth floor to find my target.

When I arrive at the room she looked up at me and started crying. She was laying in the bed with only a hospital gown on. She read my mind then quickly pulled the covers over her body. "Aww, why are you crying?" I asked. I walked over to her bedside.

"Happy to see you, Bolo,"Teresa said. She extended her arms out to me. We embraced.

"I'm happy to see you too," I said. "That's why this teddy bear and balloons are for you."

"Thank you Bolo," she kissed my lips.

"They match those beautiful lips of yours."

Teresa laughing. "Give me my teddy bear, Bolo," she snatched the teddy bear from me then embraced it. I sat on the bed beside her.

"When will your ass be getting out because you and I have some unfinished business that we have to take care of?"

"We do, don't we," she said. "Because the last time I saw you Bolo was at the swimming pool party, then I got shot."Teresa placed the teddy bear and balloons on the nightstand. She pointed to a small calendar with the words *Going Home* on the day of Wednesday.

"What you have for lunch?" I asked.

"Nothing yet," she responded, laughing.

"Well, I have to use the bathroom," I stood up. "Why don't you order us something to eat, please?"

"I will," she reached for the phone. "What do you like?"Teresa yelled.

I shouted, "ORDER WHAT YOU WANTNME TO HAVE, BUT NO SEAFOOD, PLEASE."

"Bolo, what happened to the guy they were shooting at?"

"They pronounced him dead on the scene, Teresa," I said while resting my head next to hers.

Teresa turned the television back on. She said, "I saw you on the eleven o'clock news Bolo." Her arm wrapped around my waist. "I guess just because they call you Delaware's Top Captain and you're untouchable, they try to tie you into every murder that happens in Wilmington."

"It seems that way, Teresa" I whispered. We looked at each other than started kissing once again. Teresa fell asleep in my arms. I left a note for her to call me then went on my way.

That night before I headed home, I drove passed Twenty-Seventh and Jefferson Street to see Mrs. Watson taking her groceries in the house. There were no parking spaces nearby so I had to park around the corner in the Jefferson Apartment complex parking lot. "Hello, Mrs. Watson," I said. "Let me help you with those bags ma'am."

"Hello, Bolo," she smiled, handing me two large white bags. "Thank you so much son."

Moments later as I was about to leave the house I noticed something dangling from the mantle that I had given the men in my organization. A special necklace reminding me of when someone wanted out of the organization knowing that they fucked up. "Mrs. Watson," I said.

"Yes, Bolo," she kindly answered. Her small, petite body stood over top of a glass cocktail table.

"I once told your son Felix that when he joined my organization to never steal from me. Because if he did then his family will be my family," I paused. "Therefore, you belong to me, Mrs. Watson."

Mrs. Watson tilted her head to the left. "Huh!" she said. There were two red spots appearing from beneath her light blue blouse. They were under her left breast. She fell crashing onto the glass table.

Sunday morning, Dawn and I decided to take an early stroll at the Brandywine Park before temperature reached a hundred degrees today. Not a soul out but a man standing alone at the riverside throwing rocks into the water. Dawn has on a pajama set that's brown in color.

I turned back to head to my car because I had forgotten my cell phone. She stood there looking at the man while patiently waiting for me. Just as I began walking back towards her, she comes up to me asking if I had my gun on me. "Yes, why?" I asked.

"Give it here," she snatched it. Dawn ran down towards the white man. He had blonde hair, tall medium build.

I started running with her. "Dawn, what the hell?" I yelled.

Dawn then shouted, raising the gun, "THIS IS FOR MY GIRL CONSTANCE, MUTHAFUCKER."

Boom! Boom! Boom! He fell forward into the water. It was Chris. Dawn told me when we arrived at my penthouse.

Chapter 20

3715 North Monroe Street. Door opens. "Yes, may I help you please?" asked a white woman. She stepped in front of a huge antique Cherry wood fashion door. Her straight blonde hair touched the tincture of her shoulders. She has a personality of a magazine model ready to be escorted down the runway. Her dark green dress reached slightly above her knees. Her hazel eyes were hypnotizing.

I stepped forward. "My name is Bolo, may I speak with Detective Johnson, please?"

"He isn't here right now." Her eyes surveyed my muscular body from head to toe.

"Then I'll just wait for him."

Sarcastically. "Oh no, the hell you won't!" She yelled, stepping back. *Shit, Delaware's Top Captain.*

Pushing my way into the house, gun pressed against her chest. "Shhh! Now sit your ass down," I whispered my eyes met hers. She was frightened.

She almost fell backwards. "Please, we don't want any trouble, Bolo," her voice weakens as she sat down.

"We," I paused. "Who else is here?" I asked, pressing the gun beneath her left breast. "Your name is?"

"Kelly," she answered. "M – m – my daughter, Katie, she's twenty-one years old and she's about to come back up from the basement."

"Mom, who were you just yelling out to?" Katie asked.

She and her mother could pass for twins. Katie's hair was much longer. She was wearing a white T-shirt with burgundy jean shorts.

"Hello Katie. Why don't you have a seat over there next to your mother." I said motioning her to sit down.

She sat in a separate chair paying me no attention. "Mom, what is going on here?" Her eyes widen as she followed my gun.

"Baby, he just wants to have a talk with your father, that's all." Kelly said. She grabbed the television remote then turned the silver plasma TV on.

"Talk to dad with a fuckin gun in his hand!" Katie yelled, rolling her eyes at me.

"You have a bad mouth young lady," I said, shaking my head.

"Whatever."

I stood up, then walked over to her. "You have any respect for your parents?" I asked, pressing the gun to her temple.

Katie cried, "Please don't shoot." She balled into a fetal position.

"WHAT, SMART ASS? NOTHING TO SAY NOW. YOU LITTLE BITCH ASS WHORE." Silence. "I THOUGHT NOT." Her head jerked from the butt of my gun.

Detective Johnson surely has been spending some kind og money. His house was decked out with brand new furniture. Everything appears to be brand new in his house.

Kelly yelled at Katie. "This isn't the time to be getting smart, Katie." She said. Kelly then looked at me. "Bolo, you care to tell me why you need to speak to my husband?"

"Mom ask him is it about some money dad and Felix have been spending lately," Katie whispered to her mother.

Katie just confirmed that Felix may be in town and that her father has been out on a shopping spree with my money. They both had to go to the bathroom so since I don't trust them, I escorted them both upstairs. Once upstairs, Katie turns around to look at me shaking her head. "Mom, we're in for a long night tonight," she said. Her hand held the door handle.

I said, "No, you're not Katie, I just wanna have a word with your father."

She smiled at me then went into the bathroom.

"Bolo, what did my husband do?" asked Kelly.

"Kelly, he'll tell you and Katie whenever he gets in."

Seconds later, Katie comes out the bathroom zipping her shorts then watched her mother go in next. She stood face-to-face touching our noses together. "Why are you doing this, Bolo? You have everything that you need and want." She asked as she backed away when she heard the door open. The tip of her tongue lightly brushed the bottom of my lips.

We headed back down to the living room. Katie sat back down to where she was sitting. She kept rolling her eyes at me. Kelly sat down next to me then pressed the play button on the remote. The movie was *Waiting to Exhale*.

Forty-five minutes into the movie, Kelly rested her head on my shoulder. Katie is sound asleep. Kelly began moving her hand up my shirt then down my shorts. I moaned, "Kelly we can't do this," I said. "Your husband might walk in."

"So what, this is what I want, Bolo."

"Oh baby, yes Kelly," I whispered experiencing the warmth of her tongue. I began running my fingers through her silky blonde hair.

After climaxing and deep throating her, she asked me to return the favor so I did just that. Katie awakens to find her mother pulling her skirt down "Mom, dad didn't get in yet?" She asked sitting in the Indian style position. She rubbed her eyes to gain better focus.

Door opening. "DADDY." Katie shouted. She angrily stared at me.

"SIT THE FUCK DOWN, NOW KATIE!" I shouted. We all looked at Detective Johnson close the door behind him. "PUT THE GUN DOWN, DETECTIVE...NOW!" I quickly stood up and reached for my other weapon. He noticed that I had a gun pressed against Katie's temple.

"Bolo, what the fuck are you doing in my house!" he yelled. His hand on his weapon ready to draw.

"PUT THE FUCKIN GUN DOWN, NOW AND SIT THE HELL DOWN!" I motioned him to sit in a brand new brown Lay-Z-Boy chair. I snatched both his guns away from him as Katie started to cry.

Kelly said, "Baby, do what he says, please."

"You have everything that you need, Bolo," he said. His eyes shifted back to his wife then his daughter then back to me. "We provide you with everything that you need to know.

"Where's Felix asshole?" I asked.

"I just left his ass smoking crack," said Johnson.

"WHERE'S MY FUCKIN' MONEY? MY TWO POINT FIVE MILLIONS DOLLARS, YOU MUTHAFUCKERS STOLE FROM ME!" I shouted pressing one gun into his temple then shoved my other gun into Katie's mouth.

Kelly screamed, "you bastard, I hate you. I hate you, you bastard!" she continued crying while watching her daughter suffer with hard steel submerged into her mouth.

I began slipping on my black leather gloves then wiping my fingerprints off both guns.

"YOU STOLE MONEY FROM ME. NOW DOES THAT GIVE ME A FUCKIN REASON TO BE HERE UNANNOUNCED," I paused. "YOU SAID THAT YOU WANTED TO ROB ME AND YOU DONE JUST THAT. YOU WORK FOR ME, YOU BASTARD," I yelled, hitting him in the head.

He said, "Bolo, please don't hurt my family."

"Oh, I'm not, trust me Detective Johnson," I said as I walked over to Kelly.

Kelly looked up at me. She asked, "Bolo, what are you about to do?"

"It's not what I'm going to do, Kelly," I said bending down. My lips hovering over her ear. "It's what your about to do, sweetheart," I whispered.

"You bastard, I just sucked your dick while my daughter was asleep," she angrily said. She pushed me away.

Both Katie and Detective Johnson began yelling at Kelly, telling her how much of a whore she was for doing what she did to me. He said that he could have my money back next week, which I wasn't going for. I shoved the gun into Kelly's hand.

"Bolo, please no," Kelly cried.

"Shoot him now, now," I said. She felt the gun pressed against her temple.

She looked at Detective Johnson, "I love you Jack," said Kelly. She pulled the trigger and watched her husband's body quickly jerk back as his head leaned to the right side. He was dead. Katie began screaming as she balled into a fetal position.

Kelly threw the gun down looking at her daughter shaking her head and crying. They both watched me reload the gun with two more bullets. "Kelly," I paused standing over top of her. "Now, it's your daughter's turn," I said. She pushed the gun away.

Rocking back and forth, crying. "No Mom, no Mom, please don't kill me," Katie's eyes widened. "Please don't kill me, Mom!" She continues to beg for her life.

I can sense the love between Kelly and Katie. Motherly love. We could smell the death of a dead man. Once again, Kelly pushes the gun away. She said, "Bolo, not my daughter," Kelly cried out. "I can't kill my own daughter."

I pulled her hair back then whispered, "What if I kill her, Kelly?" I asked, shoving the gun into her hand.

"Katie, I love you," Kelly said. She watched her daughter cover her face with both her hands. Rocking back and forth, "Mommy loves you."

"I love you too, Mommy," Katie cried.

"Bolo, please don't make me," cried Kelly. She looked up at me. Kelly raised the gun to Katie's chest.

"Now Kelly," I said. We both watched Katie's body hit the floor. She landed between her father's feet.

"Oh my God, Katie!"

"Finish her off, Kelly!" I said. "She isn't dead. FINISH HER DAMN IT!"

Kelly cried out so loud that she thought her neighbors were gonna hear her. She shot Katie one more time in the back. We watched Katie's body go into convulsions. She was dead. Kelly threw the gun on the floor.

"Oh my God!" she screamed, shaking.

"Your turn Kelly," I placed another gun on her bare thigh.

"Bolo, please," she looked up at me. *Don't make me do this.* "You had me kill my family," her body trembling.

I yelled, "Now join them bitch!" Walking towards the door.

She shouted, "I HATE YOU. I HATE YOU MUTHAFUCKER!" she cried. "I HATE YOU SO MUCH, BOLO!" she yelled, staring at me through the antique gold framed mirror.

I whispered, "I'm hated by so many Kelly," I said watching her place the gun to her temple.

She stood over top of her daughter and husband blowing her brains away. Her body fell onto Katie's, *her daughter*, but partially onto her husband's legs. They were one dead family.

That net morning, the Johnson family was found murdered in their home by Detective Johnson's partner. They rule the homicide as a double-murder suicide while stating that Kelly and Jack had filed for a divorce some months ago. Case closed. The funeral of the Johnson family will be held next week.

Several days later, while relaxing at a luxurious suite at the Taj Mahal in Atlantic City, I made a few calls back to Delaware to check on my Aunt Ann. I leaned back to enjoy a bubbly glass of Dom Perignon while puffing on a cherry flavored Black & Mild. Instrumental jazz playing in the background. "Sophie, where is everyone?" I asked, as she walked over to me. She had on an all-white terry cloth robe with white high heels on. Her hair loosely hanging down to her shoulders.

"What do you mean, Bolo?" She asked. "The guys are out doing their own thing," she reached for my glass then took a sip of champagne.

I leaned forward. "What the hell," I paused reaching for the phone. "Let me call and have them come join me."

Choking, "No, no Bolo, please," said Sophie. She handed the champagne glass back to me while holding my hand down from picking the phone up.

"Why, Sophie?" I asked.

"HAPPY BIRTHDAY, BOLO," said Brandy and Dawn. Their loud sexy voices came from the Jacuzzi area. They were also wearing white terry cloth robes.

"What are you two doing?" I asked. They smiled watching me pour myself another glass of Dom Perignon. "Where are the rest?"

Sophie said, "There they go sweetie," she motioned her eyes to the burgundy ruffle curtains. *You're in for a big one, baby.*

Constance, Crystal and Diamond stepped from behind the curtains smiling. They were all dressed in white terry cloth robes. "Happy Birthday, Bolo," they all spoke at once standing side by side. They stopped dead in their tracks. Hands on their hips with feet spread apart.

"DAMN, Y'ALL LOOK GOOD," I shouted. All six women begin walking over to me as slowly leaned back into the recliner chair I was sitting in.

They all stood directly in front of me. Constance held the CD remote in her hand. She looked over left shoulder at the sound system mounted into the wall then tossed the remote. *This is a Man's World* by James Brown came screaming out of the four wall speakers. *What the hell am I about to experience here with these ladies, I don't know.* Slowly they begin encircling me while removing their robes then letting them drop to the floor.

"OH SHIT," I shouted. My eyes begin rolling from left to right. I quickly hoisted myself admiring all the women sporting different color lingerie sets.

Pink, silver, yellow, red and gold. They were all satin. What really caught my eyes was the black-laced lingerie Constance was sporting. She had the word "Bolo" engraved on the front. She stuck her tongue out at me then looked downward.

Dawn yelled, "well ladies," she then paused. "What should we do with him next?" They all looked at Dawn and nodded their heads.

"Dawn?" I watched her giving a single head nod to Diamond and Sophie.

"No time to be talking now, Cousin Bolo," she said.

Diamond and Sophie walked over to me. Raised both my arms then kindly removed my robe. I was now sitting butt-naked in front of all six women staring at me. They all stared at my fifth limb and the hardness it displayed. Each woman in this room knows that when I get aroused the way that I am now. It's time for some serious foreplay and fucking.

I started pouring champagne on my hardness while watching them all wiggle their panties down to their ankles. Next they removed their bras, nipples hard, as they want to be.

"Excuse me ladies, but..."

Dawn interrupted. "Shhh!" Her index finger pressed lightly against my lips.

"This is your birthday, baby," Constance said. She looked over at Crystal standing over top of me. "I dare you!" She blurted out laughing.

Sophie and Brandy shouted, "LET'S GETTHIS MUTHFUCKIN SHOW ON THE ROAD."They watched me and Constance enjoy a wet kiss. Crystal stooped low while swallowing my dick whole.

"Mmm," I moaned. The wetness of her mouth was driving me crazy. I could feel the warmth of her tongue teasing the tip of my hardness as she traced slowly. She swallowed it all. Once I climaxed, the escorted me over to the bed covered in red, white and yellow rose petals. Sophie climbed onto the bed placing her pussy smack on my face. "Ohhh , yes" I moaned. The feeling of someone sliding their clitoris onto my stiff hardness. She began moaning heavily. It was Constance.

"Bolo – Bolo, yes, Bolo," she moaned. "I'm cummin, I'm cummin," Constance screamed as her bod tightened. Sophie climaxed right behind her.

Moments later while everyone was enjoying themselves in the swimming pool.

Arriving back in Delaware, early the next morning I prepared myself to pay respect to a fallen detective and his family.

"Would anyone care to join me?" I asked.

They all shouted, "HELL NOOO," shaking their heads.

Laughing. "I'll see ya scared asses later on then." I pulled away.

Dawn thinks that I'm losing my mind because of the many police officers that will be at the Johnson's family funeral. It's open to the public so therefore I have the right to pay my respects.

I arrived at Cornerstone Fellowship Baptist Church on Market Street and Lea Boulevard. There were so many squad cars and unmarked police cars parked outside. Some were in the parking lot across the street. I spotted Detective Johnson's squad car which had a writing on the window, written in white, that read *R.I.P Detective Johnson and Family.*

The second I walked into the church everyone turned their attention on me. I was sporting an Armani two piece suit with a black pair of Armani sunglasses as always when I view someone's body. A plain clothes officer walked up to me and said, "you're not welcomed here, Bolo." He crossed his arms above his chest blocking me from taking another step. Detective Walker. He was Detective Johnson's partner who worked for me. He had a tear fall from his eyes. *Please don't come after my family* was his thought.

"Looka' here, Detective Walker," I paused then tilted my sunglasses below my eyes. "It's open to the public so I'm here to pay my respects," I said. He watched me fasten the few buttons on my blazer.

He stepped to the side. "You bastard," he whispered.

What is he doing here? He probably had something to do with the murders. Click – Click was the nly sound I heard as I slowly walked up to view Detective Johnson and his daughter's body. From my peripheral vision, I could see several officers has their weapons drawn. Moving along to admire the beautiful wife of the fallen detective. Kelly had on a silk black dress with her beautiful, blonde hair nicely draped down her shoulders. I placed the back of my left hand on her cold forehead. I whispered, "sorry but I don't leave witnesses," without moving my lips.

A woman cried, "Hurry and get outta here."

"I'm done, thank you ma'am," I spoke politely. She rolled her eyes at me so hard that I felt her hand on the trigger wanting to pull it. She brandished a chrome .380.

I wondered what would have happened if my crew came. That night my face was broadcasted all over the news that I was at the Johnson's family funeral paying my respects.

Chapter 21

One of the many places that I've done business. The old building on Miller Road that once housed the department store, *Ames*. Our last time meeting at this place before it gets torched. "Well gentlemen," I said. "This will be the last time we see this place," I paused. And do business."

"Bolo, man," said Kev. He stopped to admire the structure of the building. "We have so many memories to cherish here." He began checking the clip to his black Smith & Wesson 9mm hand gun to see if it was fully loaded.

Laughing. "Y'all remember a few back when Jay mention this joint to us?" I asked. Then paused. "Damn, I was gonna turn this place into a strip club."

The weakness in my voice alerted Kev, Monte, Leon and Dexter of how much I was missing Jay. Someone all over one of my own family. "Hey, Bolo," said Monte. We stood face-to-face. "Here's the twenty million doctors in cash that you requested from Constance." He held high-five black leather briefcase.

"Thank you, Monte," I held my composure. "It's appreciate of you, sir."

"Thank you, sir," he answered.

"Are you ready?"

He smiled. "I been ready," he stepped back while brandishing a chrome .357 with a black rubber grip.

"You look ready, too, nigga," Leon said. He definitely lifted our spirits by making us all laugh.

We all stepped inside the emptiness of the old run down building. The coldness felt as though winter was just lurking around the corner. Mildew gave way to the unoccupied years of the building.

"Too bad the women couldn't be here to join us, Bolo," said Dexter. We stood in front of the two grayish steel tables.

"Gentlemen, it was for there…" I paused watching Monte and Leon place five briefcase on the table. "Safety," I paused again to light a Black & Mild. "Trust me, they have what it takes, but today we're up against some of the most dangerous men from New York, so no telling what they may have up their sleeves."

"We heard that, Bolo," said Kev. He stepped forward to my right acknowledging that he's my right hand man. "We're ready for whatever they want to bring."

"Leon and Dex, we have all the material to torch this muthafucka after the deal is closed?" I asked. Slightly looking over my left shoulder.

"Yes, sir," they replied, moving to step forward to my left.

I leaned forward to watch Monte step to Kev's right. All are in their rightful position. I opened all five briefcases making sure the money was properly neat and stacked.

Everyone standing side by side sporting black two-piece Armani suits. Oyster Perpetual Yacht – Master Rolex watches on. A stray bird continues to fly about.

Door open. "Gentlemen, good evening," an Italian man yelled. He wasn't much tall in height. His silk shirt opened displaying growth of hair on his chest. He had two men on each side of him.

"Welcome gentlemen," I said. My men crossed their arms resting them above their chest. "Sweet temptation awaits you," a quick gesture motioning my extended hands over the briefcase.

"DELAWARE'S TOP CAPTAIN, IT'S NICE TO FINALLY MEET YOU, SIR" he shouted as he approached the table to shake my hand. My men looked at me as if something was about to ablaze. I shook my head in a motion to stand down.

"Mr. Amillio, I have all five briefcases." I opened every briefcases to show my money. "Four million dollars apiece in each totaling twenty million dollars as requested."

Laughing. " I didn't think that you could come up with this kind of money," he said nodding his head.

I leaned forward to whisper, "Delaware's Top Captain, what ya think. I'm worth over eighty-million dollars and counting," My men and I watched his eyes protrude while looking to his left then right at my men.

"Wow, that much?" asked Amillio.

"I take it Amillio that you're not even close to half of what I have in these black leather Louis Vuitton suitcases," I paused. "Which will be yours and all ours once our deal is closed."

"Hello," said Kev. "Cat gotcha tongue muthafucka," he blurted out. We all laughed.

"Bolo," Amillio paused. He searched his men then mines. "I'm a little short here," he said.

I forward myself one-step, "wait, wait, wait, what the fuck do you mean," I pause placing both my hands flat on the table. "You're a little short?"

"I couldn't provide all the guns and drugs that you requested," he said smiling. The small stray bird stood afar watching our every movement as if he knew something was about to go down. He smelled death in the air.

Shoes tapping. It was Kev alerting me something was definitely wrong with this picture. I looked to my right then to my left while clearing my throat. A signal for my crew to draw their weapons.

Click – click – click – click. Everyone drops back two steps raising our weapons to chest level. I thought the little bird was here to stay, but he flew away at the sounds of our guns cocking. "I'll tell you what gentlemen, why don't we just forget this day ever happened and go our separate ways," I paused. Swaying. "We can do this like gentlemen or we can do this my fuckin way."

"Whoa! Bolo. We only came here for the money!" He yelled. They all stepped back. Guns raised. Amillio's mind was set on me and my crew given in to him.

I shouted," MY FUCKIN MONEY. NOT NOW, NOT TODAY, NOT ANYTIME," they watched me close all five briefcases.

"Sorry Bolo, but my boss Amillio told us not to come back to New York empty handed," he paused. Then said, "shall we do this politely or shall we do this with fire?"

They definitely didn't think twice about their surroundings before they entered into their death sentence. Not knowing that this will be their last day alive. Death wish written across their faces. I never met Amillio. Talked to him on the phone a few times.

He was about to blaze when someone shouted, "ME AND MY GIRLS PREFER TO GO OUT WITH FIERCE FIRE MUTHAFUCKAS," she paused. "WHATTAYA SAY CAPTAIN?" Sophie asked. Crystal and Diamond accompanied her. They were in all black clothing with their weapons raised to their chest ready to blaze.

"Wow gentlemen, what are we to do now?" I asked lowering my weapons. "Nice to see you, ladies."

"Ah shit, Bolo, we were just joking with you man," he said swaying his head. His shoulder bouncing up and down.

"SHUT THE FUCK UP," I shouted. "HERE'S WHAT I'LL DO. SINCE YOU ONLY CAME HERE FOR MY MONEY. WHY DON'TYOU LEAVE YOU WITH FOUR MILLION DOLLARS," I then paused. Grabbed four briefcases and left on the table open. "SO YOU AND YOUR BOYS CAN SHARE."

"Damn, thanks sir," he excitedly said. They all watched me smile then walk away.

"Ladies and gentlemen," I turned back around. Looking around once again, I looked up and nodded my head at the small bird chirping. He came back for the action. "Please torch this muthafuckin place after you're done here with Mr. so calls himself Amillio and his sorry ass crew.

They cried, "Bolo, Bolo, Bolo."

I looked up to watch that little bird disappear into a small fissure. I then shouted to Kev, "GET AMILLIO ON THE PHONE. I WANT HIS LIFE BECAUSE IT BELONGS TO ME."

"Yes sir!" He yelled.

That next morning I was chilling over my aunt's house talking to Brandy and Dawn when Channel 6 News interrupted our cartoons. We were watching Tom and Jerry.

"*Five unidentified victims were pronounced dead at the scene of a fatal fire on Miller Road. The old building that once housed Ames department store. The office of the state Medical Examiner is expected to identify the victims and the fire's origin and cause remain under investigation,*" she said.

My Aunt Ann rushed into the living room from the kitchen to find out more of what was happening. She looked at me shaking her head. *You had something to do with this.*

Brandy and Dawn sat up to get an ear full. They glanced back at me periodically. The anchorwoman continued with her story. "*The fire spread, causing damage initially estimated at about one million dollars in damages. Also Wilmington's Fire Company discovered an undisclosed amount of money lying next to a black leather Louis Vuitton briefcase. According to investigators, the building was equipped with hard-wired smoke detectors, but they had not determined whether the alarms were activated during the fire. The owner of the property is the notorious Delaware's Top Captain, Lance 'Bolo' Jones.*"

All eyes turned towards me shaking their heads knowing that that was my work and money. "Look, it was a big deal going down last night," I said. "They came to rob and kill me. What was I supposed to do, let them kill me and my crew."

"How much, nephew?" Aunt Ann asked, standing over top of me. Her hands placed on her hips.

My head tilted down, chin in my chest. "I torched their asses along with the four million dollars." I looked at Dawn and Brandy from the corner of my eyes.

"FOUR MILLION DOLLARS," they shouted.

They damn near blew my eardrums out. "Well, just consider them going out in a conspicuous style which they fuckin deserved," I said.

"I heard that, Cousin Bolo," said Dawn

"What you did, you had to do baby," Brandy said.

I grabbed both of them around my neck then pulled them closer to me.

We all looked at Aunt Ann still shaking her head. She said, "Oh my gosh, I have the three murderers sitting right here before my very eyes," she paused. "Those two are getting just like you, your attitude and everything about you, Bolo." Aunt Ann rolled her eyes at us.

"Anyway, Cousin Bolo, its this white girl that saw your picture at the college," said Dawn. "We talked and she said that she'll do anything you want her to do."

"Her name is Heidi, Bolo!" Brandy yelled. She sat up. Her eyes focused on Aunt Ann.

"We told her that she has to come out to the penthouse," Dawn smiled at her mother.

"Time to go, cause I know where this conversation is leading," Aunt Ann headed back upstairs.

"Whatever, Mom," said Dawn.

Brandy yelled, "Come on back dawn her, Mrs. Ann!"

"HELL NO," she shouted. Her bedroom door closed behind her.

Dawn an Brandy began giving me all the details about Heidi and a description of her. From what they told me, Heidi's about 5'7", petite with hazel eyes and long brown hair. I left the house leaving them pondering about what next step I'll take.

Moments later, I approached Eden Park to spend some quality time with them. Maybe take them to see some real live shit. Since the women took control of Southbridge housing projects, business went well along with eliminating at me when I pulled up. "Okay, what I do this time!" I yelled out the window.

"Hello, Bolo." They had the sexiest voiced when they spoke to me. I believed they wanted to seduce me on the spot.

"I must say ladies," I paused. Sophie opened the door for me and Crystal held the lighter out, ready to spark my Black & Mild. "You three made one helluva entrance last night," I said. Diamond closed the car door for me.

Sophie rolled her eyes. "Your ass should've stayed for the fireworks last night," she said laughing. "They were begging for their lives."

"That so called Amillio, he wanted to take my money, he was so happy," I shook my head, "that we were leaving him with four million dollars." We all watched a short, black man punch a woman twice his size in the face. I looked at the women and they looked at me. *Damn, we're in trouble. Please don't tell at us, Bolo. We'll handle his black ass.*

Crystal broke the silence. "Did y'all see the smiles on their faces?" she asked. "He wanted fire and money, so we gave him the money on fire." We all laughed.

Diamond asked it the men knew they were coming as our back up plan. They all began laughing as the guys were driving up in Kev's white Mercedes Benz.

"Well, I told them that you ladies weren't cut out for this job, so I had to leave y'all out this one," I said.

"Why is everyone staring at us?" asked Monte.

"I plea the fifth fellas," I laughed. We all high-fived with a brotherly hug, laughing.

"We asked Bolo was y'all expecting us ladies to show up as a back up plan," Sophie said. "The expression that y'all had on y'all faces was like '*oh shit, where the hell they come from*'." She began making a flustering expression with her face.

"Check it out y'all. I have to be somewhere in about a half an hour, but I want everyone coming along to see the excitement," I said. I hopped back behind the wheel of my car. Crystal closed the door for me.

"Bolo," Crystal paused. She rested both hands on the door while bending down to look at me. "A movie or something?" she asked. Sophie's standing in the back of Crystal rolling her eyes at one of us. Her facial expression is deadly.

Smirking, I said, "depends on how you look at it Crystal, some movie shit or some real life shit." I wanted to reach behind her and smack the shit out of Sophie, sensing some type of jealousy about Crystal. I don't hit women. I assassinate them.

"MORE EXCITEMENT," Kev shouted. He leaped high off the ground.

"Ladies, in the car with me, please!" I said. Sophie jumped in the passenger seat, Diamond and Crystal in the back.

Once en route to our destination I give Kev a call and have him to place me and the girls on his speakerphone. "Bolo, what the hell is going on?" Kev's voice echoed through my car's speakers. We passed Wilmington Police Department as I noticed Detective Walker nodding his head at me.

Detective Walker was partners with Detective Johnson whom wished to stay on my payroll or shall I say that I have him by the balls. One small fuck up and I'll kill his entire family. His parents also.

"Okay," I paused. All are silent. Jazz is barely seeping through the speakers. "Now tell me something ladies and gentlemen," I said. I turned to look at Diamond, Crystal and Sophie. Stuck my hand out the window to wave at the guys to follow me. "Have y'all ever seen a live movie in broad daylight on the streets of Wilmington?"

"HELL NO," they all shouted. Diamond damn near blew my ear off when she leaned forward.

"DON'T WORRY," I shouted. "WE'RE GONNA SIT BACK AND ENJOY SOME WESTERN SHIT," I yelled. I then pulled over to park my Navigator between Rodney and Broom Street on Fourth.

Sophie asked, "Bolo, what's going on?" She leaned to the left resting on her elbows. Her chin in the palm of her hands. *Thank you for not snapping on me earlier.*

I yelled through the speakerphone to telling everyone to tell Sophie to be patient. They did just that.

"Guys, listen up!" I yelled. "There goes Felix," I pointed to the corner of Fourth and Rodney Street. There were a few people standing outside the Chinese store selling drug. Then there were several people outside the laundry mat drinking and selling drugs.

Click – click – click. Everyone displaying their weapon ready to leap out the truck. Felix was just standing there snorting something into his nose. He looked so dirty I began to wonder what the hell he did to my two point five million dollars. I had to calm everyone down because they all wanted to get Felix.

"Y'all see those three knuckle heads that's getting out that black Honda Accord?"

"Yes," they all answered.

"The previews just ended," I paused. "Now let the movies begin."

"Oh, shit, they all have guns y'all!" Crystal yelled. She pointed to three black males. They were all dressed in black double gauge shotguns.

Incessantly, Weapons raised. "Boom! Boom! Boom! Seconds later, the three gunmen retreated back to their vehicle, but not until they watched Felix lifeless body fall motionless to the ground. He had only half a face. Brain matter and tissue plastered over the Chinese window.

We pulled away making a U-turn back down Fourth Street. Ambulance and police cars racing to the crime scene. "Monte's voice came through the speaker. He asked, "hey Bolo," he paused a second. "How long have you known Felix was hanging out here on the Westside?"

"For a while, Monte. For quite some time now," I said while looking through my rearview mirror to see them turn up towards Fifth and Adams Street. I took the women back to Southbridge to pick up their cars.

That night I headed over to Constance place to relax in her Jacuzzi. Whine down while drinking Dom Perignon. She joined me. "Here, have a piece of cake, sweetheart," she said.

"Hmm, thank you, honey." We both smile at each other then I handed her a champagne glass.

"Bolo, what time are you, Ann and Dawn heading out to the cemetery tomorrow?" asked Constance. She gulped the champagne then poured more into her glass.

"Around eleven o'clock," I said, submerging my body into the water.

"Will you call me afterwards?" She joined me.

"Sure I will, Constance."

"Bolo, can I ask you something, please?"

"Ask me what?" I placed her leg on mines.

Her hands begin massaging my hardness. "Can we have a baby someday in the future?" She climbed on top of me while waiting for my response.

"A baby," I said, losing my train of thought not knowing what really came out her mouth.

Constance broke my daze. "Yes, a baby, Bolo," she grabbed my chin. "You need to think about your future," she said.

Constance was right about me and my future. On the other hand a baby would be nice to bring into this world. Someone to leave my money to. " I will Constance," I said. "What would you name him or her?"

"Well," she paused, kissing my lips. Her smile became sunshine. "If it's a boy I woud name him Lance Cornelius Jones, Junior. A girl, I would name her Lacy Constance Jones." She held my hand to follow her to the bedroom.

"Damn you look delicious!" I yelled, tapping her ass. She smiled. Laid flat on her back while pulling me on top of her.

Constance," I whispered

She looked into my eyes while sliding my hardness into her warm, wet pussy. "FUCK ME," Constance shouted.

That next morning at the Riverview Cemetery, Me, Dawn and Aunt Ann stand over top of my mother's tombstone with a dozen roses each at hand. Dawn bent down on both knees crying and talking to my mother, then Aunt Ann placed her hand on her shoulder and bent down beside her. I stood standing. "Joyce," my Aunt Ann paused. She was crying. "Would you look at your son and how he's grown," she said. I placed my hand on your shoulder.

"Aunt Joyce," Dawn looked up at me. Her tears flowed like a stream, "thank you so much for being Cousin Bolo's guardian angel." She turned away from me.

I know what Dawn was talking about when she asked my mother to continue to be my guardian angel. The life that I'm living requires some type of protection from up above. I believed that my mother agreed with me. Sun came peeping from the dark gray clouds. Wind slightly blowing the little bit of leaves nearby.

"Joyce, all our years together, we never ever broken a promise to one another," Aunt Ann placed some roses down at the tombstone. "Here I am, a promise kept," she said placing her hand on mines.

I kneeled down as if I were a child about to say his bedtime prayer.

"Mom…every day I bleed inside thinking about you constantly. The rage and pain that I carry deep inside me is unbearable. I have no respect for another man's life," I paused. "I know that you're somewhere up there watching over me," I looked into the sky. The feeling of tears slowly walking down my cheeks. "I remember the last time we saw each other…" Choking. "I – I miss you so much, our holidays together, our birthdays that we shared all the time together. I need your help, Mom. I'm slowly dying and don't know it," I cried. "I love you."

Chapter 22

"Two days ago, I saw you at the cemetery visiting someone. You were crying," I said to Sophie. She looked down at her chocolate cake.

"Yes, I was there. I go from time to time," said Sophie. Tapping her fork on the saucer. *Fuck the questionnaire, Bolo.*

I asked, "Someone passed away?" There were kids in the background crying.

"Miguel Lopez," she paused. "He's my brother, Bolo. Someone killed him in his own home." Sophie's eyes blazed fire.

She began crying out tome telling me that she's gonna do everything within her power to bring her brother's killer to his knees. Her brother. My ex-partner in crime. I wonder if she knows that I was his right hand man. He never mentioned Sophie, not once when I was protecting his family. Does she know that I killed her brother to be in the position that I'm in today? *That mothafucka was only paying me ten thousand dollars a month.*

I left her at a Red Lobster talking to a family member. They stayed with her while I headed out to handle some business.

Cell phone ringing. "Hello."

"Hi, Bolo," a woman's voice sounded through my car speakers.

"Penny," I paused. "Is that you?"

"Yes, Bolo, it's me," she said.

"I thought that I would never hear from you again," I made a sudden stop at a red light.

"Well, I've been crying most of the time, Bolo."

"Why is that?"

"Various reasons," she answered. "I cursed you out, took my house key back from you. Told you to get out of my face and my office."

"You were so cruel to me, Penny." *Damn light, is it ever gonna change.*

"I know, I was crying and stressing so much," she inhaled air through her nostrils.

"Where are you now?" I asked. The light finally turned green.

"At work," she replied, sniffling. "You told me from the start Bolo, that you were dating other women besides me." I can imagine tears trickling down her face. She continued, "You treated me like a queen and I threw it all away."

"Penny, you're a beautiful woman," I said. "Very intelligent, you have charisma as well as great potential." I pulled into the parking lot of AstraZeneca.

"Bolo, I wanted to tell you so much that I was pregnant with your baby," said Penny.

"You were pregnant!" I yelled not meaning to scare her. I almost hit a parked car.

Sobbing. "Yes, I was pregnant with your child," she then paused. "I was stressing so much that I had a miscarriage. Please forgive me?"

I forgive you, Penny, baby," I walked into her office. She was staring at a portrait of me that I've given to her. My hands were stretched out to her as she looked up at me.

Penny threw the phone then ran to me. "Bolo, Bolo," she cried. "I miss you so much."

"It's okay, baby," I held her clos to me. She continued to cry. "It's not your fault."

I left Penny in the comfort of her co-workers. My cell phone began vibrating, alerting me that it was an emergency. Come to find out, some niggas from the Hilltop section of Wilmington decided they wanted to have a shootout with my men.

I arrived at Trina's house across the street from the "Bucket" housing projects. A mother and her child were caught in between the crossfire. Hilltop, the Westside of Wilmington will be dealt with sooner or later.

Trina was standing up shaking her head at the blue detective car, as it turned left onto Thatcher Street. "You heard what happened, Bolo?" she asked. She sat down on the steps, I sat beside her.

"Yes, I received a call about twenty minutes ago," I said. "And I can't stay because I should've been at this meeting a half an hour ago, so I'll call you tonight."

"We need to handle our business soon, like yesterday." Trina smiled, placing her hand on my thigh to hoist herself. "I'll be waiting, Bolo." She whispered that she had no panties on. Her pussy was calling for me.

Later that evening, at one of Constance's hideaway houses. Everyone acknowledged my presence by raising their glasses to the ceiling. They were drinking Dom Perignon. Some were drinking red wine. "Well ladies and gentlemen," I paused. Constance kindly stood up and lit my Black & Mild. "The summer months have passed, we lost and we gained," I paused again, noticing that Crystal wasn't present. "Has anyone called or seen Crystal?"

Dawn said, "I called her last night Cousin Bolo and she said that she'll be here."

"Thank you, Dawn."

"Bolo, we had one helluva summer," said Diamond. She placed three large, black duffle bags on the table.

"Girl, time flies," Brandy smiled.

"Okay, here is what I need," I sat between Sophie and Constance. Sophie reached for an ashtray then placed it in front of me. "I need everyone to report to me what they brought to the table, starting with Sophie.

"I have here a total of three million dollars and not a penny short." She opened each briefcase one by one.

Diamond said, "Bolo, I have two point five million dollars here," She began unzipping the black duffle bags. I watched Constance press a button on the CD changer remote.

"Definitely six million here, Bolo," Kev pointed to four large black heavy trash bags. Jazz began seeping through the homemade speakers.

Dexter had a total of two million dollars while Monte only had one point five million with him. Leon pulled in a cool four million dollars. Constance was steady punching number pads on her Panasonic high-tech calculator.

She said, "Bolo," her eyes widened. You're at a total of nineteen million dollars, which added to your overall worth," Constance paused. She searched everyone's facial expressions. "Two hundred thirty-four million dollars."

Damn! Everyone yelled.

Constance motioned everyone to calm down then made an announcement that New Jersey, Baltimore and my stocks are definitely bringing in money.

"Constance, sweetheart, since I have a wonderful crew and it's almost Christmas time in two months, why don't you write everyone two million dollar check, on me," I said. They were all so excite, but so sad that I had to leave on short notice. Crystal wasn't present today so I'll head over to her place. I know she had to be somewhere with her mother and hope everything went well with the family situation that escalated two weeks before.

Seven days later, watching my black butterfly lay in a pearly, white coffin. She's so beautiful. Her low-cut black hair. Her black-laced dress trimmed with fine embedded white flowers. "Who the fuck could have done this to you," I mumbled under my breath.

Everyone's eyes are on my organization line up to pay our respects to Mrs. Russ, Crystal's mother. I watched Kev embrace and kiss Mrs. Russ on her forehead then walked away. "Mrs. Russ," I said. She looked up at me. "I'm deeply sorry for your loss."

Her right hand opened. *Smack! Smack!* "DAMN YOU!" she shouted. "YOU WERE SUPPOSE TO PROTECT MY LITTLE GIRL!" Her body quivered. She cried endless tears.

In my organization, I bond a special connect with my crew and their family members. They become so obsessed with material things that life has to offer them because it's all free. Not knowing the consequence that their loved ones have to face in my organizations. Families get together and claim that you're the son they wished they had but when sudden tragedy happens to a loved one…it's all my fault that the death of a loved one happened. *I can understand the pain that she's going through.*

That' night, me and the guy's head on out to the workers' night out at the Longshoremen's Hall over in Southbridge. "Hey guy," I paused. "I have to handle some persona business before we head on out."

Kev spoke for everyone, Cool, Captain, handle your business," he said.

They all watched me walk up to 402 Bethune Drive in New Castle. "Clear!" Monte yelled.

Door opened. "Hey Bolo, come on it," Ron said, he motioned me to step inside. He was 5'4", dark-skinned and stocky. His two partners were sitting down snorting cocaine. Ron stood by their side to listen to what I was about to say to them all.

"I stopped by to congratulate you guys on a job well done blasting Felix in broad daylight for me," I said.

"No problem," they all said. They watched me open the door.

I turned to say. "Thanks," I paused. Gun cocking. "Muthafuckas," I whispered. Brain matter and tissue decorated the entire living room for the month's 1st Halloween party. No witnesses.

I decided not to hang out with the fellas, so I went on home to relax and see what else I could get into. I took a quick hot shower then headed out to my balcony. Gazing at the Wilmington's skyline puffing on a Vanilla flavored Black & Mild and drinking the finest champagne, Dom Perignon.

My front door swung open. I reached for my weapon that was resting on the outside balcony table of my penthouse when Brandy and Dawn walked in wearing black terry-cloth robes. Both had black high heel pumps o match.

They stood there in silence for about five minutes, smiling at me not saying one word. Their hair style in two long plaits reaching the tops of their asses. Since I had a mix CD in my CD changer, I pressed number four on the remote as the Whispers began singing *This is What I'll Do to Get You in the Mood* through the mounted speakers on the wall. Surround sound. They both took a few steps forward while dropping their robes then slightly looking back over their shoulders.

Seconds later, Heidi steps between them, smiling. She was picture perfect as described. Petite, long brown hair also styled in two long plaits touching the tip of her ass. She has hazel eyes and definitely had all the right curves a man is looking for. Heidi was wearing a pink Bill Blass floral silk robe and bikini perfectly blended in with her cream color skin tone.

"Good evening, ladies," I said, taking a sip of champagne.

"Hi Bolo," said Brandy.

"Cousin Bolo," Dawn said. "This is Heidi and Heidi this is my Cousin Bolo."

Heidi smiled. "Hello handsome. It's a pleasure to meet you," she said, in her sexy tone of voice.

"Same here, Heidi," I paused. They each took a glass of champagne. "The three of you look so gorgeous." I said while admiring their nakedness before me. I motioned them to come join me out on my balcony to watch the lovely Wilmington skyline.

"It feels so great up here." Said Heidi. She watched Dawn move to my left and Brandy to my right.

"You won't mind if I caress your breast would you?" I asked.

Heidi stepped forward so we were face-to-face. "Be my guest," she said.

I began to slowly caress her hard nipples listening to her moan, wanting me to suck on them. My tongue slowly traced her nipples. She heard me moan out her name as she grabbed my hardness then fell to her knees and began to slowly wrapping her lips around my fifth limb.

Chapter 23

November 2002. Two o'clock that morning at Kimberton Apartments out in Newark. Trina and I slowly creep into apartment twenty-seven zero nine to find a petite, black woman, butt naked laying on her back. She held not one string of hair on her vagina. She was hairless. Her clitoris protruded. "Damn," I mumbled, shaking my head at the size of her pussy lips.

"Watcha mouth, boy," Trina said, pushing my shoulder and rolling her eyes at me.

"Sorry baby," I paused. "Wake that nigga up outta his sleep," I said. There was a man laying down on his left shoulder sleep. He was butt naked.

Dirk and his girlfriend has sex and were snorting drugs before they feel asleep. Sex aroma filled the air.

"Hey, mothafucka, get the fuck up!" Trina tapped Dirk on his bare naked ass.

"Shhh! Bitch, don't say a word or you're dead," I placed my index finger on both her lips while holding my gun to her head. She immediately pissed herself. I thought she was having an orgasm.

"What the fuck is this!" Dirk yelled, he was covering his face from Trina smacking him repeatedly.

"Please, please don't hurt us," the woman began begging.

"Bitch, Michelle," I paused looking at her gold colored necklace around her neck. "Shut the fuck up. We came here for ya man," I said. They both sat up in the bed. She pulled the green and black strip blanket to their waist while placing their hands on top.

"Bitch, we didn' come here for you," said Trina. "I-came-here-for-your-cheating-ass-boyfriend-that's-how-I-got-your-apartment-key...you like calling me a bitch!" She knocked him in his mouth so hard that his head jerked back, slamming into the headboard.

After every word she said, Trina whacked Dirk with the butt of the gun. He bled from his head and eyebrows. She broke his nose and several of his teeth fell out. Michelle covered her face with both hands crying. *Please don't hit me,* she thought to herself.

Dirk started spitting blood out all over. He said, " damn, I didn't mean it."

"You know what…get the fuck up! You too, bitch!" Trina yelled, pressing the gun against his temple. She rolled her eyes at me because I helped Michelle out the bed.

Once in the living room Trina started giving me orders, orders to duct tape Dirk. She's the type of woman I wouldn't mind running my organization. I laughed and did as I was told to do. Michelle quickly curled under Dirk's right arm as she sat down next to him.

"No need to cry now bitch, it's ya man's fault," she handed me a grey roll of duct tape.

"Trina, I didn't mean…"

I interrupted Dirk. "Shut the fuck up, nigga." I pressed a strip of tape to his mouth.

"I'm going to put you in so much pain in front of your bitch, nigga," Trina pointed to Dirk's penis then pulled the trigger. Blood splattered everywhere.

"Do his ass Trina, so we can get the hell outta here," I said.

"Noooo!" Michelle screamed. She watched Trina send two slugs into Dirk's chest. "Please – please, I don't have anything to do with him threatening you two," she cried. Michelle looked at me. *Please don't let her kill me too.*

I said, "He didn't threaten me, sweetheart." I kindly backed away from her, shaking my head watching Trina thrust her gun into Michelle's mouth.

"That's right bitch, open your mouth," Trina shoved the gun further into Michelle's mouth looking at me rolling her eyes. *You want this bitch now?* "Keep your mouth shut bitch, or I'll come back and kill your whole family," she paused. "You hear me?"

Michelle nodded her head while balling into a fetal position. She was sucking on the steel, black silencer. *Thank you so much,* she thought.

"I mean it bitch," said Trina. We both backed up towards the door. "Then again, I changed my fuckin' mind."

Pop! Pop!

Michelle looked at us in silence. She felt two slugs into her chest, not knowing the third one directly to her forehead. Brain matter and tissue covered the back wall.

We made a quick exit from the apartment only to see a black couple quickly turn away from us pretending to be kissing each other. "You see that shit, Bolo?" asked Trina. "How all of a sudden they all focused on each other?"

"Every move they made, baby." I said.

Trina stopped. "Excuse me?" she said.

"Yes, what's up?" The man asked. His right arm wrapped around the woman's waist.

"I intervened. "Y'all didn't see us coming from that apartment?" I asked. Paused. "Did you?"

He answered, "Man, we didn't see shit." His voice frightened.

Trina said, "We know." Then she emptied her clip on both of them. *Pop! Pop! Pop! Pop!*

The next morning, Constance called me to come over to her place, so I took a quick shower. Made a few calls then headed on out the house. What is so urgent that Constance needed to speak with me early in the morning?

Once I arrived, I noticed two of my guards standing at the window of Constance bedroom. They were peeking inside while shaking their heads. She mentioned to me that she was gonna shower first before making breakfast.

I stood watching them for about a half hour then waited for them to remain back into position. They noticed me pulling into the driveway, then quickly stood in the parade-rest position. Feet spread apart with their hands behind their backs.

"Gentlemen," I paused. My car came to a complete stop. "How's the perimeters?"

"Fine" said Tony.

"Cool, Bolo," Art said. They both responded fractiously.

"You're both relieved of your duties until further notice," I handed them both a manila envelope containing ten thousand dollars apiece. "Have a nice day and I'll definitely see y'all soon."

"Thanks sir," they said watching me pull away. They gave each other a high-five. Tony and Art then embraced a brotherly hug.

Constance was standing in the doorway of her dining room. She had breakfast already on the table. The food was on hot plates. I kissed her lips then we sat down across from each other. She had a facial glow. I could see why Tony and Art were peeping in on Constance. She's picture perfect. Her body was all that and some.

"Thank you for joining me, Bolo, on such short notice," said Constance. She positioned herself firmly in the chair.

I said smiling, "Welcome sweetheart." We both then said grace as she passed me my favorite homemade blueberry muffin.

"I'm pregnant, Bolo."

"Huh?"

"You heard me, I'm carrying your baby," Constance reached across the table to hand me a piece of black and white plastic with a crazy design on it.

"You're having my baby!" I yelled, quickly jumping to go rub her stomach. "How many months are you?"

She motioned for me to pull a chair closer. "Two months. And Dawn and I will probably have our babies around the same time."

Constance was so happy to tell me about the baby, our baby, that I couldn't object to her happiness of her wanting to have my baby.

Now Dawn for some apparent reason, she's hesitant about me meeting her unborn child's father. Maybe because I'll kill him then talk her into getting an abortion. After all, she once stated that I owned that sweet, good pussy she has. I'll do some investigation and then have that nigga killed.

Constance and I finished breakfast then we both cleaned the kitchen together. I followed her to work then went my way.

That evening, I picked up Heidi from Delaware Technical Community College then we headed on over to my house on Augustine Cut-off. Once there Heidi helped herself to a self-tour. I called everyone reminding them all about the meeting that I'm having tomorrow afternoon. Just as I hung up the phone, Heidi comes walking into my extra bedroom that I got custom made. She was wearing one of my black Armani robes.

"What?" she asked, stepping directly in front of me smiling. "You said to make myself at home, so I did just that."

"Are you comfortable?"

"Yes, I will be." She let the robe fall to the floor then motioned me to undress myself. Without hesitating, she dropped to her knees stroking her tongue up and down my hardness. I could feel the warmth of her saliva running down my hardness and onto my nut sack. "Ummm, Heidi baby," I moaned.

She reached up to grab both my hands placing them on her head, up and down my dick emerges knowing that I'm about to explode. Heidi pulls back and climbed on top of my hardness. Moments later we both exploded.

I had to end our session to attend a very important meeting that I've scheduled a few weeks back. I took Heidi home.

That same week at Brandywine Park with Kimberly. "Bolo, I haven't been down here since you brought me and Naomi down here," said Kimberly. She wrapped her arms around mines. It was chilly outside.

"Really?" I said. We started to walk. "It's cold out here."

She clinched my hand. "My, it is, so we'll keep each other warm.

"How about you and Naomi, Kimberly?"

"What about us?" she asked. Kimberly stopped us dead in our tracks. We were standing in front of the zoo.

"Your house, Naomi's house. Your new cars."

"Bolo," she paused. "We truly thank you for all that you're doing for us, we really do." We began laughing, watching a little black girl chase a squirrel up a tree.

"Look how cute she is," I said.

Kimberly looked me in the eyes. "Yes, she is Bolo. That's why I would love to have a little girl someday, so she and I can do our girlie things together," she paused while looking at the little girl "So when a man lets me down, I'll have my daughter to keep me strong. I'll braid her hair in all types of different styles."

Giggling. "I know that's right Kim."

Kim kept going on and on about how she wanted to have a baby. "She and I will dress alike and have so much fun together." We began walking again. Kim smiled at the little girl then the little girl shot a smile back at her.

Just by that little girl smiling back at Kim really boosted her confidence on wanting a baby. "Look at the two of you."

Smiling. "Dawn is having a baby. Constance is having your baby...damn. Bolo, they're having them around the same time, too."

"That will be quite a surprise, won't it Kim."

"Yes, but don't you want to at least have two kids of your own?" Kimberly asked, motioning me to have a seat on the wooden picnic table.

Why the hell did you ask me that question? "Only if you want that only one," I said. *I can't believe what the hell just came outta my mouth.*

"So," she paused smiling at the little girl rolling around in the fall leaves. "Does that mean I can have your baby, your second child?"

"One day Kim, we'll sit down and talk about everything."

She quickly jumped up catching the little girl's attention. Her mother stood there watching and smiling at us.

Standing over top of me. "We'll have a beautiful little girl," said Kim. "She'll be half African-American and half Chinese with our looks and our intelligence."

I interrupted, "your long, silky, black hair and gorgeous Chinese eyes." I watched the mother and kid get into a bright red Mercedes Benz then drive away.

"Wouldn't that be nice, Bolo? A little Kimberly or a little Bolo running around the house."

"No child support!" I yelled standing to my feet.

Laughing. "Shut up, Bolo, our baby will be well taken care of with no problem."

"Damn right, Kim. Stocks and bonds everywhere, girl."

"Did you make up your mind about Naomi and me joining your organization?"

"Wait a minute, I stepped away from her. "What happened to the baby that you want to have?" I asked.

"I'm sorry, sweetheart," she watched me jog backwards.

"Where are you going?"

"Running away from you, crazy ass."

"GET BACK HERE, BOLO," she shouted.

"You'll have to catch me, Kim!" I yelled. She started running towards me.

"Wait for me, please Bolo."

"Come on slow ass," I slowed down.

Seconds later I allowed her to catch up with me as we began sharing a passionate kiss. No one seem to be at the park. They all left, leaving Kim and me stranded to do whatever we wanted. "You better stop playin with me, Bolo." We kissed with non-stop movement.

"Damn, you kiss so good girl."

So do you, baby," Kim said. She was looking or peeping over my right shoulder. She opens my coat slowly. "You have your guns on you?"

"Shit, what the fuck is going on?"

"Don't move, trust me, don't move baby," she quickly grabbed both of my nine millimeter glocks.

"Kim," I said. She stood on her toes then placed her chin on my shoulder.

Boom! Boom! Boom! Boom! Boom! Boom! I fell to the ground while following Kimberly's eyes only to see two black men laying in a pool of blood. Guns several feet from where they lay dead.

Shaking my head, she helped me off the ground. "Damn, baby," I paused. "Kim you saved my fuckin life."

"Come on, let's get the hell away from here, Bolo." Kim yanked my arm as we began running to my car.

Boom! Boom! Glass shattered. I felt the heat sensation quickly spread through the coldness of my body before she shoved me into the car.

I ended up behind the steering wheel of my car looking pass Kimberly. She shot an old white man in the head. He was sitting in his blue Ford pickup truck. That explained where the heat sensation was coming from when she pointed the gun at me.

Chapter 24

Fearfully, they all watched me as I walked into my meeting room at my penthouse. Everyone has a glass of red wine in their hand. I noticed two new familiar faces at my table, Kimberly and Naomi. They were bobbing their heads to the sweet, mellow sound of jazz from my wall speakers. The rest of my crew was shaking their heads knowing what was on my mind and that I was about to explode. "Hello everyone," I said. My eyes glued to Naomi and Kimberly.

"Hey Captain," they all responded at once. All wine glasses landed on the table. Naomi and Kimberly notice what was happening, so they quickly placed theirs down, spilling some on the table.

"Kimberly and Naomi, what are you two doing here at my meeting?" I asked. "Let alone at my fuckin' table!" I yelled. They startled, almost knocking the wine glasses completely off the table.

They sat straight up giving me their undivided attention, placing their hands on the table in front of them. Kimberly spoke for the both of them. She said, "Bolo…"

I interrupted, "CAPTAIN!" I shouted bending over Diamond's right shoulder. She lit my Black & Mild.

"Captain," Kimberly paused, choosing her words carefully. "Sophie and Diamond said that – that we should be here at the meeting today," she said tilting her head downwards wanting to be rescued by someone.

Sophie came to her rescue. "Cap't, did they get the confirmation from your to attend?" Sophie shot them both a killer look then rolled her eyes and sat back down.

"HELL NO," I shouted. "SO WHY THE FUCK ARE THEY AT MY MEETING?" I paused. "ANYONE CARE TO EXPLAIN," they all jumped when I banged on the table once. Red wine spilled everywhere.

"Capt., neither one of us has any idea about them two attending the meeting," said Kev.

I stood over top of Kimberly's right shoulder. I could hear every breath that she breathed. Her heart was pumping irregular beats. Hands trembling. "JUST BECAUSE YOU SAVED A LIFE AT BRANDYWINE PARK," I paused taking a puff off my Black & Mild. "DOESN'T MEAN YOU CAN DO WHAT THE FUCK YOU WANNA DO. YOU HEAR ME?" I yelled louder.

"Hmmmm," Kimberly mumbled.

"What!" I yelled. "Answer me, damn it."

"No, Bolo," she paused. "No Capt., I don't think that." She stared at me with teary eyes. *Why are you treating me like this, Bolo?* Kimberly thought to herself.

"What the fuck did you just mumble under your stinkin ass breath, Naomi?" My attention was now focused on her. She watched me slip on my black leather gloves.

"Nothing, Capt.," she answered. Her childish eyes lead her to imagining running out that door screaming for her mother.

"Monte, Dexter, Kev and Leon," I paused, stopping behind Naomi and Kimberly. They dare not look up at me. "Sophie and Diamond, what should we do with our unwanted guests?" I asked, placing my gun to Kimberly's temple. She jumped from the coldness of black, steel pressed against her tender flesh.

"Bolo, we're sorry, we didn't mean to come here," Kimberly words cracked. She begins begging for her and Naomi's life.

"No need to beg now, this is something that has to be takin care of, right here and right now." I said.

Naomi cried. "Bolo, please, we're sorry," her hands flew to cover her face. She quickly them both back on the table when click of gun sounded. Tears rushing down her cheeks like a river.

"SHUT UP. YOU FUCKED UP," I shouted grabbing my weapon off the table. "YOU FUCKED UP TOO, KIMBERLY," I whipped out the other gun then pointed it to her head. She jerked back.

Kimberly cried out, "Bolo, we're sorry."

"You are?"

"Yes Bolo, we're truly sorry," Kimberly said. She spoke for herself and Naomi. Naomi was rocking back and forth crying. She motioned with her lips. *Please help us please* to Sophie and Diamond. For a minute they all watched me leave the room then walked back in.

"I'm sorry Kimberly and Naomi," I paused. "It's time to get what you came here for."They watched me pluck the air bubbles out the clear syringe that I had. "You have two choices, one in the heart or six CC's in your veins!" I yelled, nodding my head as everyone drew their weapons.

Screaming, "Oh my God, please don't do this Bolo. Please don't kill us, please!" Kimberly jumped up and down in her chair. Her mother can't save her ass now.

I yelled at Kimberly, "didn't I say shut the fuck up?"

"Yes, yes," she answered. Her hunter green cotton shirt was filled with tears.

"Ladies and gentlemen, take care of them both," I pause. All eyes focused on me as I walked to the door. "Then throw their stinkin bodies in the Christiana River."

"Bolo, please don't do this to us," Naomi cried. *Please let us live, please.* Her facial expression. Kimberly just cried knowing that their time was up. Time for the two of them to die.

"NOW," I shouted. Turned my back away from them.

Click, click, click, click, click, click. Everyone pulled the trigger then shouted out, "WELCOME TO OUR ORGANIZATION, DELAWARE'S TOP CAPTAIN." They all stood there watching Naomi and Kimberly stand to their feet crying.

"Bolo, why you scare us like this?" cried Kimberly.

"Bolo," Naomi said. The both ran to me crying and embracing me.

Tears started rolling down Sophie and Diamond's cheeks. I could tell they were missing Joy, Crystal and Bianca.

"C'mere my two cry babies," I wrapped my arms around their necks then placed my weapons on the table.

"Yes," they continued crying while wrapping their arms around my waist.

"Time and time again, you ladies asked could you join my organization. Too persistent, the both of you," I said. "I like that in both of you, you're full of energy."

My plan was to set both of them in some concrete then leave them down in Brandywine River.

"Guys, one month Kimberly and I took a stroll down Brandywine Park." Everyone focused on Kim. "We were talking when suddenly she reached in my coat for my weapons while gunning down two men who tried to kill me," I said. They welcomed them to the family once again.

They all remember the incident then began congratulating our new family members, Naomi and Kimberly. I left the penthouse so they can continue to celebrate. They are to explain to Kimberly and Naomi all about my likes and dislikes and what I expect out of them living in the family of my organization.

Soldiers, I remember Kimberly and Naomi ask me to come to their neck of the woods in Dover, Delaware. A housing project called Capital Green. That night they took me over to this black sister's crib and left me there for about a good two hours. She had a body with all the seductive curves a man hollered out. Sandy brown hair sported and styled by Nia Long. Full bloomed lips that could and would suck a dick for hours. Her name was Precious and Precious had a champion suck game on her.

I was just relaxing, watching TV when Precious came downstairs wearing nothing but an all black fishnet. Next thing I know she was giving me all the brains that I wished for. That was, until Naomi and Kimberly walked in from the kitchen and blew her brain matter and tissue all over the place. You would have thought that I fucked Precious three months straight while on her period.

That was the night they proved themselves to me, so I made up my mind to welcome them both into my family, "Delaware's Top Captain" organization. They had the audacity to take me to a nearby hotel to clean me up then fuck the hell out of me. We all agree to a menag a trois.

Tony and Art. Doors opened. "Come on in, Bolo" Tony said. He held the door open for me until after I completely stepped inside. Art was sitting down leaning over a square, glass table. He looked up at me then spoke while snorting three straight lines of cocaine. He had about seven more to finish. Tony then sat down to join him.

"Hey guys," I said. They only nodded their heads in response. "Remember the last time that I saw the two of you?" They again nodded their head, pissing me the fuck off.

On top of that, this living room is full of aroma from marijuana. Since they're acknowledging my fuckin presence, as they should be, I'll get this party started the way I run things. "Why in the hell were you two peeping through Constance's bedroom window when she got out the shower?" I asked. Their bodied jerked back into the position of attention.

"B – B – Bolo," Tony stuttered, looking at Art from his peripheral vision. *Damn nigga, we're in serious trouble now,* his thoughts

"N – N – Nah Bolo," said Art. His words barely came out of his mouth. He was focused on the last line of cocaine he wanted to snort.

I interrupted, "YOU DISRESPECTED AND VIOLATE THE BOTH OF US," I shouted. They both stared down the barrel of my nine-millimeter weapons. "YOU SON OF A BITCH," I yelled. Three slugs went into Tony as he leaned to the left. I pumped five slugs into Art, jerking him forward. He finally snorted that last line of cocaine he ached for.

Looking at my watch to see that it was two o'clock in the afternoon already so I headed on over to Eden Park in Southbridge. Naomi and Kimberly smiled when they noticed me pulling into the park. "Look at my new family members," I came to a complete stop.

"Hey, Cap't," said Naomi. "Hello handsome," Kimberly said. They both turned their heads to the Wilmington Police squad car driving pass.

"Where's Diamond and Sophie?" I asked as I grabbed my full-length leather coat.

Kimberly responded first. "They left us here to see how well we can handle our business ourselves."

"We're going pretty damn well too, " Naomi said. She nodded her head at someone who was working under her to complete a transaction. I just nodded my head while alerting suspicion in our surroundings. Kimberly reached into her car to turn the music up. TuPac's *All Eyes on Me* was sounding through her speakers. She stopped to say, "Cap't these bitches over in Riverside keep grittin on us, too."

"Y'all know what to do, Kimberly," I paused. "Get those bitches where it hurts. Handle ya business if you know what I mean."

"Then we'll do just that. Handle our business, girlfriend." Naomi walked up to Kimberly for sisterly hug. They both turned to me then smiled rolling their eyes at me.

"Ladies, why don't y'all look around then tell me what you see."

Shaking their heads, "nothing," they said.

"So if someone was to run on the both of you, maybe robbed or tried to kill your asses," I paused. Naomi reached into her jacket pocket then pulled out a gold lighter to light my Black & Mild. "You two would have had no knowledge of what would take place."

"Cap't, what are you talking about?" Kimberly asked stepping back beside me.

"Just take a real good look."

Naomi stepped back to my left side. "Cap't, you're scaring us," she said.

"Both of your lives are on the line as we speak, ladies." I leaned back on my Navigator. "Now Sophie and Diamond have been gone for approximately two hours."

"H – H – How did you know that?" Naomi said. *Damn girl, what the hell we do wrong?* Her thoughts as she looked passed me to focus on Kimberly's facial expression.

"They called me to explain what they were doing," I paused. "But don't worry about it now, Naomi and Kimberly, because the two of you are both dead." I wrapped my arms around their necks, smiling. "Now, why don't you look behind that bush were that red car is on the right side and wave to Sophie," I point in Sophie's direction. She waved back at us."

"Damn," Naomi mumbled. Kimberly in silence.

"Ladies, now feast your eyes on Diamond," I spun the both of them around. "That's Diamond under the hood of her car." I pointed to Diamond signaling her to wave at us. She did just that. Kimberly and Naomi barely lifted their arm up to wave back.

Seconds later, I gave a lecture to Naomi and Kimberly, as Diamond and Sophie listened as well. I told them to keep in mind that safety is more important than the money they were making as long as they're in my family. Also, to be aware of their surroundings coming in and out of dirty Southbridge.

"This is not the Capital Green Projects in Dover," I said. "It's much more dangerous here in the city. Lesson learned, so use it daily or your lives will be taken away from your in a blink of an eye. "They all watched me jump behind the steering wheel of my Navigator.

"We're with professionals, Naomi, so let's be professionals along with our family," Kimberly said, motioning a sign of group hug extending her arms out. They waved at me as I drove away. They all went shopping in Philly.

Not a day goes by without these sorry ass detectives wanting to pull me over. I pulled over about twenty yard before I was about to make a left onto Twenty-Third Street.

"What the fuck do you clowns want with me this time?" I asked.

"Get the hell up against the car!" Detective Walker yelled at me as he snatched me out my car.

"Dumb muthafuckers."

"Keep yelling at us, while we frisk you," his partner said to me.

I continued to follow their orders as they were telling me about Monk and Biz shouting at me a month ago. Word is that they're hating on me. So their job is to kidnap Monk and Biz' entire family and bring them to me.

Chapter 25

Rockford Park. One of many late night parks in Wilmington that Sophie loves to relax at night. We were standing at the top of the tower when we witnessed a falling star dashing across the sky. She closed her eyes for a minute or two wishing that her desires would come true. Temperature in the low forties. 43° to be exact. Sound of a dog echoing from afar. Sophie held my hand that glanced into the midnight skies. "Sophie," I said. She turned to face me, "Why didn't you tell me that Crystal was in the studio recording a song baby?"

"Bolo," she giggled. "You know what honey, it slipped my mind," said Sophie. She grabbed my other hand.

"She sings very well. That was her dream, to become a singer and I believed that she would've been successful at it."

"Yes, she would have been. I miss my girl so much, Bolo," she rested her head on my chest.

I could feel the emotions about to rise so I decided to jump to another subject. "Naomi and Kimberly, I'm placing them over in Riverside because that's what they want," I paused. "What's your opinion on that?"

She said, "Bolo, they have what it takes, I think it's a good move for them anyway."

"Thank you." We walked back over to the open of the tower. "It's so beautiful out here tonight."

She looked up. "Bolo, the stars and the night glow that they give..."

"Sophie. What do you think about family? The organization?" I asked. She gently let my hands go, then walked away from me.

"The family," she paused. Sophie turned to face me. "I love the family, Bolo," she said.

"To what extent, Sophie?"

"To the extent that I would do anything for them," she answered while pushing her hair off her face.

"You will?"

"Yes, Bolo."

I walked to her. We were face to face. "Anything… you mean like… kill someone that you truly love?" She felt the steel coldness of my nine millimeter pressed against her throat.

"Bolo, what's the meaning of this sweetheart?" her eyes begin filling with tears. Her fingers softly ran across my cheeks.

"You know what I'm talking about. Why you do it? She had a fuckin life and you ended it for what reason I don't know," I said.

"I WAS JEALOUS OF HER BOLO! CRYSTAL MADE ME JEALOUS OF HER!" Sophie shouted, stepping back with tears flowing from her eyes.

I yelled. "Jealously doesn't run in the family, you know it. The many years that I've been in this business, I've never seen anything like it except…" I lowered my gun.

"EXCEPT WHAT, BOLO," Sophie paused. She wiped her tears. "THAT YOU KILLED MY BROTHER, MIGUEL LOPEZ," she shouted, walking up to me until we were face to face. "JUST TO GET WHERE YOU ARE TODAY!" she cried.

"Sophie," I said. She interrupted.

"I WANTED TO KILL YOU THE FIRST TIME I MET YOU AT THE HOTEL DUPONT," she paused to catch her breath. "THAN I SAID TO MYSELF…I'LL KILL HIS FAMILY ONE BY ONE."

"It wasn't personal, Sophie, it was business," I whispered. "He was only paying me ten thousand dollars a month to protect him and his family and run his business," I cried.

She walked to the ledge. "I guess this is the last of us," she said, looking downward.

Cocking my gun. "I never thought I would have to terminate the women in my family. You fuckin had everything, Sophie, but Crystal's voice."

"I'm sorry, I'm sorry, I'm sorry," she cried out.

"I won't kill you, Sophie. I'll give you the death wish that you placed upon yourself, sweetheart."

"What are they here for? They work for you?" she asked, as Detective Walker and Detective Owens pulled up, then go out to leave up against their car.

"What do you think? You remembered Detective Johnson...well he was working for me also, but I had to kill his family for sharing the money that Felix had stolen from me."

"So everyone is on your payroll?"

"From the Senator on down, Sophie. They will all have their day sooner or later."

"I always admired how you handled your business, Captain," she shook her head.

"Sophie," I walked over to her. She watched my endless tears.

"Captain, will you tell the others that I'm sorry. That I will always love them." She then paused. "Will you remember me?"

I cried like a baby. "Y-Yes."

She pointed. "What about them?"

"They will join you Sophie because they didn't have to mention none of this shit to me."

"You have a good heart, Captain." She began wiping the tears from my eyes.

"Sophie..."

"Shhh!" she kissed my lips. "I love you, Captain Lance 'Bolo' Jones. I love you," she closed her eyes while falling backwards.

"Noooooo – SOPHIE!"

Seconds later while talking to the detectives over Sophie's body. "She's still alive, sir."

"Leave her," I said. Her eyes were closed. "She'll die slowly."

They agreed then asked when could they received their million dollars I promised them. "You could've kept this one to yourselves. Next week you'll get paid."

"Damn, next week!" Detective yelled.

"Yes...after they bury your asses next to your families," I said, as I watched both their lifeless bodies fall onto Sophie's.

Later that night, at my penthouse I pressed the CD changer remote button to hear Jackie Wilson's *Lonely Teardrops,* loudly coming from my wall speakers.

I took a big gulp of Hennessey than reached for my nine millimeter weapon to place it to my temple.

"THIS LIFE I WANT TO LIVE NO MORE," I shouted. "THIS ISN'T MY LIFE," I cried.

Boom!!!!!!

Chapter 26

"Mom, what time is the funeral? What about everyone else, are they gonna be there?"

"Dawn, sweetheart, this is what Bolo wants. You know how he wants everyone to be on time, and yes they all have to be there."

"I remember when Cousin Bolo took me over to that warehouse on 26th and Market Street."

"Warehouse?"

"Yes, Mom," she paused. "Once we got there, the two niggas that beat me into that coma were there hanging butt naked from ropes for their dear lives, but of course, Cousin Bolo had me to handle my business. So I done just that and killed them muthafuckas."

"WHAT THE FUCK DID YOU JUST SAY?"

"Sorry Mom, but it was strictly business."

"Anyway, Dawn, we have to go pick up about five dozen roses, you know how much your Cousin Bolo loves them roses."

"Gotta go, so I'll see ya later."

Door opened and closed. "Hey, nephew."

"Hey Aunt Ann," I said, kissing her cheeks. "Where is Dawn running off to?"

"Bolo, I have the slightest idea. I told her that we were gonna go pick up the roses you wanted for Sophie's funeral."

"Does everyone know what time to be there?" I sat down next to her.

"Yes, I called them all, Bolo," she said.

"Thank you," I said, voice weakened.

"You have been crying, haven't you?"

"Yes, how you know?"

She said, "Because when you were younger, you would always place your chin in the palms of both your hands, with your elbows rested on your knees."

Smiling. "You know me too damn well Auntie."

"I should. I took care of you all of your life Bolo, and watched you become the man you are today," Aunt Ann paused. She turned the television off. "Sophie was the one who killed Crystal."

"How you know that?" I asked.

"Bolo, at every event that you had, Sophie always became jealous of Crystal when she started singing. Remember the family reunions when we all applauded Crystal."

I interrupted. "That's when it all started?"

She turned to face me. "Bolo, if looks could kill, Crystal would've been dead that very first day Sophie rolled her eyes at Crystal…they had dragon's fire coming from them." Aunt Ann handed me a Black & Mild.

Aunt Ann knew everyone in my organization better than I know them. She's very observant. Everyone thinks that I'm the backbone of the family. Me, personally, it's Aunt Ann. I'm just the crazy guy that they all look up to and I don't take any shit from no one."

"In this business that you're in nephew, there's always a bad apple in the bunch which could spoil the whole batch, it's obvious what you had to do to Sophie."

Crying, "Auntie."

"It's all about business, Bolo. You had to watch her commit suicide because you couldn't kill her yourself. For one, she's a woman, which you have emotions for. One the other hand, you don't have a problem wacking them men in your organization."

"I can't believe this happened." I said, sobbing.

"Bolo, your mother always said that you would always love your family no matter what, bloodline or non-bloodline," she paused, wiping my tears. "That day we couldn't stop laughing, you were imitating some gangster."

"I miss my mom so much Aunt Ann."

"Me too, Bolo. That following week she passed away in the hospital right in front of us. You were cuddled up under her."

"Next month is her birthday, so Dawn and me are taking flowers out to her grave stone. You're more than welcome to come," I said.

"I'd love that, nephew. I would really love that," Aunt Ann cried, while reaching to embrace me. We cried together.

Four years later. Summer of 2006.

Dawn and I had just finished eating dinner at my penthouse. She called her mother to check up on her daughter. She gently laid on top of me. "Guess what?" she asked.

"What, Dawn?" I smiled.

"My daughter is really our daughter," she said.

"WHAT THE FUCK DID I TELL YOU?!" I shouted; she fell on the floor when I pushed her off me.

"IT'S NOT WHAT YOU WANTED BOLO, IT'S WHAT THE DOCTORS TOLD ME," she shouted back at me. "THEY SAID THAT IF I GOTTEN ANOTHER ABORTION, THAN I WOULD HAVE FUCKIN DIED," Dawn screamed at the top of her lungs.

I pointed at her. "Get the hell out of here!" I yelled.

She started to get dressed. "I would have died, damn you."

"JUST GET THE FUCK OUT OF MY HOUSE, DAWN…NOW!" I screamed. She quickly ran out my bedroom, topless and crying. I heard the door open then slowly close.

Heidi: *Hello Bolo. Just wanted you to know that I miss you so much, just last week you and I made love and now this. I wanted so much for you to see me graduate from law school in two years. You taught me how to become a woman, how to be strong and now I'm standing here crying. Crying my heart out wishing you were here with me.*

Kev: *Hey, what's up Captain. That was your Aunt Ann escorting Heidi to her seat. We're all here, still standing as one big family man. Damn we miss you so much. Captain, you said that in this game everyone will witness this someday soon, as all of us will. You should see the many fans that you have here.*

Constance: *Hey you. I can't hold back these tears anymore, Bolo. I miss and love you so much baby. I'm still taking care of business like you would want me to. Always will for you. Come here Lance Jones Junior (Yes Mommy) come kiss your daddy and tell him that you love and miss him.*

Dawn: *Constance*

Constance: *Dawn, I have to do this. It's what Bolo would want and you know it.*

Bolo's son, Lance Jr: *Hi daddy. I miss you and (kissing forehead) love you very muh. Okay me and mommy love you daddy.*

Dawn: *Cousin Bolo, you look sharp in your Armani suite like always*

Dawn's mother: *Dawn, the service is about to start.*

Dawn: *Yes mom, a few more minutes with my Cousin Bolo. Please Hey Cousin Bolo, that was your Aunt Ann. She's been crying since. Me, I miss you very much. We had so much fun together. Everyone misses you…can you believe that they're calling me Delaware's Top Captain…Second in command that is. I'm sorry for the way that I took your life Cousin Bolo, truly I am. You taught me well. (Mommy) yes baby, come here (yes mommy) tell daddy that you love and miss him.*

Bolo's daughter, Lacey Jones: *I miss you and love you too daddy (Give daddy a kiss-kiss).*

Dawn looked back at her mother forming her hand over her mouth, shaking her head and crying, not trying to believe what she was hearing.

My name is Dawn Brown, Bolo's cousin. I had to terminate my cousin because I became impregnated with his baby six times. The doctors said that on my seventh pregnancy, I would have to carry the baby to full term. If I had gotten another abortion, I would have died. Cousin Bolo would have disapproved of carrying the baby.

That same year at our daughter's birthday party, my mother confessed to me that my Cousin Bolo wasn't my real cousin and that she promised her best friend Joyce, Bolo's mother, that she would take care of him and watch him grow up to be the man that she wanted him to be. That's why our daughter Lacey is so healthy today. Our blood type was different.

"Hey, bitch."

"Hey Kimberly and Constance."

"What's up Dawn?"

"Nothing. What's up with you Kimberly?"

"Waiting for next month to come so I can have Bolo's daughter, his third child."

Constance and Dawn walked over to Kimberly, then started rubbing her stomach. They share a laugh together watching the baby's movement.

Rest in Peace.

Lance (Bolo) Jones...

Lightning Source UK Ltd.
Milton Keynes UK
UKOW04f0215170316

270361UK00001B/136/P

9 781432 775476